The Revenant

The Revenant

Sonia Gensler

All rights reserved. Published in the United States by Ember, an imprint of Random House Children's Books, a division of Random House, Inc., New York. Originally published in hardcover in the United States by Alfred A. Knopf, an imprint of Random House Children's Books, New York, in 2011.

Ember and the E colophon are registered trademarks of Random House, Inc.

Visit us on the Web! randomhouse.com/teens

Educators and librarians, for a variety of teaching tools, visit us at
RHTeachersLibrarians.com

The Library of Congress has cataloged the hardcover edition of this work as follows:
Gensler, Sonia.
The revenant / Sonia Gensler. — 1st ed.
p. cm.
Summary: When seventeen-year-old Willemina Hammond fakes credentials to get a teaching position at a school for Cherokee girls in nineteenth-century Oklahoma, she is haunted by the ghost of a drowned student.
ISBN 978-0-375-86701-9 (trade) — ISBN 978-0-375-96701-6 (lib. bdg.) —
ISBN 978-0-375-89732-0 (ebook)
1. Cherokee Indians—Oklahoma—Tahlequah—Juvenile fiction. 2. Cherokee National Female Seminary—Juvenile fiction. [1. Cherokee Indians—Fiction. 2. Cherokee National Female Seminary—Fiction. 3. Indians of North America—Oklahoma—Fiction. 4. Haunted places—Fiction. 5. Teachers—Fiction. 6. Boarding schools—Fiction. 7. Schools—Fiction.] I. Title.
PZ7.G29177Re 2011
[Fic]—dc22
2010028701

ISBN 978-0-375-86139-0 (tr. pbk.)

Book design by Melissa Greenberg

Printed in the United States of America

10 9 8 7 6 5 4 3

First Ember Edition 2013

For Steve

The Revenant

Part I

Impostor

August 1896

Chapter 1

I THOUGHT BY THE TIME I'D TRANSFERRED to the Kansas and Arkansas Valley Railway, this foolish tendency to jump at every sound, to blush each time someone looked me in the eye, would have subsided. If Papa had been sitting next to me, he'd have patted my hand, his mustache curving into a smile. "All the world's a stage, Willie," he'd have said, "and you're playing your part out of necessity, as have many before you."

But Papa was dead, and the space next to me was empty. Staring at that void, I knew in my heart I was something much worse than a player on the world's stage. And more than the summer heat made the perspiration trickle down the back of my neck. I jumped and blushed and perspired for good reason.

I was a liar and a thief.

The conductor called all passengers aboard, and I breathed a sigh of relief. But before I had time to celebrate my solitude, a young man bounded up the steps of my car and slid into the opposite seat. I stiffened, bracing myself for the prying questions strangers asked so freely of young ladies traveling alone. But he only removed his hat and, with a quick nod to me, slumped against the window with his eyes closed. The train jerked into motion with a great metallic screech, but even this did not rouse him. Grateful, I turned back to the window and studied what I could of Van Buren, Arkansas, branding my memory with details of the landscape before we entered Indian Territory.

What had I expected to find outside the train windows when we'd crossed the Arkansas border? Men with crow-black hair riding painted ponies and throwing spears at buffalo? Women in buckskin tending the fires outside their tepees? I knew it could not be so wild or so quaint as the stories I'd read, but I'd expected something . . . else. I never expected to find the terrain so *familiar*. The trees weren't quite as tall here, but otherwise we might as well have been traveling through Tennessee, what with the densely wooded hills and crisscrossing rivers. It should have been comforting to me, this familiarity, but instead it made my heart ache and I had to turn away from the window.

More than an hour had passed, and yet the young man across from me slept on, his mouth hanging open slightly. Something about him reminded me of Papa after a night cozying up to his whiskey bottle. No doubt he'd spent the previous evening carousing with gentleman friends. He *was* a gentleman, I felt sure. His clothes were much finer than mine—they fit his rangy frame as though tailored rather than ready-made.

A barber had trimmed his smooth brown hair, and though his tanned cheeks were covered in stubble, the skin itself looked accustomed to careful tending. I studied his face, noting his strong features and handsome cheekbones. Papa would have deemed it a good face for the stage. "Some folks," he often said, "have delicate features that seem pleasing up close but look mushy from a distance. An actor needs bold features and sharp angles to his face. The audience needs something for the eye to grab hold of."

The face across from me would have made a fine Cassio, I thought, with those handsome features slack with fatigue after a wild night. Or perhaps a Demetrius—there'd been a haughty quality to the young man's bearing when he leapt upon the train and sat down without the merest "How do ye do." But not a Hamlet. There was nothing tortured about his face, no inner turmoil written there.

At that moment, he opened his eyes and looked directly at me. His mouth curved.

Then he winked.

I turned my head to the window so quickly that my neck bones nearly cracked. My cheeks flushed with heat. Such an impish sparkle to his eye! He must have thought me quite common to stare so openly. Surely he would think it an invitation to pry and flirt.

But he said nothing. When I risked a peek at him, he seemed to be asleep once more. My toes tingled with a longing to kick him. He could have at least shown me the courtesy of being aware I was ignoring him.

Two more hours dragged on, and the champion sleeper

barely stirred. When we reached Gibson Station, I leapt to my feet as soon as we came to a stop, heaved my bag off the floor, and headed for the door without a backward glance. But once outside, no one would meet my gaze long enough for me to ask directions. The letter had provided no details about this part of the journey, and I was overwhelmed again by the brazenness of my scheme. I stood alone as the press of people continued past me.

A sudden and powerful gust of wind tore the hat from my head. I whipped around to follow its flight through the air until it fell at the feet of . . . the smirking young man. He reached down, catching it before the wind tossed it again. My heart sank to see him hold the crumpled thing in both hands.

His eyes met mine. "Miss?"

I wanted to turn my back to him, but he held the only hat I owned.

"Yes?" I gripped the pinned coil of my hair as the wind gusted again.

"Pardon me," he said, "but are you on your way to the female seminary in Tahlequah?"

I blinked. "How did you know?"

He smiled, though gently this time. "You look the scholarly type." He pointed past the platform. "You'll find the stage-coach just beyond the station house. It will take you to the school. There'll be other young ladies from this train heading the same way. May I help you with your bag?"

"Thank you, no," I said quickly, reclaiming the offered hat. "It's not terribly heavy." His brown eyes were warm and no longer impish. I stifled the urge to say more, for fear of speaking foolishness.

"I wish you good day, then." He tipped his own hat and turned away, strolling easily and not looking back. I set the bag down to pin the hat more securely to my head. Then I slipped my fingers into my purse to count the few remaining coins, praying they would be enough to cover this final leg of the journey.

It was early afternoon by the time my bag was stowed and I'd taken my seat in the coach. A dark-haired girl in a simple dress and bonnet sat next to me with her head down and hands clasped in her lap. I could not see much of her face, but the skin of her slender hands was light brown. She was Cherokee—most certainly a student. I'd not expected the Indian girls to dress . . . well, to dress much as I would.

"Do you travel to the seminary?" I asked, though I knew the answer.

She turned her broad face and dark eyes to me, her expression guarded.

"Yes."

"How long a journey should I expect?"

"Two hours," she said flatly, before returning her gaze to the hands in her lap.

I didn't mind her shyness. I was relieved—relieved to have someone to follow and also glad the girl wasn't given to chatter and questions. Free to gaze out the window, I took in the wooded scenery and imagined what sort of place awaited me. A female seminary in the middle of Indian Territory must be something like a mission school, I thought. Rougher living than I was accustomed to, but much preferred to living with *her* and taking care of her brats—and watching her playing wife to the likes of *him*. My blood boiled at the very thought.

As a distraction, I imagined myself a heroine out of Shakespeare. *As You Like It* seemed best suited to my wooded surroundings, so I became another Rosalind. Life at court had grown dangerous, and thus I must flee to a simple, rustic life. I would trade court intrigues for a quiet existence among the forest people, who would be grateful for my wisdom and company. I only lacked a dear cousin to be my bosom companion. That, and a father waiting for me at the center of the forest.

My stomach growled, as I'd not eaten since that morning, but the warm air and rocking of the coach soon lulled me to sleep. When I woke, damp with perspiration and blinking at the light, the forest had given way to the outskirts of a town. Moments later, the coach jerked to a halt and the door swung open. I scrambled out to collect my bag from the driver, and then I sought the girl who'd sat next to me.

"May I follow you? I've never been to the female seminary."

"I thought so." She pointed at my bag. "Is that all you have?"

"Yes, it is." I blushed, for it was indeed very little. Yet it was everything I had in the world.

"I didn't think to meet someone with less than me. My trunk will be sent separately. Will you follow me?"

Despite her blunt manner, I was grateful to have someone in the lead so I could look about me. Tall, elegantly bricked storefronts lined the main street, including two general stores, a druggist, a livery stable, and more. Distracted by a pretty park area with a burbling creek, I did not look into the distance ahead of us until the girl spoke again.

"That's it—up there on the hill."

I looked up and nearly stumbled. This was no lowly mission school cobbled together with the labor of poor folk who wanted their children to learn numbers and letters.

This was a *castle*.

I turned to the girl. "It's not at all what I expected," I breathed.

She ducked her head, saying nothing.

The school was enormous, intimidating and elegant all at once. A three-story, redbrick structure, it boasted two fairytale turrets at the center, framing the entrance, and at the right a handsome clock tower reaching up to the sky. A walkway made of wooden slats led to a wrought-iron gate that arched in front of the building. Two lampposts stood just beyond the gate. I couldn't have been more surprised if the school had been surrounded by a moat and we'd been forced to enter by drawbridge.

In truth, I felt emptied out when looking upon it. There was barely anything left to keep me from blowing away in that relentless wind. No food in my belly, no bravery in my heart. Barely a thought in my head except for wonderment.

The girl walked on, undaunted. We climbed the steps and passed through the brick archway of the building to stand before the large double doors. The girl boldly opened one door and walked through, not bothering to stand aside for me to enter. I followed her into a large vestibule with a bricked fireplace at the right and a handsome staircase with polished wood banisters to my left.

I'd set my bag down to take in these impressive surroundings when the silence was interrupted by a crash and piercing scream in the next room.

The girl frowned. "Someone's in the parlor."

I followed her through the corridor to a well-furnished sitting room. Three ladies stood by a low table set for tea, their faces stricken. They were teachers, fashionably dressed and quite lovely to look upon. My heart sank a little, and I shivered at the strange chill in the air. On second glance, I saw that one lady's fingers were bloodied, her bodice soaked with tea, and the shattered remains of a cup and saucer lay on the floor by her skirt.

Her eyes were wild as she looked to us. "It fell to pieces in my hands!"

The lady next to her, who was taller and possessed a bolder beauty, tossed her head. "She wasn't handling it roughly."

"Miss Crenshaw is going to blame us anyway, Fannie." The third lady was plump and bespectacled.

"But it wasn't my fault!" The injured lady paled as she stared at her bloodied hand.

The plump one gripped her arm. "We know whose fault it was," she hissed. "But *she* won't believe us."

Fannie sighed and pulled a handkerchief from her sleeve. "Wrap this around your hand, Lelia. If we throw away the broken pieces, Miss Crenshaw might never know." She turned to us, her eyes narrowing at the girl next to me. "Unless *you* say something, Lucy Sharp."

My companion's spine stiffened at the lady's imperious tone. I could do nothing but stare at Fannie, mesmerized by her deep green eyes. Surely I needed to speak, to introduce myself, but my tongue stuck in my throat.

Just then, a tall figure in black swept into the room. Everyone but me lowered her head. The woman, older and plain but with a commanding presence, surveyed the damage in silence. The moment stretched on for a small eternity before she finally spoke.

"Lucy, help them clean up—they seem to have worked themselves into a tizzy over nothing."

The three ladies relaxed visibly, but Lucy's face was grim as she knelt to retrieve the shattered pieces of porcelain. My stomach chose that time to growl most hideously.

The woman in black turned to me, her eyebrows raised in question.

"May I help you, young lady?"

I choked back a gasp.

I'm Willie Hammond, and your bulldog face doesn't scare me.

Straightening my spine, I stifled that thought and cleared my throat.

"I am Angeline McClure, ma'am. Your new English teacher."

Chapter 2

I KEPT MY EYES ON THE WOMAN but could feel the ladies turn to me as if they were trying to get a better look.

The woman's stern expression did not change, though her eyes narrowed in appraisal. "My goodness, you are young," she finally said, without offering her hand. "I was not certain when you would arrive. I am Harriet Crenshaw, principal of the Cherokee Female Seminary."

The lady they called Fannie drew near, her eyes bold. "Miss Crenshaw? Lelia is looking rather peaked. She has cut herself upon the broken porcelain. Might we send for Dr. Stewart?"

The principal shook her head. "Of course not. He has better things to do than tend to clumsy girls. No doubt you are all so excitable today because you have cinched your stays too tightly." She gestured at Fannie's elegant figure. "I expect you in uniform, Fannie. No more of these ridiculous and unhealthy refinements. You know the rules."

Fannie dropped her gaze demurely. "Classes do not begin until Wednesday, Miss Crenshaw."

"Yes, but new students are arriving already, and I expect seniors to set a proper example."

I turned from the ladies to Miss Crenshaw. "Seniors?"

The principal stared at Fannie, ignoring my question. "Do you hear me, Fannie Bell?"

Tension thickened the air. After a moment, the lady's stiff shoulders softened. "Yes, ma'am."

Victory in hand, Miss Crenshaw swept out of the room. I had no choice but to follow. I grabbed my case in the vestibule and scrambled up the stairs after her.

"Are those young ladies *students,* Miss Crenshaw?" The question came out in gasps, for I struggled to keep up with her. "I felt quite sure they must be teachers."

"They are indeed students, and officers of the Minervian Literary Society," she replied evenly. "They met today to plan the year's events; otherwise, they would not yet be at school. They are only seventeen years of age, but they give themselves airs. You must not let them intimidate you."

How could I not?

"But, Miss Crenshaw, I thought this was a school for Cherokee girls only. That is what I understood from your letter."

"They *are* Cherokee. Indeed, they are from one of the foremost Cherokee families in this territory." She paused on the landing to turn and look at me. "You wonder at their fair skin and light eyes? I was surprised too when I first arrived. They are mixed-blood. And they think highly of themselves for it."

"Are you . . . ?" I couldn't think how to ask it politely.

"Am I Cherokee? No. There has never been a Cherokee principal of the seminary. Only now, after forty years of operation, are we finding qualified Cherokee teachers." We'd reached the second floor, and she turned to face me. "You should know, Miss McClure, that the Cherokee are well nigh *obsessed* with education. This seminary was the first institution of higher education west of the Mississippi. I'm certain you'll be satisfied with our high standards."

I gulped, having no idea how to respond. She merely raised an eyebrow before turning away and leading me to the first door on the right. Opening it, she gestured me inside.

The room was made large by the narrowness of the bed at the center. A small desk and wooden chair stood against the opposite wall near a cast-iron radiator—something I'd only seen in the most recently constructed buildings back home. My eyes were drawn to the golden light streaming through the bay windows. A large chiffonier stood between the windows, but even so, I could see the wall was curiously curved. I gaped like a child. This curved bay was formed from one of the turrets I'd marveled at when walking toward the school.

By no means was it an *elegant* room, but compared to what I'd grown accustomed to, it was quite spacious and well appointed. And wouldn't Papa have been delighted to know that his princess lived in a turret?

"I trust this room is sufficient?" asked Miss Crenshaw after a moment.

"Yes," I breathed. "Very much so."

"It *was* a student room. Four girls slept here in two beds, but we've had changes in enrollment and those girls are now situated elsewhere. I thought it would make a spacious dwelling for our new teacher." She gestured toward the windows. "You'll get a nice breeze during the warm months, and steam heat keeps us cozy enough in the winter."

"I am very grateful, Miss Crenshaw."

We stood in awkward silence for a moment. Had I not thanked her sufficiently? Fortunately, I was saved by the sound of swishing fabric at the door. We both turned to find a lady standing there—surely *this* was a lady teacher and not a student, for though she was much younger than the principal, she had the stiff spine and graceful bearing of one who held authority. Her eyebrows, however, were arched in surprise.

"Ah, Miss Adair," said Miss Crenshaw. "Meet your new colleague, Miss Angeline McClure. She hails from Columbia, Tennessee, and is a graduate of their Athenaeum."

The lady's vague alarm melted into a smile as she stepped closer. Her eyes were dark and prettily framed by long lashes. She took my hand and grasped it firmly.

"Olivia was once my student, and a very fine one at that," said Miss Crenshaw. "She is one of a select group of Cherokee ladies who have both studied and taught at the seminary. So you see, Miss McClure, how far these girls have come from their humble beginnings?"

Miss Adair lowered her head. It wasn't clear whether she was pleased or embarrassed by the principal's praise.

Before I could speak, Miss Crenshaw lifted her brooch

watch and clucked her tongue. "There is so much to do and already it is nearly time for supper. Olivia, will you take Miss McClure on the tour?"

Miss Adair led me back downstairs and paused first at the parlor door. The room glowed softly in the late-afternoon light. I stepped inside, bracing myself for the eerie blast of cold air. But I did not shiver, nor did gooseflesh prickle my arms. The room was quite warm. Had I imagined the earlier chill?

"The girls do not spend much time here," said Miss Adair, "unless it is to clean the room or, more rarely, to receive family or visitors from the male seminary."

"There is a Cherokee Male Seminary as well?" I asked.

"Oh yes. Its enrollment is not as high as ours, and their building is much older, but it's a fine school. You will see the male students in town, and they will visit here from time to time."

Across from the vestibule stood a library with handsomely arching windows and endless shelves of books. Tables and chairs gleamed in the warm light, and I was certain a gloved finger traced along the wood's surface would remain pristinely white. We moved on to view several classrooms full of wooden desks, the sight of which made my stomach flutter. At the far end of the building was a high-ceilinged chapel, full of desks rather than pews, that extended into another large room set up as a study hall. We completed our first-floor tour by making our way to the other end of the building, past more schoolrooms and around the corner to a grand dining hall that could seat hundreds of girls.

Rustic mission school, indeed.

On the second floor, Miss Adair pointed out the cavernous lavatories with their rows of sinks and curious water closets with flush toilets. We even peered into a student room comparable in size to mine but crowded by two larger beds and additional furnishings. The windows were shaded with pretty gingham curtains, while crocheted doilies brightened the desk and small side tables.

"Are all the rooms furnished with such homey adornments?"

Miss Adair smiled. "The students often bring items with them. Some of the more fortunate girls bring their own dressers and beds. These girls knew they would be coming back to this very room, and so they left some of their decorative furnishings behind." She closed the door. "It's a little different upstairs."

"Are there more students upstairs?" I asked as we continued down the corridor.

Miss Adair frowned. "Yes. The primaries reside above and take their lessons there as well."

"Primaries? They are little children, then?"

"Some are small children. A considerable number are country girls over the age of twelve who are not quite as . . . *advanced* as the other students. Their circumstances are less fortunate, and thus they must work for their tuition. Miss Crenshaw keeps them upstairs together to protect them. The girls from town are not as gentle with them as they should be."

"I well remember how it feels to be teased and condescended to as a charity case," I said absently, then cringed at my own stupidity. Angeline McClure had never been condescended to in her life.

Miss Adair looked at me searchingly for a moment before continuing. "The infirmary is upstairs as well, though many of the upper-school girls loathe to go there. They think they'll catch lice from the primaries." She paused by a door. "This is my room."

The door opened to a room smaller than mine—the same narrow bed, a wooden chair and desk, but a single window rather than the curved bay with two windows. Books were stacked unevenly on the desk and beneath her window. A small dresser stood near the door. The room was crowded and stuffy, but she'd enlivened it with a cheerful bed quilt and white curtains edged with lace.

"It's charming," I said.

Miss Adair shrugged. "Most of the teachers have rooms like this. You were given a room meant for four or more girls." She did not look at me as she spoke, and her hands fluttered as though she were nervous.

"Is there a reason I was given a student room?"

She met my gaze then, and something in her expression made the back of my neck tingle. Sorrow darkened her eyes, but also . . . fear? She opened her mouth, and I leaned forward, expecting something lurid to pour from her lips.

"Well," she said, and then lowered her voice to a whisper, "it may not be my place to tell you—"

Footsteps thumped in the corridor, and Miss Adair clamped her mouth shut. I turned to find Miss Crenshaw gliding toward us, her petticoats hissing on the wood floor and a frown on her face.

"Whispering in the corridors already, ladies? Surely Miss McClure wishes to rest before supper."

"Yes, Miss Crenshaw," said Miss Adair. She turned to smile at me. "I look forward to speaking with you later." With a nod to the principal, she entered her room and shut the door.

Miss Crenshaw walked me to my room, following closely as if I might bolt at any moment. "Supper is at six," she said briskly as we walked. "Our gathering will be small and informal. As for tomorrow, we ordinarily rise at five-thirty sharp, but as classes are not yet in session, the bell will ring an hour later than usual. Breakfast will be served in the dining hall at seven o'clock, followed immediately by Chapel." She paused before my door. "Until supper, then."

"Yes, Miss Crenshaw." But she was already walking away, and I was not sure she even heard me.

Supper was quiet, with teachers and students seated together at one table. The girls from the parlor were not there, and I breathed a little easier in their absence. Miss Adair kindly made introductions, but I was too tired to do more than smile and nod. I forgot the names almost instantly. A negro man called Jimmy served us a baked hash with bread and vegetables, the smell of which made my stomach groan in anticipation. Eating so preoccupied me that I said little to the others at the table. I would strive to make a better impression the next day.

What a relief to finally retire to my very own room for the

night! I opened the windows of my turret and sat in the evening air. The breeze wasn't much cooler than the still air in the room, but it was fresh and smelled of cut grass. I stared out onto the boardwalk that led down toward town but could see little. Faint lights sparkled in the distance, but the seminary lamps had been extinguished. All was dim and quiet outside this fortress.

When I felt cooler, I unpacked my case by lamplight. It was a rather pathetic collection of items. A nightgown, which I placed on the bed. Two shirtwaists and one skirt. Very worn underclothes, patched in a few places, but soft from many washings. A heavy shawl, which made me sweat to look upon it. The last item was a fine black cape with a ruffled collar and a satin bow at the neck. I placed it around my shoulders and studied my reflection in the chiffonier mirror. Very handsome it was, and very unhandsome I'd been in taking it. I shrugged the cape off and folded it carefully, placing it with the other items in the chiffonier.

All that remained in my bag was my father's three-volume set of Shakespeare's complete works and, within the first volume, a faded tintype of him in full costume as Orlando in *As You Like It*. He was very young when the photo was taken—he'd not yet met my mother and surely thought himself quite the dandy. I sat upon the bed and gazed at the image, wanting to touch it, as though petting a photograph would bring me comfort. But I did not wish to cause damage with my sweaty hands.

I placed the photo back between the pages of the volume.

That was everything I owned. Father's gold watch had been sold, as had my good coat. I'd needed the money for the train fare and one night's stay at a respectable inn along the way.

I glanced at the white paper peeping out of the third volume of Shakespeare's works—the collection of his tragic plays. How fitting. The letter had all the makings of a tragedy unfolding. But it now signified a tragedy averted, for rather than drawing me to my doom, it had spurred me to action. I pulled the letter out and smoothed it open on my lap.

Dear Willemina,

Your father's dream was for you to have a fine education, and you've worked hard to stay at the Athenaeum when I had no money for tuition. You've made me proud. You frown and shake your head as you read this, but I write the truth.

We need you home now. My heart is heavy as the ink blots this page, because I feel your disappointment like a weight even though you're so far from me. I am with child again. It is a blessing, to be sure, but right now it seems like a wasting disease has come upon me. I can barely rise from bed. The food won't stay down, and I get sicker by the day. I can't get the housework done, and it's nearly killing me to chase after the boys.

Willie, you are seventeen, with many years of schooling behind you. I need you at home. I wouldn't ask if I weren't so desperate. Mr. Toomey will come for you on Saturday. I beg you not to be rude to him. He's been very good to us.

*When the child is older, perhaps we'll get you back
to school, though by then you might feel too old. By
then you might be ready to marry and start your
own family.*

I can barely sit up long enough to finish this letter.

Mother

That letter was delivered to me at the Columbia Athenaeum four days prior, and I'd immediately hidden it in the pocket of my apron. All that day, despair had clutched at my innards, its dull ache nearly doubling me over. I'd dreamed up a thousand different ways to avoid returning to that farmhouse, where my father's laughter had been replaced by the howls and crashings of twin boys. I'd offered to work at the school during the summer for paltry wages—most of which I sent home—just to avoid the place.

I'd been sweeping the floor in the Athenaeum's dormitory, sluggish under the weight of my doom, when fate intervened in the form of Angeline McClure's golden head popping through her doorway to beckon me.

Angeline was a young lady of refinement who kept her person perfectly tidy. Her room, however, always looked as though Mother's little boys had been locked inside to run rampant. That day was no exception—the only difference was that two elegant trunks lay in the midst of the chaos. Apparently, Angeline was packing. When I entered the room, she stood next to one half-filled trunk, her eyes nearly bulging with excitement.

She wanted me to ask why she was packing. Her entire body quivered with the yearning to blurt her news. I crossed my arms and waited for the eruption—I would not call it forth myself.

"Willie, I am getting married!"

Angeline had been courted all summer by a well-to-do landowner, so this did not surprise me. She was only telling me because there was no one else around. She'd never taken much interest in me, for I was younger and a charity student. I knew her disdain and tried to stay cool, but the small sentimental part of my heart perked up to be singled out by her.

"Congratulations," I said softly.

She clapped her hands with glee, then shoved a stack of papers off a chair and gestured for me to sit. Still smiling fatuously, she settled herself upon the bed without bothering to move the clothing scattered upon it. Then she held out her hand and wriggled her fingers so that I could not miss the sparkle. I murmured my admiration.

"It took some maneuvering on my part to secure this proposal, let me tell you."

"How romantic," I said, knowing the irony would be lost on her.

"In fact," she continued, "I had to accept a teaching position to force his hand. And from quite a curious school! Can you imagine what sort of school it was?"

I shook my head.

"A seminary for Cherokee girls in *Indian Territory*! Is that not a scream?"

I tried to imagine Angeline, in her prissy clothes, demanding recitations from a group of sullen Indian girls. "Why did you want to teach there?"

"Gracious! Can you imagine *me* teaching *Indians?*" She frowned thoughtfully. "Accepting the position was the only way to push Jarvis into action. He was far too complacent before he knew I might leave for the back of beyond. It wasn't until he set his eyes upon the letter offering me the position that he realized he might lose me."

"Quite a gamble," I said.

"Not really." She tossed her head. "I knew it would work." She looked at the disorder around her and sighed. "And now I must gather all this together, for on Saturday I leave for Arkansas so that Mother and I can prepare my wedding trousseau. But I'm already late for lessons with Reverend Wilson's girls." She tilted her head and scrunched her pale features into a pleading expression. "Would you mind, Willie—would it be a terrible inconvenience if I asked you to post a letter for me? I fear I shall forget."

This was why she'd asked me in—not to share news with a friend, not just to crow over her "victory." She needed me for an errand.

I forced a smile. "Of course. Give it to me and I will take it when I run errands for Mrs. Wilson."

"Oh, it's written, but not yet placed in an envelope. I really must dash. It's all there on the desk—would you mind finishing it up for me? I'll return the favor somehow, I promise."

And with that, she was gone to teach her lessons. I stood up and waded through the clutter to the desk. Fortunately, her letter was on top of the pile of papers, so I folded it and poked around for an envelope. She'd not addressed one, of course, and I would have to beg coins for postage from Mrs. Wilson.

The letter from the school lay underneath, and I copied the address onto Angeline's envelope. Angeline hadn't for a moment intended to teach at this simple charity school, and I felt a flash of sympathy for the principal who would receive her letter declining the position.

I was about to leave when something caught my eye in the letter from the seminary. It was a number—a number that leapt off the page and slapped me in the face.

$450.

I grabbed the letter and looked closer. "Room and board are provided, and the salary is $450 per annum."

Four hundred and fifty dollars? With none of it going toward food? And a room of one's own—surely a teacher would have her own room. Her own bed, at least. Four hundred and fifty dollars to teach a group of simple Indian girls?

My heart began to pound.

I rifled through the papers on Angeline's desk. At the very bottom was her teaching certificate, newly signed that summer. After staring at it for a moment, I added the certificate to the letter and envelope. Then I gathered the remaining papers into a neat pile on the desk. But of course she would notice that and wonder. So I set my small bundle of papers down and looked about me. I would have to tidy the entire room. I could leave a note telling her it was my wedding gift to her, for I knew how busy she was. Hands hot and trembling, I collected the clothes from the floor and bed and folded them neatly. It was so easy I could not see why she couldn't manage it herself.

When I beheld the cape, with its high ruffled neck and satin ribbon, my heart expanded. It was the most beautiful thing I'd ever seen. And Angeline had many things like it—elegant clothes for which she cared so little that she would toss them upon the floor. Would she miss this beauty? In her fleeting gratitude for my tidying labors, would she miss this one cape?

I decided not and carefully stuffed it into my drawers.

I need you at home. I wouldn't ask if I weren't so desperate. Mr. Toomey will come for you on Saturday.

The next day—my first full day at the seminary—would be Saturday. I smiled to think of Toomey arriving at the Athenaeum only to learn I'd vanished. His jowls would sag with confusion, his eyes narrow and piglike as he stared at Mrs. Wilson. She'd grow uncomfortable under that gaze of animal stupidity. Finally, he would shake his head and turn away, leaving her sighing with relief to have him gone from her parlor.

I folded the letter and returned it to the volume of Shakespeare's tragedies, where it marked act 3, scene 4 of *Hamlet*.

"Mother," I whispered, "you have my father much offended."

Part of me had wished to put a match to that letter. After some consideration, however, it seemed better to keep it. I would read the letter when doubt weakened my resolve. I would turn to it when worried that my lies and deceits were corrupting me.

Mr. Toomey—Mr. *Gabriel* Toomey—was my stepfather. A red-faced man with a lumpish body and little learning. Our neighbor when my father was alive, he was free with his advice on farming and raising livestock. Apparently, he was free with my mother as well. Why else would they marry so soon after my father's death? She gave birth to twin boys a mere eight months later. And now another was on the way.

I would not—could not—return to that.

Chapter 3

CLASSES WERE TO BEGIN ON WEDNESDAY, and each day brought a new wave of girls to the school. Many arrived on the stagecoach as Lucy and I had; others were brought by wagon or simply walked from the far reaches of town. There were fair-skinned, smartly dressed girls like Fannie and her friends, but many of the girls were plainly attired and darkly handsome. The rural primaries were easy to spot, for they looked more than a little ragged as they huddled together in the vestibule. Miss Crenshaw saw to them herself, quickly ushering the girls upstairs to join those who were more like them.

I kept to my room as much as possible, reviewing the texts Miss Crenshaw had provided for me. I'd thought to be teaching basic skills to rough Indian girls, but as I pored over McGuffey's *Sixth Eclectic Reader* and Swinton's *Studies in English Literature,* I knew a battle lay in wait. This was no charity school for girls needing instruction in proper speech and manners. This was an institution of higher learning, and the students thought too much of themselves to be grateful for anything I had to offer. The part I played had become more challenging, but there was no turning back.

The night before classes were to begin, I sat on my bed and stared at the wall. I'd read through the textbooks until the words blurred on the page and I'd despaired almost to the point of tears. Perhaps it was childish, but sitting still and tracing the wallpaper pattern with my eyes seemed to smooth out the jumble of my nerves.

A knock came at the door, making my heart leap.

"Come in?"

The door opened and Olivia Adair peered around the edge. Relieved, I waved her in. After a moment's hesitation, she sat next to me on the bed. It would have been very cozy had I not felt so ill at the thought of teaching the next day.

"Miss Crenshaw asked me to pay you a visit." She took my hand very solemnly, concern widening her eyes. "Are you nervous?"

"I am absolutely terrified!"

She sighed. "You *are* a kindred spirit. I knew it the moment I saw you."

"Is that supposed to reassure me?"

"It didn't sound reassuring, did it?" Her eyes sparkled. "I meant that you are feeling exactly the way I felt the night before my first day as a teacher. And I did not die of terror, so neither shall you." She squeezed my hand. "I'd be worried if you *weren't* nervous, because that would mean you were setting yourself up for disaster tomorrow."

"All this talk of death and disaster is souring my stomach, Miss Adair."

"I have a little suggestion that might help you tomorrow. It's a trick, really."

I leaned forward. "Please share it."

"No matter how carefully you prepare, when you face your first class, you will feel like a schoolgirl with no authority. It happens to every new teacher."

But I am a schoolgirl.

I shook my head, banishing the thought. "Do go on."

"You must prepare yourself by remembering the sternest teacher you ever knew. Can you think of one?"

I considered my recent teachers at the Athenaeum. "Well, Miss Kirtley was rather fearsome."

"Good. Identify the qualities that made her so."

"That's easy enough. She was thin as a rail with the pointiest elbows you've ever seen—so pointy you'd cut yourself if you brushed against her. And she was terribly vain and prissy. But her most fearsome quality was her mean tongue. She never said anything unseemly, but when she was disappointed in you, her words sliced you open like a knife."

Olivia grinned. "Excellent! Now, tomorrow when you face the class, you must imagine yourself as Miss Kirtley. Not that you must flay the girls with your words—just pull Miss Kirtley's authority around your shoulders like a cloak. I promise it will help."

"Truly?"

"I wore the cloak of Miss Morton for weeks—we called her

Monstrous Morton during my school days—and it served me well. You'll be fine, Miss McClure. And I can't wait to hear all about it."

She returned to her own room shortly after that, leaving me slightly less terrified than I was before. It wasn't until I was settled into bed that I remembered—she'd still not explained the mystery behind my spacious turret room. Why was I given a student room meant for four when more senior teachers made do with less? If I survived the first day of classes, I would ask her.

The morning bell was to ring at five-thirty on Wednesday, but I woke hours before dawn. I kept my eyes down during breakfast and Chapel, lifting my head only when Miss Crenshaw made her announcements and teacher introductions. When she declared my name and whence I'd come, I held my chin high and tried to look fearsome.

Recitations began at half past eight, and I started the day with the seniors. It was a small group—only eight girls—but each wore a crisply ironed apron over her striped blouse and narrow skirt. My own limp shirtwaist and skirt were shabby by comparison. These girls were the same age as me, but clearly more refined. Were they smarter? If they were, I couldn't let them know it.

I called roll with a moderately steady voice. Two girls had Bell as their surname, and one used it as a middle name—these three were the ones I'd met in the parlor on my first day at the seminary. Were they all cousins? The two prettier girls sat together at a desk three rows back, their heads held high. The third one sat nearer to the front, her eyes dark and eager behind thick spectacles.

Lucy Sharp, the quiet girl who'd sat next to me on the stagecoach, now sat at a desk in the front row. I'd learned from Miss Crenshaw that she was the only full-blood girl in the senior class.

Once the roll was called, I picked up our reader, gripping it tightly to disguise the tremor in my hands.

"Ladies, if you will now turn to page eleven in your readers—"

A hand shot up in the air. Fannie Bell, the tall and elegant girl from the parlor, was hailing me.

"Yes, Miss Bell?"

"Aren't you going to tell us about yourself, miss?"

I stared at her stupidly.

"That's what new teachers do at the beginning of the year."

Of course they do. I hadn't prepared a speech. Why hadn't I prepared a speech?

"What do you wish to know?"

Their faces instantly told me what a sorry response that was.

"You seem very young," said Fannie, her demeanor prim but her green eyes flashing with mischief. "How long did you teach before coming to the seminary?"

I knew this trap only too well—I'd seen girls set it at the Athenaeum. As soon as they knew a teacher had come straight from school, their respect plummeted dramatically. They began to calculate the pranks they could pull. Why hadn't I thought of this?

"I think you know, Miss Bell, that before arriving here I was at the Columbia Athenaeum in Tennessee." That was vague enough. They might actually believe I'd been teaching there. "Now, if you'll open your readers and turn to—"

Fannie Bell was raising her hand again, and this time she didn't wait for my acknowledgment before she spoke.

"How do you like your room, Miss McClure?"

What was she playing at? "I have a lovely room."

"Do you hear anything at night?" Her eyes widened. "Have you seen anything *strange?*"

A nervous titter arose from some of the girls, while others squirmed in their seats.

I took a breath and spoke slowly. "I haven't heard or seen anything, Miss Bell."

"I ask, Miss McClure, because . . ." The girl next to her—Lelia, the one who broke her cup in the parlor—shook her head vigorously, but it only seemed to fuel Fannie's ardor. "I ask because that room belongs to a dead girl."

Several girls gasped. Lucy Sharp put her head down on her desk. With great effort, I closed my gaping mouth. I needed to put a stop to this, but the back of my neck was tingling and curiosity got the better of me.

"What do you mean, Miss Bell?"

"Ella Blackstone lived in that room for three years, but she drowned ever so tragically last spring. There are some who say she haunts the school." She held my gaze, challenge in her eyes. "Have you seen her ghost, Miss McClure?"

Someone laughed—a high-pitched, hysterical sound—and a strained silence followed. I felt certain my face was red, that perspiration must be staining my underarms, but as Fannie boldly stared at me, I took a deep breath and gathered my courage.

"I've not seen or heard a single thing. I do not believe in ghosts, Miss Bell. And I will not tolerate you, or anyone else, speaking of them in my presence again."

Fannie Bell frowned mightily but said nothing.

"Now," I said, my voice pitched a little too high, "if you all will turn to page eleven of your readers, we will review the elements of proper elocution."

The remainder of that class was a terrible bore, but at least there were no more interruptions. The instant the bell rang, the girls leapt from their desks and pushed their way out the door in a most unladylike fashion. Should this be allowed? Was it regular? I wasn't certain. I did know I needed to be stricter in the future . . . and much less of a ditherer.

It wasn't until the sophomores walked in that I finally remembered the cloak of authority. No wonder I'd been such a ninny with the seniors! I was playing *me* instead of a teacher. I turned my back to the class under the guise of arranging papers, but in truth I took a moment to meditate upon Miss Kirtley. When I turned around, I hadn't merely stepped into her cloak—I'd stepped right into her pointy little body.

I played Miss Kirtley to the hilt with the rest of my classes—so cold and stern that they gave me no problems. Perhaps it was because they were younger. Perhaps it was because these groups didn't have a Fannie Bell to pollute the atmosphere. Whatever the reason, I was grateful.

The day's labors concluded with the afternoon constitutional—an hour-long walk around the grounds of the school. The girls lined up, two by two, and marched forward as though part of a military drill. I fell in with Olivia Adair, glad to have sympathetic company for the first time that day.

"Did Miss Kirtley come to your rescue this morning?" she asked with a grin.

"I forgot her during my first class, but she performed very well afterward. Tomorrow I must call upon her if I'm to impress my authority upon the seniors." I looked about to make sure Miss Crenshaw was nowhere near. "In fact, Miss Adair, I must ask you about something that occurred with the seniors today."

She smiled. "Please call me Olivia—the students are too distracted to hear us now."

"Oh, and you must call me Willie." Her friendly charm had so disarmed me that it came out before I could think. "Willemina is my middle name," I said quickly when she raised her eyebrows. "I've always despised the name Angeline. My dear papa called me Willie, and I should like for you to do the same."

"Of course, Willie. What is it you wish to ask?"

I lowered my voice. "Fannie Bell told me something very curious. She said my room belongs to a dead girl."

Olivia looked down, her shoulders drooping. "Ah, she speaks of Ella Blackstone."

"She drowned?"

"She did, and it was devastating. She shared a room with Lucy Sharp, whom you know from the senior class, along with two other girls. Lucy would not stay in the room afterward. In fact, each of the remaining girls made it clear that she did not wish to sleep in that room any longer."

"A drowning death is very sad, but why avoid the room? It's not as though she died *there*."

Olivia looked away for a moment. "Many of the girls believe poor Ella was murdered by her beau, who then ran away."

"Murdered? How intriguing!" I sobered at Olivia's dark expression. "I mean, how dreadful. Simply horrible, of course. But I still don't see how this concerns the room I was given."

"Some believe her spirit cannot rest because of the violence done to her. They think she haunts the school—that she haunts *your* room."

I snorted. "They said something like that in class. You can't possibly believe in such things as ghosts!"

Olivia's face was stony. "I prefer the word *revenant*."

"What?"

"It's an old word my grandmother used. French, I think, for *one who returns*." Her expression softened slightly. "We lost Ella, but her spirit returned to the place where she was happy and beloved. Now her spirit is confused."

I could only stare at her for spouting such idiocy. Papa had often scoffed at the weak-willed and easily led, but I hadn't truly known what he meant until that moment.

"I am sensitive to these things," she continued, "and I have felt a presence—there are cold spots in the building, strange rapping noises, and water faucets that turn on when no one is nearby."

"You can't be serious!"

"I am. Don't you believe in spirits that become trapped in the earthly plane?"

"No, I do not. There are plenty of ghosts in Shakespeare, but my papa always insisted they were born of the characters' fevered minds, and would only be taken for spirits by the poor and ignorant. He loathed such superstitions."

Olivia sighed. "You would not be the first doubter I've encountered. People close themselves off to what the spirit world tries to tell us, and when they do experience something out of the ordinary, they are quick to dismiss it as the work of imagination or fever."

I shook my head. "My dear papa died most tragically, and if anyone had a reason to come back and haunt his family, it would be he. And if he were to communicate with anyone, it would be me. Yet I've *never* felt his presence, nor heard his voice. So, no, I can't say I believe in spirits that visit the living." I laughed. "In fact, I find this notion of spirits very backward."

"You needn't be so dismissive. I will not speak of it again." With those words, she drew away a few inches, and I knew she would have walked off had we not been in formation. Instead, she retreated into herself, her face drawn with disappointment. We walked in silence for the remainder of the outing.

I dreamed of Papa that very night—the first time since those sad days right after his death. In the hazy murk of the dream, he was sitting by the fire in his study, surrounded by shelves crammed with books. Joy flooded my heart. Papa was not dead! He'd merely been resting in his study—waiting patiently for us to realize our mistake. I bounded into the room to embrace him, calling out to him. But no matter how loud I cried, he did not look up. My feet turned to lead and my arms grew heavy at my sides. I could not reach him. I called and called, but he only looked into the fire, his eyes sad and mustache drooping.

I woke with an ache in my stomach, an emptiness that had nothing to do with hunger. Why wouldn't Papa look at me?

Mother had erased Papa's presence from our house. His study was now the boys' room. His clothing, pipes, toiletries, and books—almost all had been sold or burned. I'd begged her to let me keep his Shakespeare books and pocket watch, but the rest was lost. The last time I'd stood in that room, I could no longer smell the sweetness of his pipe tobacco. Instead, the air was ripe with the stench of soiled diapers.

I thought of Papa's cold face in the dream. Had he refused to look at me out of *anger*? Did he blame me for leaving Mother?

I shook my head. Papa was dead and couldn't be angry with me.

Mother was angry, to be sure. She begrudged the hours of labor she'd planned to extract from me, for she couldn't afford to pay someone else to do the work. I was valuable to her, if only as a workhorse. Was I so valuable that she'd send the law after me? Would they be able to track me down and drag me back to the farm?

A tap near the window jolted me upright in the bed. I sat still and listened. Another tap. I drew back the covers and moved slowly to the window to pull the curtain aside. All was darkness. If there was someone underneath my window, I could not see him. Or her.

Had the noise come from inside the room? My arms prickled with gooseflesh.

Perhaps a ghost was standing next to me.

I shook my head, laughing at myself. I was acting as fretful as Brutus upon seeing Caesar's ghost, but it was only the dream of Papa that had me twitching. I got back in bed and pulled the covers to my chin. All was silence.

Tap, tap.

"Stop it!" I whispered harshly.

Silence.

Shivering, I buried my face in the pillow and pulled the covers over my head.

Chapter 4

MY GOAL FOR THE WEEK was survival. I had to keep the performance going, even if the members of my company were threatening to rebel. Fortunately, my younger students proved compliant. It was only the seniors who whispered, rolled their eyes, and dozed during class.

On Friday, however, the girls were all smiles as they walked in. When the bell rang, they sat quietly in their seats, looking at me expectantly. Their faces were radiant.

I called roll. Each girl responded promptly. I asked them to open their books. Each one did so without complaint.

"You are all in fine form today," I said, rather pleased that my cloak of Kirtley authority had finally brought them in line.

"We are excited about tomorrow, Miss McClure," said Alice Bell Johnston, the plump and bespectacled girl from the parlor. The plainest of the three Bells, she'd set herself apart from the others as the class busybody.

"Tomorrow? What happens tomorrow?" I saw Fannie Bell smile slyly at Lelia and pounced on her. "Fannie? Will you tell me what is so wonderful about tomorrow, aside from the fact that there are no classes?"

"On Saturdays we are allowed to go into town, Miss McClure."

"But only if we have no demerits!" cried Alice. "So we are trying to be especially good today." She bit her lip when Fannie frowned at her.

"What does one do in town?" I asked.

"Oh, there's so much to see at the stores," Alice gushed. "New fabrics and trimmings, new hats and stockings."

"And the nicest treats," said Lelia, her pretty face widened by a grin.

"Cookies and ice cream—"

"Or salted peanuts!"

My stomach growled.

"And don't forget the boys!" Fannie Bell batted her eyelashes. "That's the best treat of all."

"I'm sure *you're* keen to see Eli Sevenstar," said Alice.

Fannie yawned dramatically. "Oh, I've moved on to better things."

"Moved on?" Alice frowned. "Why didn't *I* know about this?"

"Who is Eli Sevenstar?" I was so taken by the talk of treats and boys that I'd leaned against the desk and let them prattle on. At my question, however, the whispers and giggles immediately ceased as each girl faced forward to stare at me. My cheeks flamed. A *teacher* never cared about boys! I stood straight and clapped my hands, as Miss Kirtley was wont to do. "All right! Enough of this mooning about. Set aside your fancies so we can get on with our lesson."

All at once, the enthusiasm drained out of the room. Shoulders slumped, the girls bent to their books. But the thought of town must have lingered in their minds, because they gave me no cause to issue any demerits.

That night the tapping started up again. I checked the windows and even peered behind the chiffonier, but I was none the wiser for having done so. To settle my thumping heart, I told myself some creature had nested within the wall between the chiffonier and window. And that seemed sensible in theory, but why would the creature *tap*? Mice scurried and scratched— as far as I knew they did not sling tiny hammers when building their nests. The noise kept me awake until the early hours, when finally I fell into a restless sleep full of dreams about my frowning papa, who would not meet my eyes nor answer my pleas.

I went to Chapel the next morning weighed down by fatigue and foreboding.

After announcing academic assignments and domestic chores for the upcoming week, Miss Crenshaw dismissed the students and called the teachers forward. It was time to dole out the first week's wages. Maybe it was exhaustion taking its toll, but I nearly wept when I beheld those banknotes. I clutched them lovingly, fighting the urge to bring them to my lips and breathe in their scent. Wild thoughts of extravagant purchases crowded my brain.

But when I remembered my dream of Papa, I sobered quickly. I knew what must be done.

"Miss Crenshaw, I wish to accompany the girls to town today."

"It will be a large group," she replied with a nod. "I might have called on you anyway, but it's always good to have chaperones who are willing rather than resentful."

After the midday meal, I returned to my room to prepare for the visit to town. I looked at my plain shirtwaist and skirt with despair. There was nothing to be done about them. So I took down my hair and brushed it until it crackled, taking more than the usual amount of time to carefully smooth and pin each strand into place. I pinched my cheeks and bit my lips until they turned pinker. My gaze lingered on Angeline's cape for a moment before I shook my head and folded it away. It was too warm to wear such a thing, and I did not feel worthy of it anyway. So I did my best to plump up my hat before pinning it securely to my head.

My scalp aching, I sat down at the desk and composed a short letter. Without reading it over, I folded the paper and sealed it in an envelope, then made my way downstairs.

The girls were clustered into groups in the corridor and vestibule, chattering with excitement. My heart sank to see them so splendidly dressed, their crisp blouses and dark skirts replaced by bright gingham and calico, their hats adorned with flowers and ribbons. Miss Crenshaw walked among them with her hand in the air, and they gradually quieted. Then she began to arrange them into groups and assign chaperones.

As luck would have it, I was assigned to the Bells—Fannie,

Lelia, and Alice Bell Johnston. The three girls roomed together and were, in fact, cousins. Alice's kinship to Fannie was not so near as Lelia's, however, and the two closer cousins seemed inclined to remind Alice of that from time to time. At that moment, Fannie and Lelia had their heads together as each exclaimed over the other's handsome dress. Alice stood a little apart, reading a small book and pretending not to notice the snub.

As I approached them, Fannie turned to me and smiled.

"How nice that you will be with us today, Miss McClure!"

I should have been disdainful of her snobbery toward Alice, but deep down her words warmed me. I'd never been a fashionable or popular girl, but I'd known plain teachers who were considered favorites among their students. If the Bells were going to be friendly, this might be a good day after all.

"Thank you, Fannie," I said primly.

"You must spend some time in the shops," she continued. "You'll surely want to see all the new clothing available at Foster's store. He has ready-made items, you know."

I blushed. Easy enough for her to stand before me in her finely tailored dress and tease me about my cheap shirtwaist and skirt. I turned away and pretended to glance about the room as we waited for Miss Crenshaw to finish assigning the chaperones. Lucy Sharp stood by the staircase, looking uncomfortable in a plain cotton dress and straw hat.

"Miss Sharp!"

She looked up at my call, her eyes wide.

I turned back to make sure Fannie was watching. "Come join our group, Lucy."

Lucy blinked and did not move. Was she waiting for Fannie's permission?

"We didn't invite *her*," spat Fannie.

"I'm inviting her now," I said, waving Lucy toward us. She kept her head down as she stepped our way, no doubt avoiding the sight of Fannie's mouth pursed in disdain.

And so our group bristled with resentment as we made our way down the boardwalk, but faces brightened as we neared the town. The main street, a long stretch of packed dirt, bustled with activity. Harnesses jangled and wheels creaked as wagons passed. Men lifted their hats and women paused in their chatter to wave as we walked by. The cloudless blue of the sky seemed to stretch on forever, and for once the wretched wind had calmed to a pleasant breeze. I would have been quite cheerful if only I could have loosened the pins that held my hat to my head.

We first visited Foster's store so that Fannie and Lelia could study the new selection of lace and kid gloves. Apparently, their tailor-made snobbery could not withstand the lure of fine machine stitching. Alice browsed the stationery and pen selection, a distracted smile on her face as she touched the elegant bundles of paper. Lucy and I walked about and glanced at the wares from a distance, neither of us stopping to pick up an item. Clearly, neither of us was much accustomed to making purchases. I had money now, and would get more, but most of it was to be saved. The remainder was guilt money. I clutched my purse tightly, feeling the letter crinkle within.

I followed the girls into more shops until finally we met with a more intriguing distraction.

"Look, there's Larkin," said Fannie, changing course and stepping up her pace toward the opposite side of the street. I followed close behind, mindful of my chaperone duties.

"And he's with Eli," said Lelia with a knowing smile.

Lucy was at my side, frowning as the girls greeted the two young men.

One of them looked very familiar. My heart lurched, threatening to fall straight through to my stomach. Was it . . . ? Yes. The very one who'd sat across from me on the train and caught me staring. I looked down, feeling my cheeks grow hot.

"Sister!" The other young man kissed Fannie on the cheek. Curiosity getting the better of me, I looked up to see Fannie's brother. He was tall like his sister, with the same green eyes and flawless skin. His hair was a little darker, but otherwise, he could have been her twin. Like her, he was fashionably dressed, his checked jacket matching his vest and his striped trousers fitting snugly.

With a glance at Lelia, Fannie whispered to the boys. Larkin laughed, and the four of them stepped a few paces away. Shut out of their circle, Alice stood staring for a moment. Then she moved closer to Lucy, her mouth drooping with disappointment.

"Is Larkin Bell twin to Fannie?" I asked, not caring that I sounded like a gossiping schoolgirl. Hadn't I been one only two weeks prior?

"He is older," said Alice, her eyes glittering behind the spectacles as she looked his way. "By almost two years. But he doesn't seem eager to graduate." She glanced at me. "He's smart enough, Miss McClure. I once heard him say he's not ready to travel far away to college. But I've also heard that his father threatens to work him as a field hand if he doesn't graduate this year."

"And the other one?" I couldn't help myself. "He is Cherokee as well?"

Alice nodded. "His name is Eli Sevenstar, and everyone knows he has a pash for Fannie." She eyed me. "That means he's fond of her—you know, as in *passion*."

"Oh my," I murmured, knowing full well what a pash was and hating to think the young man would have such poor taste. "Is *he* an idler too?"

"He likes his fun," said Alice, "but he's a more serious student than Larkin. Eli plans to go to law school."

I chuckled. "An Indian in law school?"

Both girls frowned at me so fiercely that I stuttered an apology.

At that moment, Eli Sevenstar looked our way. Was it my imagination, or did his eyes seem to brighten when they settled on me? Perhaps the expression was one of amusement. He'd recognized me and was thinking how best to tease. My face grew hot once more.

"Alice and Lucy," he called out, "why are you standing back? Bring your new friend forward and introduce us."

He thought I was a student. Well, why wouldn't he?

"She's not our friend, Eli," simpered Fannie. "She's our new teacher."

Eli laughed. "Don't tease me. I knew her at once for a student."

Fannie turned to me and gloated. "I *said* you seemed young for a teacher, didn't I, Miss McClure?"

"She's right, Eli," said Alice. She looked at me a little nervously. "Miss McClure, please allow me to introduce you to Mr. Eli Sevenstar of Sallisaw."

Eli stood still for a moment, his expression now sober. Then he reached out to take my hand. "I'm pleased to make your acquaintance, Miss McClure." His grasp was confident, but his eyes were still puzzled.

"Pleased to meet you," I mumbled awkwardly.

"Miss McClure was at the Columbia Athenaeum," said Alice.

"You're from Tennessee, then?" he asked.

I nodded and then checked myself. "My schooling was in Tennessee, but my family lives in Van Buren, Arkansas."

Please don't say anything about the train. Please, please, please.

He started to speak, then bit his lip. "Well," he said finally, "the Cherokee Nation welcomes you, miss. I hope you are settling in at the seminary."

"Are we going to stand here jabbering all day," demanded Larkin Bell, "or are we going to get some ice cream and sit in the shade? It's damned hot in the sun." He glanced at me and pretended to look embarrassed. "Pardon my language, Miss McClure." He offered one arm to Lelia and the other to Alice, who squealed happily, and off they went. With one last glance back at me, Eli took Fannie by the arm, leaving Lucy and me to trail behind.

I could not keep my eyes off the back of Eli's head. I tried to look away, but he talked so animatedly with Fannie, and she responded with vivacity. So much for having "moved on." Their flirtation was mesmerizing . . . and somewhat sickening. I tossed my head. Why did I care about a Cherokee boy?

I knew why. He was more gentlemanly than any boy who'd ever tried to court me in Columbia. And he'd seemed pleased to see me. Surely his eyes had brightened when he recognized me. But now I was no longer a girl to him. I was a teacher. A spinster in service. A frump.

The young men purchased treats for the girls from the ice cream saloon. Nothing was offered to me. My purpose was merely to hover at the edge of their party like prissy Miss Kirtley, ready to shake my finger at any pair who dared sit too close or speak too intimately. I followed them to a large and handsome brick structure—the sign told me it was the capitol building—bordered by a grassy lawn shaded by trees. As if long accustomed to this routine, the cousins sat together under a tree, arranging their skirts carefully, while the young men sat a cautious distance away. Lucy stood behind the girls, arms crossed at her chest. I leaned against a nearby tree, wondering if I should fly up to a branch to perch over them, vulture-like. Instead, I sighed, prepared to be thoroughly bored.

"We had a run-in with the ghost last week," said Fannie cheerfully, as if speaking of a friendly encounter on the street.

"Fannie!" gasped Lelia, her eyes darting toward me.

"Oh, don't get in a tizzy, Lelia," said Fannie. "*She* won't say anything. After all, she *lives* with it."

Eli looked toward me, his eyebrows raised in alarm. "What are you talking about, Fannie?"

"Miss Crenshaw gave her Ella's room," said Alice, pouncing

on the opportunity to join the conversation. "None of the girls would stay there. Isn't that right, Lucy?"

Lucy merely frowned in response.

"How did Ella drown?" I asked abruptly.

There was a pause as they glanced at each other.

"That is," I continued awkwardly, "if I'm to stay in her room, I should be privy to the details."

"No one really knows," said Larkin finally. "Her body washed up on the bank of the river south of town."

"It was an accident," Eli said, fiddling with his hat.

Alice tilted her head thoughtfully. "You know what people say, Eli Sevenstar."

He set the hat down and fixed her with a hard stare. "About what?"

"About Cale."

Larkin frowned. "That's all nonsense. Cale loved Ella."

Alice held up a finger. "But they'd been at odds before she died."

"He was a wild boy," said Fannie with a sniff. "Hardly civilized at all. I'm sure he wouldn't have thought twice about holding Ella under the water when he caught her looking elsewhere."

Larkin's eyes widened. "He had a temper, but Cale never would have hurt her."

"Then why," asked Alice, "did he leave the same night she died?"

"Maybe because Ella drove him mad with her flirting and moodiness?" Eli's voice was harsh.

"Ella was not a flirt!" Lucy spoke for the first time, her eyes flashing. "She loved to have fun, and Cale couldn't bear her liking anyone's company but his own."

Fannie stared at Eli, one eyebrow arched. "How interesting to hear you condemn Ella as a flirt when you were in love with her yourself at one time."

At those words, each head snapped toward Eli, including my own. His jaw tightened. Then he took a breath and looked directly at Fannie.

"I won't deny that," he said. "The same was true for every boy at the male seminary. What does that have to do with anything, Miss Bell?"

I cleared my throat, suddenly eager to break their locked gaze. "What if it wasn't murder? Could it not also be that she . . . killed herself?"

All of them turned to stare at me.

"No," said Lucy flatly. "Ella loved life too much. Cale Hawkins had something to do with her death, and he should be punished for it."

"Cale tried to *stop* her going to the river," said Larkin, "or at least that's what the telegram said. Right, Eli?"

Eli stared at the ground, his mouth a thin line.

"What telegram was this?" I asked.

Larkin glanced at Eli in expectation, then shook his head at his friend's continued silence. "Eli got a telegram from Cale the day after Ella's body was found." Larkin spoke slowly to me, as though I were addled in the wits. "It said he tried to stop her, he was sorry, and that he was going to Texas and never coming back."

"Yes, but we've never seen this telegram, have we?" Alice turned to Eli. "Why didn't you show us?"

Eli did not raise his head. "I showed it to the sheriff. It was no one else's business."

"When you consider Cale's words," I said, "it sounds like she may have done it deliberately."

"I'll never believe it," hissed Lucy.

"That telegram doesn't prove she threw herself into the river," Larkin said. "Maybe it was an accident and Cale couldn't save her. We'll never know."

The group fell into uncomfortable silence. Fannie glanced back and forth between Eli, who still stared sullenly at the ground, and Lucy Sharp, who seemed near to tears. Which one would Fannie choose to torment? Why didn't someone speak? Remembering why I'd come to town in the first place, I brushed the tree bark from my skirt and cleared my throat again.

"I must post a letter," I said briskly. "As soon as I return, we'll make our way back to the seminary."

"Have you written to your beau, Miss McClure?" Fannie's eyes sparkled with mischief. "You must tell us all about him. Do you have a photograph?"

They all turned to look at me, curiosity written plain on their faces. If anyone had bothered to offer me an ice cream earlier, I would have thrown it at Fannie.

"I've *not* written to a beau," I snapped. "You should mind your own business, Fannie."

The others smirked, but Fannie's mouth tightened in fury. I would surely pay for my words in the classroom on Monday. Why didn't I just lie and say I *did* have a beau?

Drat them all.

I clutched my skirts and stalked away. Once free of them, I calmed myself by taking in the details of my surroundings. Men in suits and hats walked purposefully under the awnings of the finer shops, packages in hand. A lady strolled with a baby carriage, two small children skipping behind her. But in the alleys and doorways of the less genteel stores, I caught glimpses of ragged, darker-skinned men slumped against the walls, their faces drawn with hunger or hopelessness. At the livery stable, negroes sweated over the grooming and harnessing of horses, while their Cherokee boss stood to the side with friends, pausing in his conversation to bark orders.

On the post office steps sat a woman in a faded calico dress. Blue eyes stared at me from beneath the flopping brim of her bonnet. In her arms she held a fair-haired boy who breathed noisily through his mouth. Both were ragged and scrawny. A stab of pity moved me to fumble in my purse for a coin.

The woman blushed. "I ain't taking nothing from an Indian, no matter how fine you and your seminary are."

I gasped. "But I'm not—"

Before I could finish the sentence, the woman stood and carried the boy away. His vacant blue eyes stared at me over her shoulder.

The postal clerk, a sunburned man with bushy whiskers, looked as though he'd rather be anywhere but behind the counter—the sort of fellow who spent his afternoons fishing and his mornings dreaming of poles and bait. He chewed his mustache in annoyance as I once more fumbled with my purse. Finally, I set the envelope on the counter, smoothing out its wrinkles with both hands.

"I'd like to mail this."

He took my coins and counted them, slow and deliberate, into his register. He then plucked a stamp out of a drawer and licked the small square thoroughly before pressing it upon my envelope. Finally, he inked his postmark stamp.

"Oh!" I cried, clutching the envelope. "Will that show where the letter is coming from?"

He narrowed his eyes. "Have you never sent a letter before, miss? Of course it will."

"Could you . . . Would it be possible to leave off the postmark?"

He sucked at his teeth and stared for a long moment. "No, miss."

I thought wildly. "What if . . . you *smudged* it a little, just enough so that it wasn't clear where it came from? I mean, you'd still have stamped it, yes?"

"Now, why would I do that?"

I reached into my purse and drew out a few more coins. "For this, perhaps?" I put them under the envelope and slid the small pile toward him.

He frowned and made a great show of taking offense. Then his eyes narrowed again, and before I knew it, he'd lifted the envelope and swiped the coins into his hand. With a tight smile, he took the rubber stamp and made a very sloppy job of smearing it on the envelope. He raised an eyebrow at me. I nodded.

And that was that.

Mother,

I am well. Please use this money toward hiring help. It was earned by honorable means. I will send more when I can.

Do not attempt to find me. If somehow you do, I will leave this place—a place that is safe and proper for young ladies—and you'll never hear from me again.

Willie

Chapter 5

THAT EVENING AS I PREPARED FOR BED, a rapping on the door startled me. Uncertain whom to expect, I pulled my shawl about my shoulders and smoothed my hair before opening the door.

Miss Crenshaw stood there, her face grim.

"Miss?" I murmured, taken aback by her frown. "Would you like to come in?"

"I need only speak to you for a moment."

Suppressing a shiver, I stepped aside for her to enter.

"Miss McClure," she said after I'd shut the door, "I have learned something that has gravely disappointed me. I found it necessary to come to you immediately and settle this matter."

This is it. My throat constricted. *One week and already my freedom has ended.*

"Yes, Miss Crenshaw?"

"When I asked you to chaperone the students today, I entrusted their safety *and* reputations to you."

The panic I held inside came out in a rush of air. *Everything's all right.* It was all I could do to nod in response.

"And I expected you to stay with them every moment of their time in town."

"They were never left alone, miss."

"Weren't they?" Her eyes were steely. "Miss McClure, one of your students—one who shall not be named—has confessed to me that you did indeed leave the girls alone, and it was *when they were in the company of young gentlemen.*"

"I did no such thing!" I thought back to the day, retracing our movements. "Well, I did leave the girls for a brief time to post a letter. It was only a few minutes, Miss Crenshaw. They hadn't even moved when I returned."

She stared at me for a moment. "Miss McClure, I am at fault for not making something clear about this school. Propriety is of the utmost importance. Do you think Indian girls need not worry about their reputations? They must worry about them even more than white girls! If they are seen alone in the company of young men, they could be ruined by gossip. In turn, the reputation of this school could be damaged beyond repair. The parents of these girls have placed great trust in me to protect their daughters. I shall not allow a teacher to undermine this!"

Every fiber of my being longed to tell her she was being ridiculous, but that would not be playing the part of a teacher. Willie might throw a fit, but Miss McClure must be passive and repentant. So I bowed my head. "Of course not, Miss Crenshaw. It will not happen again."

She did not speak, but her foot tapped softly.

I looked up and widened my eyes in hopes of appearing deeply contrite. "I am so very sorry, miss."

"I accept your apology." Her mouth tightened into a dour smile. "Tomorrow we will have a church service in the chapel. Many of the girls will be there, but some are allowed to attend services in town if they are chaperoned by a teacher. I think it is best that you attend the service here at the school."

"I understand."

"Good night, then."

Once the door had shut behind her, I kicked it . . . gently. I'd left those girls for mere moments! Nothing could have happened in such a brief time. Miss Crenshaw was a silly old crow for squawking over nothing.

And who'd snitched on me? It had to be Fannie. I'd spoken sharply to her more than once, and for all her simpering refinement, she could not accept my reprimands with grace.

She was out to get me now, I was sure of it.

I steeled myself for bad behavior from Fannie in the days that followed, but after flashing me a triumphant look the morning after my chastisement, she turned distracted rather than vengeful. The senior class continued to be a trial, but as long as I played dagger-eyed Miss Kirtley and gave them loads of written work, the days were manageable.

Assigning compositions in class freed me from actually

having to *talk* to the students. The only problem was that written work required marking, and rather than face the fact that I had no idea how to properly evaluate their work, I allowed the papers to pile on my desk. I was in dire need of some spine-bracing advice from Olivia Adair. Unfortunately, she seemed less than inclined to talk to me.

Olivia was polite enough when I met her in the corridors, but she maintained the chilly reserve that began with our disagreement. The other teachers I learned to recognize, to greet in the corridors and exchange pleasantries with, but I did not find them kindred spirits. Their severe hair and spectacles intimidated me, as did their private jests and insiders' knowledge of the school and community. They were free enough with advice but not with friendship. I did not wish to admit my weaknesses to them.

I was alone. It wasn't a new feeling, but that didn't make it easier to endure. I'd never had bosom friends at school, but there had been kind teachers who took an interest in my progress. There'd been servants who thanked me for helping with their work. At the seminary I had no one.

One September night, a storm swept in, and the howling wind and thunder kept me awake for hours. Finally, I dreamed of water and mermaids with dark, streaming hair. Their black eyes were wide and curiously empty, and their hands reached out to me with long, spidery fingers.

I woke to the sound of tapping at the window. It was no mouse in the wall. Flesh prickling, I groped for a match and lit my lamp, cringing as the glass chimney clattered noisily against the base. I stepped quietly to the window and pulled back the curtain. Had the tapping come from outside, or did it originate in the room?

It was impossible to tell, for all I heard was the wind and drumming of rain. I set the lamp down and pulled the bottom window panel upward, gasping as the rain gusted inward and splashed my arms. The night sky was a damp, velvety darkness. I couldn't see a thing, but nevertheless, I *sensed* something. Movement? A rustling? Perhaps a bird had flapped outside the window, tapping with its spiny feet or beak. I felt around for a nest.

At that moment, the sash cord snapped and the window panel came slicing down like a guillotine blade. I jerked my hand back so fast that I slipped on a damp spot and tumbled backward onto my rump. The lamp crashed to the floor next to me, the flame flickering as the oil reserves seeped into the chimney. Quickly, I tipped it upright and blew out the flame. Then I cowered in the darkness, holding my nearly crushed fingers to my mouth and listening to the wild pounding of my heart. Wrapping my arms around my body, I hunched over and waited for the ceiling to crash, the floor to open beneath me . . . or something worse.

But nothing happened. The walls and floorboards held steady. No spectral presence oozed its way through the window glass. No one even bothered to pound on my door to ask what the noise was all about. I took several deep breaths until the thumping in my heart eased.

I had just stood on quivering legs when I heard the scream.

It was followed by a tremendous series of thumps from somewhere nearby. The staircase? My head jerked to the door at the sound of voices raised in excitement and clattering footsteps in the corridor. Feeling faint, I wrapped a shawl around my shoulders and peeked outside.

Girls were coming out of rooms in their nightgowns, holding lamps, their long hair hanging loose or in braids. Most had eyes wide with fear and confusion, though some looked eager for an adventure. I barked at them to return to their rooms, but they chose not to heed me. Apparently, my limited authority dissolved completely after midnight. There seemed nothing to do but follow them to the central staircase, where other girls looked over the railing to the floor below. I thrust myself between two of them and peered down.

It was quite a spectacle, made more gruesome by the flickering light of student lamps. A girl lay sprawled on the landing of the staircase, sobbing loudly. The girls near her seemed frozen by shock, and no one knelt to help. I'd just worked up the courage to go down to her, as a teacher should, when Miss Crenshaw swept past me and thumped down the stairs to kneel by the girl. In the light of her lamp, I could see Fannie Bell's face contorted in pain.

The principal touched the girl's cheek and then raised her lamp. "All students must return to their rooms *immediately*." She looked up the stairs until her eyes found me. "Miss McClure, come here."

I stumbled down the steps toward her, brushing past

students who'd finally been stirred to action by the principal's stern voice. "Miss Crenshaw, I tried to get the students back to their rooms, but they paid me no mind."

She sighed in exasperation. "Your youthful demeanor is a detriment, to be sure. Miss Adair and the others will get them sorted in a moment. I need you for another task. Nurse Gott is in town tonight and must be fetched to stay the night with Miss Bell." She peered at Fannie. "I suppose we must also wake Dr. Stewart in case she's suffered a broken bone."

In the light of the lamp, I saw Fannie's eyes flutter open.

"Oh, please!" she gasped. "I need the doctor."

I clutched at my shawl. "You want *me* to fetch them? I don't know where they live!"

She handed me her lamp. "Take this and find Jimmy—he'll accompany you into town and point you in the direction of Mrs. Gott's house. He'll have to go to the other side of town to fetch the doctor. Sending the both of you will save time."

I slunk away to find Jimmy in his tiny room near the kitchen. I expected him to be asleep, but instead, he sat up on the bed, his ebony face shining with perspiration in the light of my lamp. The poor fellow slept in his work clothes, and I wondered if this was his choice or if Miss Crenshaw demanded it for the sake of propriety.

"Jimmy?"

He blinked at the sound of my voice. "Trouble, miss?"

"There's been an accident. We must fetch Nurse Gott and the doctor."

He quickly laced his boots and, after lighting his own lantern, beckoned me to follow him through the dining hall to the side door. Fortunately, the rain had calmed to a light mist, but I still slipped and lurched on the wet grass as I scrambled to keep up with Jimmy. He stopped short as we neared the boardwalk.

"Do you feel that?" he whispered.

I looked around. "What?"

"Somethin' strange out here."

We were standing under my window. My scalp prickled. "What do you mean?"

"Can't say exactly, but I've felt it before and I don't like it." He shook his head. "I can almost smell it."

I sniffed the air, smelling only the rain-soaked grass and earth. "What does *it* smell like?"

He closed his eyes. "Death."

"Let's keep moving," I hissed.

Jimmy held his tongue as we walked down the hill toward the main street. I knew he was a superstitious fool, but I couldn't help looking back every few steps. Was that a footfall behind me? A shadow to my left? Finally, I fixed my eyes upon Jimmy's feet as we walked, and that seemed to help.

By the time we reached Downing Street, my flesh had ceased its crawling and I felt like an idiot for allowing Jimmy to spook me. He paused to point me toward a row of small houses several yards off the main street.

"One with the red door is the Gott house. After you fetch her, go on up to the school. Tell Miss Crenshaw I'm on my way with the doc."

I had to pound on the door before someone finally opened it. A sturdy, dark-skinned Cherokee woman in her nightgown and shawl raised her eyebrow but said nothing. I'd only seen Mrs. Gott a few times and wasn't sure she recognized me.

"I've come from the seminary, Mrs. Gott. A student is hurt, and Miss Crenshaw needs you tonight."

She stared at me for a moment, her face stern. "Wait here and let me put on some proper clothes." She shut the door then, leaving me standing alone on her front step.

"Frightful woman," I murmured, but only a few minutes passed before the door opened again and she emerged, fully dressed and carrying a small bag.

"Doctor coming too?" she asked.

I nodded and we were on our way. Like Lucy Sharp, the woman was blunt in her manner and not given to polite conversation. But her steadiness braced me as we walked back to the seminary.

We found Fannie still lying on the staircase landing, moaning now rather than weeping. Miss Crenshaw sat near her, stroking her temple. Mrs. Gott helped the principal to her feet and knelt by the girl. She put her hands on Fannie's face, shoulders, and arms, not flinching a whit as the girl cried in pain.

"She's dislocated her shoulder," Mrs. Gott pronounced.

"Can we move her?" Miss Crenshaw lifted the lamp to shine it in Fannie's face. The girl winced.

The Cherokee woman shook her head. "We should wait for the doctor to set it first."

Jimmy arrived with Dr. Stewart moments later. The doctor was tall, fair-haired, and much younger than I would have expected. He paled visibly upon first seeing Fannie's crumpled form. Miss Crenshaw smiled with relief to see him, and Fannie stared as though he were an angel even as he applied his hands to the painful dislocation.

"I need to put the shoulder back in the socket," he said. "Once I've wrapped it, we can take her up to the third floor."

"Need she go to the infirmary, Dr. Stewart?" Mrs. Gott's voice rumbled with sleepy irritation. "She got a whole bed to herself."

"But she'll need privacy for proper rest," said the doctor. "We don't want her woken during the night."

I had to look away as he shoved at her shoulder. Fannie's cries were almost as piercing as before, but as soon as the shoulder was in its proper place, the shrill noise subsided into whimpering.

"The water," she gasped. "The water was everywhere."

"What is she talking about?" asked Miss Crenshaw.

"Something about water," said Dr. Stewart.

"From the washbasins!" cried Fannie, clutching at the doctor's arm. "The water was rushing toward me. It's Ella's doing!" Her whimpers turned to sobs once more.

The doctor stared at her for a moment before turning back to Miss Crenshaw. "She should be carried upstairs now. I'll give her something for the pain once she's in the infirmary."

"I'll check the water closets," said Miss Crenshaw briskly. "Miss McClure, go with the doctor and give Nurse Gott any assistance she requires. I sent Miss Adair ahead to prepare a bed. I'll follow you shortly."

•　•　•

Once Dr. Stewart had departed and Fannie was settled in the infirmary bed with her arm in a sling, Miss Crenshaw pressed her to tell us what caused her fall.

Fannie frowned at us, swallowing hard before speaking. "I heard the sound of water running, almost as though it were gushing—so much noise that I could not go back to sleep. Alice and Lelia slept on, so I got out of bed and checked the second-floor lavatory. But the sound was coming from below."

"Why didn't you come for me?" Miss Crenshaw's eyes glittered angrily.

"Everyone was asleep. I couldn't think properly. I just knew it was up to me to turn off the water before the first floor flooded. So I went downstairs. When I walked into the water closet, all the washbasin faucets were gushing, the water flooding the edges and rising like a wave on the floor." She paused, closing her eyes with a shudder.

"And then?" asked Olivia gently.

Fannie sighed. "The wave was coming toward me, growing higher, so I ran for the staircase. I had to reach higher ground. The water was coming for *me*." Her voice failed her for a moment, and as she paused to take a breath, we all leaned in a little closer. "As I reached the stairs above the landing," she continued, "I saw the water was still rising—I was so afraid I couldn't outrun it—and that's when I slipped and fell."

Everyone was silent. Miss Crenshaw stared at the wall, frowning. I risked a glance at Olivia and saw her brow was furrowed. Fannie looked at all our faces and turned haughty, speaking in a thunderous voice.

"You don't *believe* me?"

"Child," said Miss Crenshaw, her eyes once more on Fannie, "there was a leaking faucet, but no sign of flooding in the downstairs water closets. The rain outside worked its way into your imagination, for I'm certain you were dreaming. Sleepwalking, perhaps. We once had a student fall out of a window for the same reason. Her injuries were far worse than yours."

"But I was wide awake," growled Fannie. "It was the ghost, Miss Crenshaw—Ella's ghost was coming after me. The water smelled so dank. It was muddy and dark, like the river. It was Ella!"

"There is no ghost, Fannie." The principal's voice was cold. "You were sleepwalking and dreaming at the same time. You must say nothing of this to the other girls."

Fannie shook her head obstinately.

"Do you hear me, girl?"

"Yes, miss," she gasped.

"All right, then. Let's return to our beds. The morning will be here all too soon."

Once we'd bid Miss Crenshaw good night, Olivia and I stood awkwardly in the corridor together. She did not meet my gaze, but neither did she turn away toward her room. I made a decision.

"Olivia?"

She flinched. "I should get to bed."

"Oh, not yet. Come to my room before Crenshaw catches us whispering in the halls again."

"If you wish," she said after a moment.

I opened my door and gestured for her to step through. She seemed lost in thought as she placed her lamp on the desk and settled into my wooden chair. I sat on the bed across from her, inwardly rehearsing what to say.

"Olivia," I finally said, "I know you were offended that day during our walk. You've barely said a word to me since."

She looked thoughtful. "I'm certain it was disappointment rather than anger."

"Disappointment that I don't believe in ghosts? That's what kept you from speaking to me?"

"No, it's . . ." She paused, biting her lip. "Prior to your arrival, I was the youngest teacher here. In fact, the other teachers knew me first as a student. Two years have passed, and they still treat me like a student." She broke off, staring at the hands clasped in her lap. When she finally continued, her words came slowly. "I don't have a true friend at this school. I suppose I latched on to you, thinking *you* could be that friend. So when you laughed at my beliefs, it wounded me more than it should have."

I blushed. "Oh dear. Mama used to say I was too brash, just like my papa. It's an unfortunate fault, for it's left me terribly lonely. I should have apologized long ago and brought an end to the coolness between us. But I've been overwhelmed." I gathered the fabric of my nightgown and pleated it nervously. "I'm . . . not a very good teacher."

"You're still settling in," she said softly. "It gets easier in time. And it helps to have a friend listen to your woes."

I smiled, much lighter in spirits. We fell into a comfortable silence for a moment, but then her brow furrowed.

"Are you worrying about Fannie?" I asked.

"Well, I am concerned for the poor girl. Very concerned." She paused, her cheeks flushing pink. "But just then I was thinking of Dr. Stewart. The sight of him always makes me heartsore."

"You find him handsome?" I thought of him kneeling over Fannie's body. "I suppose he is, with that fair, wavy hair. He's tall too . . . but rather thin."

"Oh, Willie! Of course he's handsome, but seeing him makes me sad. He was married to Fannie's older sister, you know. He's from Illinois, and he came to Tahlequah straight from medical school as temporary replacement for poor old Dr. Ross. But he gladly settled into the community when he married Sarah. She was so beautiful and good, and they were very much in love."

"She *was* beautiful?"

"Sarah died of cholera. And Dr. Stewart has grieved for so long. He's grown quite thin and pale with his sadness."

There was nothing like a tragedy to make a man more interesting. "My lord hath endured a grief," I murmured.

"What?"

"*Pericles,* act five. Oh, never mind." I rubbed my eyes, stifling a yawn. "That was quite a story Fannie cooked up, wasn't it?"

Olivia looked thoughtful. "I was a student when that girl—the one Miss Crenshaw mentioned—fell out the window. It was terrible. Her injuries *were* more severe than Fannie's. And it's true she was sleepwalking. But she did not remember anything about the accident. She did not remember having a dream, nor did she remember leaving her bed and walking toward the window."

"What are you saying?"

"I don't believe Fannie was sleepwalking. Laugh all you like," she said with a gleam in her eye, "but I think her visions came from the spirit world."

Chapter 6

OVER THE NEXT SEVERAL DAYS, the students dragged themselves into the classroom with dark circles under their eyes. They struggled to concentrate during recitations. The seniors were grim and silent, but the younger students confided that their sleep was disturbed by bad dreams and strange noises.

"I hear a thumping sound, Miss McClure. It seems to come from below," said one girl in the sophomore class. A few others nodded.

"For me, it's whispering. It wakes me up and then fades to silence," said another. "I thought I was going mad until Sally said she heard it too."

"I've heard a rapping sound almost every night since Fannie fell."

"Running water! I hear it, and that's what Fannie Bell heard."

So much for Fannie keeping mum.

I was still skeptical. But it was true that the tapping at my window had grown more urgent since Fannie's accident. It always waited until I was nearly asleep before starting up, only to stop again when I was fully awake. I'd taken to stuffing my ears with cotton, but it only dulled the sound.

The seniors would not speak of strange noises and sleepless nights. They merely looked stricken. In August they'd gasped and giggled when Fannie taunted me about a ghost; now they seemed shaken to the core by her violent accident. Fannie was back in class, her arm still in its sling, but her once sparkling eyes were dull with fatigue.

I didn't know what to make of it all. In truth, the dread of facing my classes each day far outweighed any concerns I might have over spooks haunting the night.

After two days of the seniors falling asleep over their compositions, I rose from my desk and asked them to open their copies of *Studies in English Literature* and find Coleridge's poem entitled "Love." If anything could distract them, surely such a subject would. But no one volunteered to read. Finally, I called on Alice. She sighed before placing her finger on the text and reading.

> All thoughts, all passions, all delights,
> Whatever stirs this mortal frame,
> All are but ministers of Love,
> And feed his sacred flame.

Her voice was flat. Several students yawned.

"Stop there, please." I cleared my throat. "Can, um, anyone

point out an example of personification in these first four lines?"

The question was met with silence. Hot with frustration, I scanned the questions in the footnotes for more inspiration.

"Perhaps someone can explain . . . how Coleridge uses the term *ministers*?"

Alice shifted uncomfortably in her seat. A few girls seemed to be straining for something to say, but the others stared blankly.

"For God's sake," I blurted, "someone in this room must have an answer to one of these questions!"

The girls gasped in unison at my blasphemy, each with eyes widened in horror. Only Fannie smiled. How I wished to dissolve into the floor! Or, better yet, disappear in a puff of smoke. I closed my eyes and willed myself to vanish. When I opened them again, the girls still stared. So I straightened my spine and tried again.

"*Anyone* have a thought to share?" I asked meekly.

Fannie raised her hand. I could have kissed her, so profound was my relief.

"Yes, Fannie?"

"Miss McClure, have you marked our compositions yet?"

I heard a scream. Did it come out of my mouth? No, it was only in my head. At that moment, I could have stormed out of the room, walked through the front door, and put my back to the seminary forever. Why work with such weak-minded fools, day in and day out? Why cope with their fears of ghosts and ghouls? For that matter, why would anyone ever dream of becoming a teacher? I finally understood why my old teachers were such lifeless automatons. It was the only way to cope with unrelenting indifference.

It would have felt like heaven to walk away from it all. Why didn't I?

$450 per annum was why.

I took a deep breath and stared once more at the textbook. I thought of Papa sitting in his chair, reading Shakespeare and laughing to himself. More than once he'd said to me, "Poets may say differently, but I believe the words never soak into your bones until you've performed them."

I smiled.

"Let's try something different," I announced, adopting a sweetly authoritative tone. "Alice, you will continue to read, but you must stand here by my desk." The girl hesitated. "Come on up here—I'm not going to bite you. Now," I said to the rest of the class, "we are going to act out this poem. Every-one in this room will play a part."

Many of the girls looked up. A few eyes brightened, while others rolled. My smile did not falter.

"I need someone to play the role of Love."

There was a pause as the girls looked at each other. Some of them simpered. My heart thudded in my chest, and yet I smiled on. Finally, Lelia raised her hand.

"I will!"

I silently blessed the girl. "Good for you, Lelia! Come up here—bring your book. Now I need someone to play an armed knight."

Lucy raised her hand. After that, more hands shot in the

air, and the girls began to grin and whisper. I cast the roles of the Lady of the Land and the murderous band that threatened her. I cast the role of the poem's speaker. That left only Fannie.

I looked hard at her, and she stared back, her eyes defiant. I longed to cast her as the "wild and hoary ruin." That would teach her to ask about compositions I'd put off marking for too long. But when I glanced at her arm in its sling, thought of her lying in pain upon the landing, I swallowed my resentment and smiled once more.

"Fannie, would you be so kind as to play Genevieve, the poet's lady love?"

She narrowed her eyes. For a moment, I thought she might decline simply to vex me. But, as I'd hoped, her vanity won out and her frown softened into a smug smile.

"Yes, Miss McClure."

Their performance was a disaster, riddled with false starts, missed cues, and laughter in all the wrong places. But the lively spirit in the room lifted us. No one thought of drowned girls, ghosts, or accidents in the dark of night. We were all caught up in the moment, living the poem instead of merely hearing it. Their indifference had vanished.

Afterward, when everyone was seated again, they shared their opinions on the poem. Good ones at that, and well expressed. Once they'd enacted the poem, lived within it, they also seemed to have something to say about it.

And I learned a very interesting thing about Fannie—a little tidbit to tuck away for later use. It was difficult to accept, but I had to admit Fannie was a natural actress.

• • •

That Friday night I went to bed early. It seemed I'd had my eyes closed only for a second when I woke to the faint strumming of a guitar. Were ghosts musical? I shook my head, dismissing it as another queer dream, but the whispers and squeals in the corridor brought me upright. Scrambling out of bed, I pulled my shawl around my shoulders before going out to see what new horror had upset the students.

But it wasn't fear on the faces of the girls. They smiled and giggled as they made their way to the wide windows in the second-floor landing. Olivia followed them, holding a lamp to light the way. She must have sensed my confusion as she drew close, for she smiled knowingly.

"Don't worry, Willie. It's only the boys from the male seminary come to serenade us."

"But won't Miss Crenshaw disapprove?"

"As long as the girls keep well covered and don't hang out the windows, she doesn't mind. After all, there is quite a distance between them and the young men."

The girls had already opened the windows and filled every available spot for viewing the scene below. It was impossible to see over them. So I stood and listened as the guitar strumming grew louder and the singing began. The young men's voices were enthusiastic if not particularly sweet, and the girls laughed and clapped their appreciation.

"I have to see this," I murmured to Olivia. "I'll just dash to my room for a moment."

She nodded. "It's quite a sight."

Once in my room, I pulled the curtain back and opened the window, propping a ruler under it to keep the heavy panel from crashing down again. There were seven boys lined up below, and the ones who did not hold guitars held lanterns. I searched the faces, ignoring the voice in my head warning me to keep out of sight. I recognized Larkin Bell holding a lantern, and, yes, there was Eli Sevenstar, strumming his guitar and singing at the top of his lungs. He was gazing intently at the girls looking through the central windows, and I turned to see that they were, perhaps, hanging a bit too far out the windows. At least they were properly wrapped in shawls. I would mention something to Olivia when I returned to the landing.

I looked down once more and allowed myself to wish, for a moment, that I were a student at the seminary and could smile and flirt with those handsome young men. Truly, there was only one with whom I wished to flirt.

As if hearing my thoughts, Eli Sevenstar turned to look in my direction. And, to my fanciful mind, it seemed he sang to me. He looked up at my window for so long—did he truly see me there? Or did he look because it was once Ella's room? Sobered by that thought, I closed my window and withdrew.

I sat on my bed for a moment, trying to calm the pounding in my heart. How could I be such a fool? He was a *student.* Now every time I saw him, my heart would thud and my face would flush. Surely the girls would see right through it and despise me all the more. And Eli himself would smirk to know that a poor and lonely teacher, a lady doomed to eternal spinsterhood, had a pash for him.

I should have returned to the landing but instead reclined upon the bed with a groan. I may have thrashed about a bit too.

A thumping noise stilled me. I glanced at the window. Nothing but the strains of guitar music and singing could be heard from outside. And then the thumping sounded again, followed by creaking and shuffling.

It came from above—the third floor.

The faint melodies of guitars and voices faded as I crept up the east staircase. I'd never heard noises above me before, and though I knew it must be the primaries, my heart skipped a few beats as I neared the third-floor landing. I had no idea who resided in the turret room above me.

I stepped softly from the landing into the corridor.

Several girls stood outside the doorway of the turret room, from which the light of more than one lamp glowed. Their faces were transfixed. I rudely pushed my way through so that I could see into the room.

Three lamps were lit on a table by the windows, which were opened wide to let in the music from below. In front of the lamps, four barefoot girls moved about the room, winding around each other in a stately dance. They took turns making elegant leaps that revealed their smooth brown legs. Their black hair gleamed in the flickering lamplight as it fell into their faces. I stood staring with the others, mesmerized by their slim, swaying bodies, until the song came to an end.

The girls looked up—and froze in place when they saw me.

"We're not doing nothing wrong, miss," said one. "We just like to dance when the boys come to sing."

"I heard thumping from below," I said. "I only wanted to know what it was."

"Did you think it was the ghost, miss?" asked a girl nearer to me.

"Well, no . . ."

"You'll not find ghosts up here," said the first girl. "We never did nothing to Ella 'cause she was one of us. She'd never haunt us, miss." The child looked down, no longer bold. "We don't want demerits. Please don't wake Miss Thompson."

Though I hardly knew her, Lucinda Thompson was widely understood to be very strict. Her room must have been at the far end of the east wing if she'd not already been woken by the music below. I had no desire to wake her. I did wish, however, to know more about these primaries who danced by lamplight. More than anything I wished they'd go on dancing, but the music had stopped.

I looked to the dancer who'd first spoken. "What is your name?"

"It's Mae, miss."

"Can I visit again sometime?"

Mae shrugged and the rest looked blank, but no one frowned or shook her head.

"Good night, then," I said quietly, and turned to leave them.

The older girls were returning to their rooms as I made my way back down to the second floor. They kept their backs to me, so wrapped up in sighs and laughter they did not think to look behind them. I waited until they'd closed their doors before stepping into the corridor toward my own.

Once in my room, I went to the window. The boys had gone and all was dark outside. I drew the curtains again and quickly settled into bed. But I kept my lamp lit long into the night, almost wishing to hear the tap at my window so I would be forced to think of anything other than Eli Sevenstar.

Chapter 7

FOR SATURDAY'S TRIP TO TOWN, I was not assigned to the Bells as chaperone. Instead, I walked with a group of freshmen excited to be making their first outing of the term. These girls were not daughters of wealthy merchants like Fannie or Lelia. They were full-bloods from the country who'd come to the seminary through the charity of the Cherokee Nation. Like Mae and her friends, they'd started their schooling later than the town girls, and thus had been grouped with the more traditional primaries. For two years they'd watched from the third-floor windows as other girls their age made the trip to town. Now that they were freshmen—at the ripe old age of sixteen—they finally were allowed to make the Saturday pilgrimage themselves.

The day was warm, but a mild breeze cooled our faces without lifting the dust from the streets. Walking with these girls put me at ease. They were close to my age, after all, and seemed anything but pretentious in their simple dresses and bonnets. Their good humor arose from companionship and a sense of adventure. I looked forward to the trip, relieved that the day would not be spent following self-absorbed young ladies. Even more so, I looked forward to an outing free of insults and condescension.

Or so I thought.

On our way to Foster's store, we saw the Bells and Eli Sevenstar. I averted my gaze, certain that even from that distance Eli could hear my blood pounding. The freshmen whispered their excitement, and I could scarcely blame them. Girls' schools were much like nunneries, after all. What could be more exciting than to break free and gaze upon handsome young men such as Larkin Bell and Eli Sevenstar?

"Larkin Bell is my distant cousin," said one girl. "Perhaps we should wish him good day?"

Her friend smiled broadly. "I think that would only be polite."

But when Larkin noticed our approach, his lip curled. He muttered something to his cousins, who giggled behind their hands. He glanced our way once more and then *turned his back to us*.

My face flushed hot with indignation—not for myself but for the students. How could Larkin be so ill mannered? Was it because they were charity students? Or did he snub all full-bloods? We stopped in our tracks, momentarily frozen. The girls' eyes flashed with anger, but they said nothing. I knew I should speak to Larkin, chastise him somehow, but . . . I was as intimidated as the students.

At that moment, Eli broke away from the group and walked toward us, chin in the air and a lazy smile on his face. "Good afternoon, ladies," he said, tipping his hat. "Shall we walk together?"

The girls greeted him with wide smiles, their cheeks flaming to pink. I could have fainted with relief . . . and gratitude.

Eli gestured toward the Bells, who were eyeing us with furrowed brows. "All they can talk about is ghosts. I've never seen Lelia so rattled, and even Fannie is flustered, though her arm is healing fine. Larkin gets a thrill from such stories, but I'd rather talk of pleasanter things." He looked down at me. "Did you enjoy our serenade, Miss McClure?"

He was smiling, but his eyes were unreadable. Was he teasing me? Or . . . *flirting*? He *had* been gazing up at my window that night. I could almost believe he fancied me. My heart soared and then sank again almost at once, falling to my stomach with a sickening thud. Did he think it amusing to play with the affections of a young teacher?

I looked away.

He strolled casually next to me, and though our shoulders were not touching, I could feel the warmth of his body, could almost imagine his arm circling my waist and my head against his chest. I breathed in his scent—a spicy, woodsy smell that reminded me of autumn nights in front of the fire with Papa. His nearness stoked a flame in my own body, starting at my chest and spreading upward to the very roots of my hair.

Everyone was looking at me. I must have turned beet-red. How much time had passed since he asked the question? What *was* the question?

Such a fool.

"Oh! Well . . . your performance was quite a spectacle, Mr. Sevenstar. The girls enjoyed it immensely." My voice squeaked oddly—sounding much like prim Miss Kirtley.

"I'm glad to hear it," Eli murmured with a small frown.

We walked in silence. The girls stared at him under their long lashes. I could think of nothing to say. I'm sure we all sighed with relief when he finally opened his mouth to speak.

"I must take my leave now, ladies." He glanced at each of the girls, his eyes twinkling. "Hope you enjoy the rest of this fine day." And with another tip of his hat, he turned to rejoin the others.

We were barely a few steps away before the girls began to chitter like chicks in a nest. What a handsome young man! So dashing! Surely he had the loveliest eyes, the softest voice, the manliest shoulders. . . .

"And he's very courteous," said one, her tone thoughtful.

"Not uppity, like some people," said another.

They chatted quite companionably as we walked on, Eli's kind attention having rubbed out the memory of Larkin Bell's snub.

Inwardly, I railed at myself for not steering them away from the Bells in the first place. I'd so looked forward to a day free of their spite, but like an idiot, I let the freshmen walk directly into its path. How could I have been so clumsy?

At the same time, I couldn't help thinking about Eli. He'd matched the Bells' cruelty with kindness—no, it was *gallantry*. Was it for *me*? Even a little? If only I could have joined the girls in their pleasant chatter. If I were a student rather than a teacher, I could have begged their opinion on every word spoken, every glance shared. *Did he seem to notice* me *especially? Was he flirting? Or was he merely being courteous to a teacher?*

Did I make a fool of myself?

But I knew those questions would only continue to echo in my brain, for there was no one to whom I could put them.

The next Friday night, the tapping woke me yet again. For the hundredth time, I went to the window and, for the hundredth time, found nothing there. The tapping would not come when I stood near the window. But I knew it would start again the instant I was comfortably settled in bed.

I thumped the window with my finger. "Why can't you let me sleep?"

There was no response.

I shuffled back to the bed and lay down on top of the covers. Slowly, I slipped my legs under and pulled the covers up to my chin. The silence continued. I settled into the pillow and imagined I was a student at the seminary, dressed in beautiful clothes and receiving Eli Sevenstar in the parlor. He was taking my hand, ready to proclaim his deep adoration, when the tapping started again.

"Oh, bother!"

I threw the covers back once more and swung my legs over the edge of the bed. After much fumbling for a match, I lit the lamp and carried it to the window. I stood there for some time, listening, and then stepped back to stare at the window . . . and the chiffonier that stood next to it. I'd found nothing behind the chiffonier, but might something have made a nest *inside it*? I shivered at the thought. The drawers had been clean and free of pests when I put my clothes in, but what about the space behind the drawers?

Setting the lamp down, I started at the top and quietly removed each drawer, setting them on the bed. The first two glided out easily, and my shoulders sagged with relief when no nests were discovered within or behind them.

The third drawer stuck halfway when I tried to pull it free.

I didn't want to force it, for who knew what blocked its path? A nest? The decayed corpse of a rodent? Holding the drawer with one hand and lifting the lamp with the other, I peered into the recesses of the chiffonier. No tiny corpse there, but also no sign of what made the drawer stick. I left the drawer hanging and set the lamp down. Then I removed the drawer underneath and set it on the bed with the others. Taking a deep breath, I knelt down and reached under the stuck drawer to feel along the sides for the obstruction.

At the left edge, my fingers found the sharp corner of something wedged between the drawer and the interior runner. Quite certain it was cardboard or paper rather than decayed flesh, I grasped the corner and gently worked it back and forth. Finally, it loosened. Taking great care not to tear it, I pulled the obstruction free.

It was a piece of thick paper folded into a small square. I sat back more comfortably and pulled the lamp near before unfolding it with shaking hands. The paper was much creased and yellowed, but it was simple enough to make out the words scrawled in untidy, slanting script.

> *Ella,*
> *My river runs to thee:*
> *Blue sea, wilt welcome me?*
> *My river waits reply.*
> *Oh sea, look graciously!*
> *I'll fetch thee brooks,*
> *From spotted nooks,—*
> *Say, sea, take me!*

The note was signed with initials in lowercase—"e.s."
Eli Sevenstar?

A phantom hand clutched at my stomach, forcing bile to my throat. My eyes traced the words again. And again.

It was impossible to deny what I read—Eli had written a passionate, poetic love note to Ella. Perhaps he'd written many, but only this one survived because it somehow became wedged between the drawer and the runner. I shook my head angrily. Why did it surprise me? On that first trip to town, Fannie had said—in front of *everyone*—that Eli once loved Ella. And he had not denied it. Everyone loved Ella, he'd said. So why was my face hot and my stomach churning?

I read the note once more and blushed even hotter. I'd read enough of Shakespeare's bawdy language to understand what it meant when a boy called himself a river and his beloved the sea. Rivers ran to the sea—*entered* the sea.

Just how well had Eli loved Ella?

A drink of water, or maybe a splash of it on my face, was what I needed. I crawled over to the bed and slid the note under the mattress. Then I pushed myself up and walked on wobbling legs to the washstand. But when I lifted my pitcher to pour, a single drop dribbled into the cup. I clutched the empty pitcher to my chest with a stifled sob.

Too lazy to fetch the lamp, I shuffled to the door and opened it quietly. The last thing I wanted was someone to find me sniffling like a fool in the dark. I inched slowly toward the lavatory and then stopped in my tracks. Something wasn't right—I could feel it like a tremor in the air. I turned in the opposite direction, toward the other bedrooms.

A faint crack of light shone through the bottom of one of the doors.

I wiped my tear-blurred eyes and stepped softly toward that crack of light. I heard low whispers. No giggles, no squeals of laughter. Just a steady stream of whispering. My scalp prickled at the oddness of it.

I pressed closer, moving slowly so as not to make a sound when I drew near the door. The whispers combined into something like a chant. Was it a prayer? Steadying the pitcher in one hand, I grasped the door handle with the other and pushed the door open.

Three girls sat on the floor, circled around a large candle that flickered wildly and threw eerie shadows upon their faces. Each held an open Bible, but I knew this was no late-night prayer circle. Their faces were not composed in prim devotion.

Rather, as their heads turned sharply toward the doorway, I saw eyes wide with fear.

"Oh, damn and blast!" cried Fannie.

"Miss McClure, we weren't doing anything wrong!" Lelia's chin trembled. Alice stared at the Bible in her hands, her shoulders slumped.

"What *were* you doing?"

Fannie raised her chin defiantly, but it was Alice who spoke.

"We were trying to lay the spirit to rest."

Chapter 8

I CLOSED THE DOOR BEHIND ME and took a seat on the nearest bed—the one Fannie kept all to herself. I stared hard at them, almost glad for this distraction from the horrid note in my chiffonier.

"Miss McClure," said Lelia, her lip trembling, "every time I go into the parlor, something breaks."

"Don't tell her anything more," Fannie spat.

"I don't care what you say," said Lelia, glaring at her friend. "I'm truly frightened. Every night you dream of that river water—I know you do! I hear you moaning about it in your sleep. *I've* barely slept since you told us about that night. I'm terrified of bathing in the lavatory because I imagine those faucets gushing with dark water and flooding the room." She turned back to me. "We had to do something!"

"You thought a séance was the answer?" I asked.

"Actually, it was an exorcism," said Fannie, her desperation barely cloaked by the bold words.

"It's Ella's ghost that's after us, Miss McClure!" Alice's soft voice was sadder than I'd ever heard it.

"Supposing for a moment there *was* a ghost," I said, "why do you think she'd be after you?"

The girls looked at each other nervously. No one spoke.

I lifted my hand in exasperation. "Did one of *you* murder her?"

Lelia gasped. "Of course not!"

"Well, then? If Miss Crenshaw finds out what you've been up to, you'll get demerits for the rest of the term." I glared at them for a moment longer, but curiosity nagged at me. "If you can explain this to me, I might let you all get back to bed without telling our principal an exorcism was going on right under her nose."

Fannie kept her eyes on the candle flame, but Lelia glanced at Alice nervously. Alice's face was hard as stone.

Lelia swallowed. "I suppose we weren't always as nice to Ella as we should have been."

"I didn't know she was one of your group."

"She was our good friend. It's just that sometimes we teased her a little."

"Your *good friend*?" It was Alice who spoke, her eyes wide behind her spectacles.

"Yes, our good friend," said Fannie, turning to her. "Are you deaf, cousin?"

Alice's mouth tightened. "You mean like *I* am your good friend? The same way a beast of burden is a good friend?"

"What are you talking about?" Fannie frowned at the girl.

"I'm saying that Ella was your friend as long as she was useful. As long as she fawned over you and did the tasks you gave her." She lifted her chin, her mouth trembling as she continued. "But you didn't really like her, did you? Just as you don't really like me!"

Fannie and Lelia glared at Alice, saying nothing. I took a breath and tried to make my voice gentle and coaxing. "Why wouldn't they like you, Alice?"

"Because girls like Ella and me were poor, and they thought us backward for growing up in log cabins with parents barely scratching out a living and grandparents who only spoke Cherokee." Tears glistened in her dark eyes. "Ella was beautiful, though. So they wanted her in their group, to keep an eye on her." She turned to me. "Miss McClure, they *hated* her for her beauty!"

"That is a lie!" Lelia spat. "Why do you say such spiteful things?"

"I'm not lying. You teased her for being a savage and for having a savage for a beau. You told her no matter how beautiful she was, she'd never be a real lady. You know what you've done, and now Ella is going to make you both sorry for it!" Alice drew a ragged breath. "And she'll come after me because I *knew* what you were doing and didn't say anything . . . because I couldn't help thinking, *Better her than me.*"

With that, she collapsed into sobs. The other two stared at her, their faces pale with alarm. Or was it guilt?

In that moment, I felt a kinship with Alice, as I had with

Lucy during that first trip to town—both were girls like me who didn't quite fit in, who were teased and bullied, but who would rather be used than ignored.

"All right," I said finally. "I don't think I'll understand all this tonight, but I *can* tell you there is no ghost. Haven't you read *Macbeth*? Do you think Banquo really appears to him and it just so happens no one else can see him? Of course not! Macbeth's imagination is plagued with guilt, just as your feelings of guilt are plaguing you."

They all stared at me blankly before looking down again.

"Clearly I need to assign more Shakespeare," I muttered.

Fannie shook her head. "You don't know what I saw the night I fell."

"Dreams can seem very real, very frightening. I know this from experience. But you can't let them drive you mad."

She raised her head to glare at me. "Will you run tattling to Miss Crenshaw?"

Oh, how I would love to, my dear. I rubbed my hands on my nightgown and stood up. Cocking my head, I stared back at Fannie. All three girls sat frozen, holding their breath until I spoke. But all I did was grab my pitcher by the handle and turn away. I moved slowly toward the door, taking my time to consider the best answer to Fannie's insolent question. I heard a collective sigh, as though they believed all hope lost. The dreaded demerits would be meted out. I had to admit I enjoyed their suffering. Just a bit.

Once I'd reached the door, I turned back to look at each of them. "If you would make an effort to be nicer to each other," I began, gesturing meaningfully at Alice, who was hanging her head again, "and if each of you tried a little harder during recitations, I'd consider not reporting this to Miss Crenshaw."

The eyes of two girls widened with hope, but Fannie frowned.

"You are blackmailing us?"

"No, I am trying to reach a compromise."

"We agree," said Lelia quickly, and Alice nodded her head forcefully. Fannie thrust her chin up and arched an eyebrow, but did not protest further.

"Good. Now blow out that candle and get back into bed." I watched with more than a little self-satisfaction as they rushed to their beds and scrambled under the covers. As soon as they were still, I opened the door—

And gasped to see Miss Crenshaw standing before me, shining her lamp in my face.

I gulped for air, my heart thudding. For a brief moment I considered shutting the door on her, but then she spoke.

"Pray tell me, Miss McClure—what are you doing in this bedroom in the middle of the night?" Her face was ghoulish in the flickering lamplight.

"Miss Crenshaw, you gave me such a fright!"

"I ask you again—what are you doing here?" She stared at the pitcher in my hand.

"I . . ." What was I supposed to say? I'd made a very advantageous compromise with the girls. "Miss Crenshaw—it's very simple. I was awoken by a sudden thirst, and when I went to the corridor, intending to make my way to the lavatory, I heard whispering in this bedroom. So I came to make sure nothing untoward was going on."

"They were eating, weren't they, Miss McClure? What sort of snack have they smuggled in now? I smell nothing other than candle smoke." She peered over my shoulder with accusing eyes.

"No, no, they weren't eating. They were talking."

"Talking about what?"

"About a noise . . . that they heard."

Miss Crenshaw frowned. "I saw a light under the door. They weren't talking about a noise. They were up and out of their beds. I'm sure of it. These late-night meetings are quite injurious to their health, not to mention their concentration during recitations. And having a candle lit so late at night is a fire risk." She leaned in, her eyes narrowed in anger. "Perhaps you did not know that we lost our first seminary building to fire."

"Yes, I'd heard that. I'm sorry, miss."

"They will receive demerits for this—no trip to town this weekend, I'm afraid."

Well, it was better than a term's worth of demerits. "Right, miss."

"And you will have to sit with them on Saturday, Miss McClure."

"But I'd planned a trip to town myself, Miss Crenshaw!"

"It shall have to wait. You are long overdue with your grade reports as it stands. This will give you an opportunity to catch up." She beckoned me forward and shut the girls' door, leaving us alone in the corridor. "You were in that room for some time,

Miss McClure." Her voice was low and steady. "By staying there and talking with those girls—and I happen to know you were in there for more than a few minutes—you were encouraging their bad behavior. I can't have this. No matter how young, teachers must never imagine themselves friends to their students. Propriety, Miss McClure! It is of the utmost importance!"

She snapped her heels together and stalked down the corridor, trailing a wake of bristling anger that nearly matched my own.

I tossed and turned that night, plagued by thoughts of Eli's letter, Ella's ghost, and Crenshaw's beastly punishment. The next morning before breakfast, I passed Olivia in the corridor. She took one look at my face and asked me to her room. It was all I could do to stifle my yawns as I sat in her chair.

"Long night?" she asked.

"If you only knew," I moaned, my mind turning again to the wretched letter hidden under my bed. I pushed the thought aside. "How much have you learned already?"

"Oh, just that Fannie and the rest received demerits for a late-night gathering. And that you are in disfavor for not bringing it to Miss Crenshaw's attention quickly enough."

"My, my. Word travels fast."

"The girls are not known for their discretion. Why were they up so late?"

I studied her kind face for a moment. Then I leaned forward. "The girls were doing more than socializing last night."

She raised her eyebrows. "Really?"

"You must tell no one, for I could get into much worse trouble for this." After she nodded, I continued in a whisper. "They were trying to perform an exorcism."

She blinked. "I see."

I'd expected more of a reaction than that. "And I caught trouble for breaking it up and telling them to go to bed. It's not fair at all. I saved them from even more demerits."

Olivia stared at the wall behind me, saying nothing.

"What are you thinking?" I asked.

"I'm sorry for the trouble this has brought you, but even more I am worried that it's come to this. The girls must be truly unsettled if they were willing to take such a drastic, and foolish, step."

"That's what I told them—that they were letting their imaginations run wild and it was driving them mad and making them do foolish things."

She turned to me, a strange urgency in her eyes. "Willie, you know how I feel about this. I don't believe this ghost exists only in their imaginations. Ella's spirit is real and restless. Somehow, it has lost its way and become trapped within the school. It needs to be shown the way home." She clasped her hands in her lap and shook her head. "But an exorcism is not the answer. Such an aggressive act could make matters worse."

"Oh, Olivia." I didn't know how to respond. I couldn't truly believe the disturbances were matters of the occult. At the same time, I couldn't deny how frightened those girls had been.

"Willie, I wish to be fully honest with you." She looked at me intently, seeming to latch on to something she saw in my expression. "I will keep your secret, but will you also agree to keep mine?"

Shared secrets were supposedly the glue of true friendship, but a flicker of foreboding kept me from smiling. After a pause, I nodded.

She reached under her narrow bed and pulled out a wooden box. She lifted the lid and removed four books, which she handed to me one by one. I read the titles—*Phantasms of the Living,* volumes one and two, *Plain Guide to Spiritualism,* and *Lights and Shadows of Spiritualism.* Dismay pressed on my shoulders like a weight.

"Olivia, are you a *Spiritualist?*"

She frowned. "You say that as though it's a filthy word. As a matter of fact, I am a Methodist . . . with Spiritualist *leanings.* And so was my grandmother, who traveled in the East and once saw the Fox sisters. You know of them?"

"Enough to know they were frauds. My papa told me Katie Fox admitted to lying about her communications with spirits."

"Only when the older sister forced her to it after arranging to have her children taken away." She lifted her chin. "And even if they were the worst frauds ever seen, I'd still believe in Spiritualism. It's certainly not something I'm ashamed of."

I eyed the box she'd hidden under the bed.

"What I meant," she continued with a frown, "is that I'm not ashamed to admit it to *friends.* Miss Crenshaw would not have hired me if she knew I'd participated in séances."

"Have you really?"

She ducked her head. "Well, only a few." When she met my

gaze again, her eyes were bright with a strange passion. "I've *watched* many, many more. Before she died, my grandmother told me I was sensitive, and that I must develop my talents. But it seemed easier to take Miss Crenshaw's offer of a teaching position than to set myself up as an untried medium."

"Your grandmother was a medium? A *Cherokee* medium? Did she host dark circles and talk to spirits?"

She looked away, her lips pressed into a thin line.

"Oh dear," I said. "Forgive me. My papa was so skeptical of those who claimed to communicate with spirits, and now his words come out of my mouth almost as though I channeled his thoughts." I reached for her hand and squeezed it until she looked at me again. "Tell me more of your grandmother."

"First of all, she was white. So banish the notion that only fools and savages believe in revenants these days."

I looked down.

"She was quite respected in our community," Olivia continued, "with both whites and Cherokee. She welcomed people in her home and sat with them, but she did not ask for money. Sometimes they would leave gifts or a few coins. But that wasn't why she did it. Her calling was to reconnect the bereaved with those they'd lost. It was her way of helping cure their grief and helping lost spirits find their way."

I sighed. "Why tell me all this when you know I don't believe?"

Her eyes grew wide and mysterious. "Because you and I must hold a séance. I need you to open your mind so we can help Ella find her way home."

• • •

Later I lay on my bed, turning over the conversation in my mind. Once, my papa had spoken of Spiritualists, his mustache bristling under eyes flashing with contempt. "They're actors, all of them, sinking to the depths of depravity to scrabble a living. They *pretend* to see spirits, changing their voices to summon their so-called controls. They read people's expressions, ask them leading questions, and sometimes steal their wallets or have a henchman go through garbage to find their secrets." He'd stroked his mustache in silence for a moment before turning back to me. "When I die, don't go to some fool medium. You'll not find me there, do you hear?"

I wondered what he'd say about sweet, caring Olivia—a respected teacher of *science*. Would he call her a charlatan?

I hadn't promised to take part in her séance, but neither had I refused. Papa had found the notion of spirits laughable, almost offensive. But I'd heard that strange tapping at night. I'd felt the cold chill in the parlor. I'd seen the fear in proud Fannie's eyes when she spoke of the dark river water rushing after her. I acknowledged all that—I just didn't know what to make of it.

Chapter 9

THE AIR WAS THICK WITH RESENTMENT in the chapel that Saturday afternoon. To be sure, there were girls who'd *chosen* not to go to town and sat contentedly reading or working on a composition. But those who were kept from town by demerits were silently seething, unable to concentrate, and sat staring at the wall clock to follow each tick of the minute hand as it traveled the distance of two hours.

I was one of the seethers. This was my first Saturday to stay at the school, and I was surprised by how much I craved fresh air and some variation in the landscape. We were allowed outside for our walk every day, demerits or no, but that was more of a chore than an escape. Without a trip to town, the seminary walls felt as though they might close in on me, and no matter where I went, it seemed Miss Crenshaw's eyes were following my every move.

And though I wouldn't—*couldn't*—admit it to anyone else,

I was mourning the lost opportunity to catch a glimpse of Eli Sevenstar. I'd looked at his letter a hundred times since the night of the attempted exorcism. It still twisted my stomach in knots, but it was more than mere jealousy that so affected me. Disgust would have been the proper response to such a note— I told this to myself again and again—and yet a part of me still thrilled at the passion it conveyed. I longed to look into Eli's dark eyes and find such a passion directed at *me*.

It was absurd, of course. I could not be Eli's welcoming blue sea. A smile or a pleasant conversation was all I could ever hope for if I wanted to keep my position. And I did want to keep my position, for though I felt trapped at that moment, the thought of leaving such independence was . . . well, it was unthinkable.

Miss Taylor, the domestic science teacher, sat in a wide wooden chair facing the desks. Though she knitted quietly, her eyes were quick to find any girl who dared whisper. I sat at the back of the room, tasked with shoring up the rear defenses.

A stack of compositions stood on the desk before me. I lifted the top composition and glanced over it—a junior essay on "Tact versus Talent." The authoress was a sweet girl who'd worked long hours to perfect her penmanship in a composition as mindless as it was tidily scripted. I placed that one at the bottom. The next essay was blotched and spattered with ink. That could wait until later too. The third was neatly penned, and the introduction unfolded in a thoughtful manner. In fact, for several paragraphs the argument struck me as beautifully clear and logical. I was giddy, quite prepared to give it the highest mark, when suddenly it entered territory that confused me.

The language was exquisite, but the meaning behind the words was muddled. Did the confusion arise from a flaw in the argument . . . or in my own reasoning? I couldn't think how to express these misgivings to the student without looking like a prize fool.

I placed that composition at the bottom of the pile.

When I checked the clock again, five minutes had passed.

Lucy Sharp—who'd received demerits for insolence in geometry class—sat to my right with her head bent over a piece of paper. She applied her pencil to it with such ferocity I feared the paper would tear. At least one of us was getting work done. I took a closer look and saw that she was drawing the same circle over and over. She caught me staring out of the corner of her eye. Frowning, she curved her arm around the page and lowered her head so that I could no longer see whether she wrote or drew.

Two desks away on my left sat Fannie, who also leaned over her work, but with pen and ink rather than pencil. Her task consisted of filling out small white cards with text that I could not make out, no matter how I squinted. After a moment, she caught my squinting, and her mouth curved in a cunning smile. I turned back to my compositions, willing myself not to blush.

During the break, she sauntered by.

"I noticed you staring, Miss McClure. I may as well give this to you now." She handed me one of the cards with a flourish of her hand. "Mama likes for me to present these early, and in person. I planned to pass them out next week, but you are here now." Her eyes narrowed accusingly. "Here with us. When we all thought we'd be in town."

"You might have been here every Saturday for the rest of term had I reported what was *really* going on last night," I reminded her, keeping my voice low.

She merely sniffed in response. I looked over the card.

YOUR PRESENCE IS REQUESTED AT A
CHRISTMAS SUPPER FOR SEMINARY FACULTY,
ADMINISTRATION, AND SENIOR STUDENTS
AT SEVEN O'CLOCK IN THE EVENING,
THE TWELFTH OF DECEMBER,
IN THE HOME OF
SAMUEL AND CORA ARCHER BELL.

"How nice," I murmured, having never attended such a function in my life. Fortunately, I had ages to pick Olivia's brain on the matter.

"We've held this party every year since I was a little girl. It's always entertaining to see the teachers in their finery. I'm sure you have something quite splendid in your wardrobe, Miss McClure." Her mouth curved into a cold smile. "I look forward to marveling at it."

I forced my own smile. "Your script on this invitation is as pretty as copperplate, Fannie. I wonder why it is that I can barely read your compositions? Ah, well, now I know what you are capable of."

She pursed her lips, and then turned as Miss Crenshaw entered the library with a bundle of letters in her hand. "Oh, look, the mail has come," she said, nodding toward the door. "Are you expecting anything, Miss McClure?" She lifted her eyebrows and waited. "I didn't think so," she said with syrupy sweetness. "I've noticed you never get mail. You post letters in town, and yet you never receive a reply. In fact, you never seem to *expect* a reply. It's very curious. I have grave doubts about this beau of yours."

My hands clenched into fists under the table. "I already told you I've not been writing to a beau."

She pouted in mock sympathy. "And not a single letter from family or friends? Ah, look," she said as Miss Crenshaw handed her a small bundle, "here are two for me!"

How I longed to tear that lovely hair from her head! She was sassy and rude, and . . . her curiosity about my mail was alarming. She was a sly one—no doubt about that. I'd need to be more cautious when posting my letters.

And I'd need *something* decent to wear to her blasted party.

That night, as I stared at the ceiling and mused on rivers and welcoming seas, the tapping started its familiar rhythm. I banged my head against the pillow, cursing whatever was truly responsible for the noise. Finally, I got out of bed with a groan and sat in the wooden chair by the desk.

The tapping stopped.

I heaved a sigh, relieved by the silence but knowing it would start again as soon as I'd returned to my bed. So I laid my head on the desk, shivering at a sudden chill near the windows.

A shriek pierced the quiet.

I leapt from the chair, and it skittered backward with a shriek of its own. I nearly fell but caught myself, knocking my elbow painfully on the desk. My fingers shook as I fumbled with the match, but finally I managed to light my lamp and carry it out into the corridor. The door next to mine opened, and a pale face peeped out. "Get back in your room and stay there," I whispered. The poor girl's face softened with relief as she shut her door. The screams continued, sounding more and more terrified. I considered a retreat to my own room. Couldn't I pretend to have slept through it all? But Miss Crenshaw would frown upon such cowardice, and she frowned at me quite enough already. So I took a deep breath and made my way down the stairs.

Crossing through the vestibule to the corridor, I listened—the screams had seemed close when I was in my room, but now it was clear they were coming from the far end of the school. I heard movement behind me and turned to raise my lamp. Olivia walked toward me, her own lamp in hand. A shorter figure followed close behind her. It seemed to be the domestic science teacher, but I was unaccustomed to seeing prim Miss Taylor in her nightgown and ruffled cap.

"Where is she? Where is the screaming coming from?" Olivia's face was strangely contorted in the flickering lamplight.

"It might be the chapel," I whispered.

"I know we must help her, but my feet are heavy as iron," cried Miss Taylor, "and I can barely catch my breath. Shouldn't we get Miss Crenshaw?"

"It's only fear that weighs us down," said Olivia. "That girl is in distress." She slipped her arm through mine and nodded toward the darkness at the end of the corridor. Biting my lip, I stepped forward with her.

The screams grew louder as we neared the chapel. Strange crashing noises filled the gaps between them.

Miss Taylor whispered from behind us. "Is she knocking over the furniture?"

"*Something* is knocking it over," said Olivia, pulling me closer as we came to stand before the door. She withdrew her arm from mine and grasped the doorknob. It would not turn. She handed Miss Taylor her lamp and put both hands to the knob. Still it would not turn.

"It's locked," she gasped.

"There is no lock on that door," cried a voice from behind us. Miss Crenshaw emerged, white-faced, from the darkness of the corridor. She carried no lamp, and her gray hair hung in an untidy braid over her shoulder.

"How can that be?" The lamp swung wildly in Miss Taylor's trembling hands. The screaming continued in the room, though the voice was growing hoarse and less piercing.

"Let me," said Miss Crenshaw, brushing past us to apply her own hands to the doorknob. When her efforts failed, she pounded on the door. "Let go of the knob! We wish to help you."

Olivia clutched at the principal's shoulder. "The screams are too far away. She can't be holding the knob."

Miss Crenshaw stepped back, her hand to her mouth. There was a final crash and a terrible cry, and then . . . silence.

"Try the door now," I said.

Eyes wide with fear, Miss Taylor shook her head. Miss Crenshaw still clutched at her mouth. Finally, Olivia stepped forward and put her hand to the knob. Each of us gasped as it turned in her hands and the heavy door opened.

Taking the lamp back from Miss Taylor, Olivia walked a few steps into the room and out of our sight. After all the commotion, the near silence was suffocating. There was a pause, followed by an audible intake of breath. Swallowing my fear, I walked through the doorway to join her.

The chapel was freezing cold—so cold I could see my breath billowing in the lamplight. Holding the lamp high, I looked about the room. It was an absolute wreck. Pictures had fallen off the walls, and nearly every piece of furniture lay on its side. Every window was wide open. And at the center, in a shivering heap, lay Lucy Sharp, her right leg pinned under an overturned desk.

Chapter 10

WHEN MISS CRENSHAW SAW LUCY'S BODY twisted under that enormous two-seat desk, she seemed to regain her wits and immediately began barking out orders like an army captain.

"Miss Taylor, you must fetch Dr. Stewart. Nurse Gott should prepare a bed in the infirmary—Miss Adair will alert her. Miss McClure, you fetch Jimmy to get this desk off the girl's leg. We'll need his help in setting the room to rights."

When we stared at her numbly, she softened ever so slightly.

"I need you all to stay calm and focused. Now please do as I directed."

I shook myself and followed the other two through the doorway, intent on finding Jimmy in the kitchen. But when we stepped into the corridor, he was already standing there.

Miss Taylor squeaked in surprise. "Jimmy! You frightened us."

"Sorry, miss," he said quietly. "Thought I heard something."

"There's been another accident," I said quickly. "We need your help in the chapel."

Jimmy nodded and stepped aside to allow Olivia and Miss Taylor to pass. I gestured for him to go ahead of me into the chapel, noting how his shoulders sagged with reluctance as he stepped through the doorway.

His dark face sweated profusely as he worked. He seemed painfully aware of Miss Crenshaw and me staring at him, for he took care not to touch Lucy as he strained to lift the heavy desk. He was visibly relieved to step away afterward. The girl regained consciousness with a gasp, tears streaming down her face and teeth chattering in the deep chill of the room.

Miss Crenshaw knelt beside her and tenderly dabbed at the tears with a handkerchief she'd drawn from her sleeve. She spoke in a low, soothing tone. "Can you speak?" When Lucy nodded, she continued. "We need to know what happened, child, before the doctor gets here. How did you come to be in the chapel?"

Lucy gulped and swallowed several times before finally uttering words. "You won't believe me."

"At this point, I'm willing to believe almost anything," said Miss Crenshaw with a tight smile.

Lucy spoke haltingly, her teeth chattering as she forced the words through them. "I heard a whisper . . . a voice calling my name . . . and I followed it here. But I stood alone in the room. The air turned cold . . . so very cold. Then the door slammed shut and everything fell from the walls. And then . . . the windows flew open on their own." She blinked away newly forming tears. "I swear that's what happened, Miss Crenshaw! I didn't open them myself."

Miss Crenshaw stroked her arm and made shushing noises. Once Lucy quieted, she prompted her to continue. "What happened then?"

"Water poured through the windows. Murky, rank water." She turned her head to the side. "I still smell it in my hair! The water rushed with such force it knocked over the desks. It filled the room and soaked the hem of my gown." Her lip trembled as her voice grew more ragged. "One of the desks fell over and pinned me to the floor. I thought I was going to die, to drown in that cold water just as Ella did!"

"But, Lucy," I said, "your hair and dress are dry. There is no water here!"

"I'm not lying," whispered the girl. "But why would Ella hurt me?" She closed her eyes and cried silently.

It took a while for Jimmy to right the overturned furniture. While he worked, I picked up the damaged picture frames and tumbled books before moving to the windows to shut them. The air outside was pleasant. In the distance I could see two separate lantern lights bobbing toward us—Miss Taylor and Dr. Stewart approached the building.

I turned to Miss Crenshaw. "What are we to tell the doctor?"

The principal's face drooped with fatigue. "I've no idea. I suppose we could say we have another case of sleepwalking, though I'm not sure how to explain the overturned desk."

She clamped her mouth shut as we heard the front door open, a sound followed by the clatter of footsteps in the corridor.

When the doctor entered, his face was grim. He nodded at the principal before kneeling next to Lucy. I could hardly bear to see Lucy's face contorting with pain as he examined her. A sudden nausea beset me, and I had to breathe deeply in order to keep my supper from ending up on the floor.

Finally, after binding the leg with a splint provided by Jimmy, the doctor stood. "Her leg is broken—a compound fracture, I'm afraid. But I can find no other injuries." He rubbed his forehead and stifled a yawn. He turned back to the principal, his face drawn with confusion and fatigue. "How did the desk fall on her?"

"We simply don't know, Dr. Stewart," said Miss Crenshaw, her voice mild.

"More sleepwalking?" His lips curved in a faint smile. "I'm starting to wonder what you feed these girls that makes them so active in their sleep, Miss Crenshaw."

The principal bowed her head.

As Jimmy and the doctor carried Lucy out of the room on a makeshift stretcher of quilts, Olivia pulled me aside.

"I never expected Ella's spirit to turn so violent. I'm afraid these accidents will only grow more terrible if we don't do something," she whispered. "It seems to be feeding on the girls' fear."

I couldn't contradict her. I'd just seen something—*felt* something—I'd never thought to encounter, and Papa's steadfast skepticism had deserted me. "What does it want? Revenge?"

Olivia frowned. "Perhaps nothing so dire. It may be desperate to make contact because it longs for peace or . . . some sort of release. We won't know if we don't ask."

"*We* ask? Why don't *you* ask?"

"As I told you before, I am sensitive. And I have the knowledge and experience. But I can't do it alone."

"Olivia," I moaned, "you know how I feel about all that Spiritualist flummery."

She held my gaze. "I wish you to help me, but perhaps I should find someone more sympathetic. Someone like Miss Taylor, perhaps?"

I straightened up, my cheeks warming at this preposterous notion. "Miss Taylor is a ninny who'd run squawking to Miss Crenshaw at the mere *mention* of a séance," I said quickly. "It'd be much safer not to involve her."

"Willie, are you saying you will help?"

I stared at her for a moment before finally nodding. "Where does one hold a séance? You're not going to make me sit by her grave, are you?"

She shook her head. "Of course not. My grandmother taught me that spirits linger in the places where they lived and loved, not where their bodies are put to rest. Ella once lived in your room. I think we should hold our séance there in order to be as close as possible to her spirit."

My stomach twisted. *This is how a teacher loses her position.*

Olivia took my hand and squeezed it tightly. "I know what I'm doing. We shall not be found out."

"Fine," I said. "Tell me what to do."

• • •

During Sunday's chapel service, the girls stared at the bare walls and whispered to each other. I frowned at them several times, warning them to be silent, and yet couldn't fault them for needing to shake off some of their gloom. I only wished I could hear what they had to say—it might have helped make some sense of this puzzle.

I visited Lucy in the infirmary afterward. Her face was gray and pinched, framed by the tangle of black hair that splayed onto the pillow. I pulled a chair next to the bed and took her hand as I sat.

"How's the pain?"

She shrugged. "Nurse Gott gives me a sleeping draught, but then I have nightmares of pain."

"I won't keep you from your rest very long. But I must ask you something about last night."

Lucy turned away. "I told you everything."

"I want to know *why* it happened." I lowered my voice. "Can you think of any reason why Ella would want to frighten you in such a way?"

She closed her eyes and lay in silence for a long time. A tear squeezed out of one eye and trickled slowly down her face. "I don't know. She knew I loved her."

"Did you have an argument before her accident? Was she angry?"

"We didn't have an argument." Her eyes opened—they were still damp, but no more tears threatened to fall.

I leaned closer. "She *was* angry, though, wasn't she?"

"No!" She wiped her face. "If anyone was angry, it was me."

"Why?"

"I don't know."

"I think you do!"

"I don't want to talk about it," she growled.

Nurse Gott shuffled in with a tray. Her heavy face sagged into a frown at the sight of me. "Lucy needs her rest, miss. You shouldn't be upsetting her with questions and such. Why, you've made her cry!"

"It's just the pain, Gotty." Lucy wiped at her face again and settled into her pillow, her hands clasped over the covers.

"I've brought you some broth—it'll settle your stomach and take your mind off the pain." She turned to me. "I think it's best you left now, miss."

"Yes, of course. I'm sorry, Lucy."

Clearly, the madness of the previous evening was getting to me. Or perhaps it was lack of sleep unhinging my good sense. How else to explain my thoughts as I left Lucy to the care of Mrs. Gott?

If Lucy won't tell me, perhaps Ella will.

Part II

Spirit Communicator

October 1896

Chapter 11

TWO WEEKS PASSED BEFORE OLIVIA AND I could conduct a midnight tryst with the spirit world. Olivia first insisted upon reviewing her library of Spiritualist material. Then she required several days to consult her journals and reread all the letters from her grandmother. She barely spoke to me as she walked the corridors with a secretive smile on her face. Finally, on a Friday after classes, she informed me she was ready to begin that very evening.

I have to admit my heart sank a little to hear it.

That night, I stood mute as Olivia moved my bedside table next to the chiffonier and lit a candle at its center. Was it fear or excitement that made her hand tremble as she touched the match to the wick? My own heart thudded as I placed my wooden chair next to hers, but I wasn't afraid of the spirits as much as Miss Crenshaw. I wanted the whole thing to be over as quickly as possible, before we were caught and I was sent away forever.

Olivia blew out her match and nodded at the arrangement. "The curtains are drawn. I'll place a cloth along the crack below the door so no one will see the candlelight from the corridor." She looked intently at me. "We must keep our voices very low. Not only will this keep us safe from detection, but the spirits prefer it as well."

I nodded and took my seat as she sat gracefully upon her own.

"Let us begin." Olivia's confidence soothed me, but only a little. "We must place our hands lightly on the table," she continued. "Relax your body and empty your mind."

I placed my fingers upon the cool wood. "What's supposed to happen?"

"If a spirit is present, the table will move."

"Truly?" I frowned, taking my hands from the table. "How are we supposed to learn anything from a moving table?"

"You must keep your heart and mind open, Willie. Once we know the spirit is present, we may ask it questions. The table's movement will communicate the answers. We will start simply with yes and no questions, and depending on the spirit's compliance, we'll move on to more complex questions."

"And you've seen this work before?"

She stared at her fingers. "My grandmother had some success with it, but I've only heard about it rather than actually seen it, for I was too young to attend the sessions." She looked up again, her eyes bright. "I've read of mediums who coaxed the spirits not only to tilt a table but also to levitate it straight up into the air. D. D. Home was famous for this, and no one ever detected trickery behind the levitations."

I placed my hands on the table, then lifted them again. "Do you ever wonder if this is a proper thing for a Methodist to do?"

Olivia smiled primly. "The Bible speaks to it in Samuel, chapter twenty-eight: 'Then said Saul unto his servants, Seek me a woman that hath a familiar spirit, that I may go to her, and inquire of her. And his servants said to him, Behold, there is a woman that hath a familiar spirit at Endor.' People have long been consulting spirits, so stop your stalling."

I glared at her as I placed my fingers on the table once more.

"Remember—you must banish all negative thoughts," said Olivia. "Keep your mind open. Look upon the candle flame, but try not to meditate upon anything in particular."

We sat very still, each of us staring at the flickering light of the candle. I tried to push those niggling thoughts aside—the unmarked compositions piling up on my desk, what dress I would wear for the party at the Bells', when I would see Eli Sevenstar again—but instead, the thoughts grew and multiplied like weeds, resisting my efforts to stamp them down.

We sat still and quiet for an eternity. I watched the wax overflow the edges of the candle and trickle slowly, so slowly, down the side into a lumpy pool at the base. My eyelids grew heavy, and my eyes burned and itched, but I could not rub them. I was blinking when the table suddenly jerked.

"Is there a spirit present?" Olivia's voice was hopeful, almost desperate.

"I think that was me," I said sheepishly, rubbing my thigh. "I had a spasm in my leg and might have kicked the table."

Olivia frowned. Then she took a deep breath, and her expression smoothed into pleasantness once more. "Shall we try again?"

This time I didn't bother trying to push the stray thoughts aside. At least they would keep me awake, and it was better than watching candle wax drip. I'd mentally scheduled all my marking sessions, considered how long it would take to sew a dress from scratch, and rehearsed several conversations with Eli Sevenstar—in which I was both cool and alluring—when a gasp from Olivia brought me back into the moment.

She shivered. "I just felt a tremendous chill."

At that moment, the tapping started.

Olivia's head jerked toward the window. "What's that sound?"

"You heard it?" My scalp prickled. "I can't find a source for the noise. Do you suppose it's pipes knocking somewhere in the building?"

"It seems to come from outside the window, almost like a branch tapping against the glass," Olivia said, her brow crinkling.

"But there are no trees that close to the building."

Her eyes brightened. "When do you hear the tapping, Willie?"

"Never during the day. It's always very late—it usually wakes me in the middle of the night. When I walk to the window, the tapping stops." I glanced at Olivia and saw her face was gravely serious. "But when I try to sleep, it starts again."

"Do you know what this means? Ella could have been at-tempting to communicate with you for some time now."

I gulped, feeling my scalp prickle as I glanced at the window.

Olivia gripped my hand tightly. "Can we try one more time? Open your mind to whatever is making the tapping sound. If it is a spirit, we may be able to converse with it."

We placed our hands on the table once more. The tapping continued for a moment, then stopped. The tingling in my scalp traveled down the back of my neck and along the length of both arms. When my fingers began to tingle, I looked up to find Olivia's eyebrows arched. Eyes still closed, she faced the window and whispered.

"Is there a spirit present?"

My fingers tingled so much I was certain the table *wanted* to move. There was an energy flowing around it, or through it. But it remained still.

We waited a long time, arms cramping as we held our fin-gers to the table. When we finally opened our eyes to look at each other, the tingling stopped. My arms felt heavy and cold. Somehow I knew nothing more would happen that night.

"It's all right," said Olivia, as though reading my thoughts. "Sometimes it takes a few sessions for anything to happen."

"I felt something—I'm sure of it," I said.

"Let's give it a few days and see how we feel." Olivia smiled. "I, for one, consider this a positive development."

I absently returned her smile, but my eyes flashed to the bed. Eli's note still lay under the mattress. My heavy limbs turned twitchy, and wild thoughts tumbled through my brain. I turned back to Olivia, searching her face. Did I dare show her? Must I keep *every* secret?

Her eyes narrowed. "What is it, Willie?"

"This tapping . . . I've checked that window many times to find the source. A few weeks ago, I searched the chiffonier, thinking something might be living in there."

Olivia's mouth dropped open, and she made to rise from the table.

"No, don't get up. There's nothing in there. I can't find a thing to explain the tapping. But I did find something else." I rose from the chair to retrieve the note from under my mattress. When I turned, Olivia's eyes had widened with curiosity. I took my seat again and passed the note across the table.

She stared at the paper a moment before unfolding it. Her brow creased as she read.

"How very interesting," she said softly.

"That's all you have to say?"

"What *should* I say?"

"Olivia, it's a *love poem* from Eli Sevenstar to Ella!"

She pursed her lips. "I assumed the initials stood for Mr. Sevenstar. That's no surprise. He did court Ella for a while, you know. But he did not write this poem."

I stared at her. "What do you mean?"

She shook her head, her eyes bright with amusement. "Sevenstar didn't write this. He may have copied it out, but a lady poet named Emily Dickinson wrote it."

"What? I've never heard of such a person!"

"And *you're* the English teacher?"

My cheeks prickled with heat. "Shakespeare has always been my specialty," I said quickly. "Papa didn't think highly of female poets."

"How unfortunate," she murmured. "Oh, don't look so fierce, Willie! I was only teasing." She laughed softly. "Dickinson is not well known. My grandmother happened upon the book during her travels and shared it with me a few years ago. Very unusual style, don't you think?"

"I can't believe a *lady* wrote it. It's so . . . *suggestive.*"

Olivia was quiet for a moment. "Why did you show this to me?"

I blushed again. I could *never* tell Olivia of my feelings for Eli Sevenstar—not if I wanted to keep my position and her friendship. I took a breath and tried to affect a lighter tone. "Fannie once said Eli was in love with Ella. I assumed it was a fleeting thing, but this poem—even if he did not write it—still conveys a great deal of passion, don't you think?"

"It's easy to get caught up in the romances of our students," Olivia said, her tone soothing. "I well remember Eli courting Ella. They were a handsome pair, and he would have been an excellent match for a poor country girl like her. But Fannie did not like Ella receiving so much attention."

"So Fannie teased Ella about her penniless full-blood beau, but then got angry when Ella attracted the attention of wealthier boys?"

Olivia sighed. "In the end it didn't really matter, for Ella always went back to Cale. They simply could not quit loving each other. It was like something out of *Wuthering Heights.*" She glanced at me out of the corner of her eye.

"Well, I *do* know that book. Are you saying he was her Heathcliff?"

"Yes, I think so."

"But Heathcliff was such an angry, violent sort of person." I shivered. "Was Cale like that?"

"I don't really know. The last time I saw him was during a gathering here at the school for planning graduation. He did seem quite stiff with anger that night, and poor Ella was quiet and pale." Olivia's mouth tightened. "A few days later, she was dead and Cale was gone." Her eyes met mine. "I know what you're thinking, and I simply can't believe Cale would hurt her."

What about Eli? I knew from Shakespeare that passion had two sides, that a shift in circumstances could turn fervent love into violent hatred. Othello was besotted with Desdemona, but Iago's manipulations drove him to such heights of jealousy that he murdered her. It was easy enough to draw a parallel to Cale. Having loved Ella since childhood, he must have agonized over the attention she received from other boys. Eli, on the other hand, hadn't known her as long, so his affection wouldn't have been deeply felt. He *couldn't* have suffered the same depth of betrayal as Othello or Cale.

And yet Eli's note spoke so eloquently, so *passionately,* even if it did borrow words from another. . . .

"It's all so puzzling," I said.

She yawned delicately. "I'm not sure what to say about that note, Willie. I suppose you could ask Mr. Sevenstar about it at the Bell Christmas party."

"I could never do such a thing! I just wondered . . . was the tapping noise pushing me to find it?"

Olivia looked thoughtful. "Perhaps." Then she frowned. "But hasn't the tapping continued *since* you found it? One would think if the intention was for you to uncover the note, the tapping would stop once you did so."

"I suppose you're right. I can't think straight anymore," I said, yawning in unison with her.

"Let's go to bed. We'll try this again soon."

Olivia seemed quite composed as she bid me good night, but my racing mind wouldn't let me sleep. It wasn't the thought of ghosts that preoccupied me. Rather, it was that damnable note to Ella. On the one hand, I was relieved Eli hadn't written it. And yet, wasn't it just as painful to think of him reading a poem and being reminded of her? Jealousy stabbed at my heart as I imagined Eli copying out the suggestive lines—words that surely had made Ella blush as she read them.

I was jealous of a dead girl. Was it possible to sink any lower?

Chapter 12

THE WEEKS FLEW BY AFTER THAT, the days full of work rather than ghostly encounters, and somehow Olivia and I never found a favorable time for the next séance. Each of us was distracted by the burdens of teaching as we drew nearer to the end of term. I'd established a fragile authority in most of my classes, but it took everything I had to stay one step ahead of the students. While Olivia diligently kept on top of her marking, I allowed the papers to stack up next to my desk, dedicating the bulk of my time to preparing each day's lessons.

At night, when I stared at those untidy piles of paper, I told myself it was easier for Olivia to manage her workload. She did not teach writing. Olivia had lab work, botany sketchbooks, and other such things to score, but surely none of those assignments was as time-consuming to mark as an essay.

However, I was never too busy for the Saturday trip to town. And by late November, my panic over what to wear to the Bell Christmas party had mounted to epic proportions. On one cold and rainy day, when few girls dared to venture outdoors, Olivia and I chaperoned a group of seniors on a trek to Foster's. It was a shivering trek of dampness, but each of us needed something for the party. Once there, I made my way to the ready-made items. Olivia kept to my side as I perused the scanty selection of dresses.

"This is a very pretty color," I said. "I adore the cape ruffle and puff sleeves." I held a smooth wine-colored wool fabric in my hands, barely resisting the urge to place it against my cheeks. "It's a good price, don't you think?"

Olivia tilted her head. "It is handsome, indeed. But you cannot wear it to a supper."

"Why not? I think it's very fine!"

"It's a tea gown, Willie. It's meant to be worn only in one's own home."

"Oh, bother!" I let go of the material with a sigh. "What should I do, Olivia? There are plenty of blouses and skirts to be found ready-made, but no dresses—at least none that I can afford. I don't have the money to purchase a tailored dress, nor do I have the skill or time to make one myself. What's to be done?"

"Perhaps if you hadn't waited so long, we could have worked on a dress together? I'm a decent seamstress."

"Now I shall have to wear a shirtwaist and skirt to a formal gathering and be laughed at by Fannie Bell's entire family. Who would have thought I'd need such fine clothes for Indian Territory?"

Olivia flinched. Then she turned her back to me, pretending to inspect a pair of gloves. I clutched at her arm.

"Oh, Olivia! Please forgive me. Was that a rude thing to say?"

"It seemed rude to me," she murmured.

"It's just that I've been constantly surprised since I got here . . . surprised at how . . ." I trailed off, unable to find the right words.

"Since you got here, you've been surprised at the heights of civilization achieved by the lowly Cherokee people?"

I bit my lip. "I suppose you have every right to be sarcastic. But you must understand that your people are nothing like what I've read or been told about Indians."

"There are many different tribes, each with its own traditions and customs, you know. And each tribe has its own idea of what it means to be civilized."

"I'm trying to understand."

She looked at me for a moment and finally smiled again. "I have an idea for your gown."

Over the next few days, Olivia and I worked together on altering one of her dresses, shortening the length and taking in the waist and bust. During those sewing sessions in her cozy little room, I learned much about her. Olivia's family lived comfortably, if not richly, as farmers. Her grandparents had come to Indian Territory by choice and not as part of the forced removal in the middle of the century. Her parents had been married twenty-one years and still tolerated each other quite well, and she had two younger brothers who worked the farm.

"I love teaching. It's a fine feeling to be so independent," she said one night. "But I sometimes wish I could teach without leaving my family. My brothers seem to grow a foot every year and soon will be men. They change so quickly during the term that we're practically strangers when I finally see them. I'm sure you know what I mean."

I hoped my nod was convincing.

"I always longed for a sister. Do you have brothers and sisters?"

What should I say? I didn't remember Angeline speaking of siblings, but was that because she didn't have any or because she was so stuck on herself she never thought to mention them? I decided on the former. Only children were much more likely to be spoiled.

"I am all the daughters of my father's house," I finally said. "And all the brothers, too."

Olivia quirked an eyebrow. "I suppose that means you are an only child. Which one is that?"

"*Twelfth Night,* of course."

"Of course," she said with a smile. "But did you wish for siblings?"

I snorted. "Not at all. I hated the thought of sharing Papa's attention with others. I preferred having him all to myself."

She nodded slowly, then her eyes brightened. "Willie, would you like to come home with me for the Christmas holiday?"

My mouth fell open.

"We don't live in a fancy house," she said quickly, "but it's homey, and Mama is a first-rate cook. You'd adore the animals, Willie. We could go riding if the days aren't too cold. I have the sweetest little mare, so plump and cheerful." She paused, biting her lip. "I do go on, don't I? You must be planning a return to Van Buren for the holiday."

"No!" I blurted. "I mean, I planned to stay at the seminary for the break. I have so much marking to do, you know."

"You could bring your work with you," she said shyly.

"Oh, Olivia, I would love to come."

"Wonderful!" she breathed, and then grinned so broadly that I saw every one of her pretty teeth.

A week later, I found myself staring in the mirror at a young lady attired none too shabbily for an evening party.

I wore no jewelry but had splurged on a pair of long white gloves and a set of decorative hair combs. A curly fringe was all the rage among the students, but I still could not bring myself to cut the front of my hair, for Papa never could abide the fashion. I did, however, take special care in pinning the greater part of my hair very high and then braiding separate strands to weave around the knot. The combs provided much-needed sparkle.

But my dress was the true triumph. Two years old and yet still very fine to me, it was made of light blue silk with velvet and lace trim at the neck and bodice. The sleeves were elegant puffs that fell almost to my elbows. An umbrella skirt, trimmed at the edge with velvet and lace, fell to the floor and swished behind me as I walked.

With one last glance at the mirror, I pinched my cheeks and bit my lips. Then I lifted the black cape from the bed and placed it on my shoulders, delighted to finally be able to wear my stolen finery.

I met Olivia downstairs in the vestibule. She looked stately in a flowing cloak that covered what I knew to be a satin gown of deep crimson. Her hair was swept up on top of her head, the thick knot cleverly decorated with sprigs of holly. I took a deep breath and sauntered toward her, clutching at the trim of my cape in anticipation of her envy.

Her eyes widened. "Willie, you are going to freeze in that thing! Isn't it a spring cape?"

I blushed. "I don't know. I suppose it might be."

"Didn't you hear that we're riding on the wagonettes to the Bell house? Those canvas flaps will barely keep out the cold night air. Don't you have anything warmer, like the coat you bought last week?"

I shook my head. "It's too cheap and plain. I'd rather be cold."

"Maybe I can wrap part of my cloak around you." She took my hand with a gentle laugh and pulled me toward the door.

Had I not already been shivering with chill upon our arrival, I would have trembled at the grandeur of the Bell home. Olivia told me the house was built before the war, back when the Bells owned slaves and were one of the richest families in the territory. Still, I wasn't prepared for the stately white dwelling with the pedimented gable and columned porch—a style much like the finest plantation homes in Columbia, Tennessee. It was the sort of home Papa always dreamed of owning.

Two young negro men in plain serving garb rushed forward to help us out of the wagons and up the steps to a porch brightly lit with lanterns. Another man opened the door for us, and I couldn't help but gasp when Olivia and I walked into a grand entrance hall decked with fragrant greenery and candles. We were greeted by Mr. Bell, a tall, gray-haired man of stately bearing, who stood next to his wife, a petite woman with porcelain skin. I could see something of Fannie in Mrs. Bell's face, but the mother's fading beauty was more delicate. Fannie's dark hair and high cheekbones bore the stamp of her Cherokee father.

Larkin stood next to his mother, looking handsome and pompous in his finely tailored clothes. Fannie, however, was breathtaking. I couldn't help admiring her white evening gown, embroidered with a thread that sparkled, her tiny waist made tinier by a tightly cinched corset.

"You look lovely, Fannie," said Olivia, echoing my thoughts.

"How wonderful to see my teachers in all their finery," cried Fannie. "And Miss Adair's dress looks quite becoming on you, Miss McClure. How clever and economical of you to make it over for tonight."

Larkin snickered, and I blushed in dismay. Olivia quickly murmured our gratitude to the Bell family and then pulled me to the side, making way for the next group to greet the hosts.

"Don't pay any attention to her," she whispered. "Only someone spiteful would judge you for wearing my dress, let alone comment on it. You look wonderful."

I took a deep breath, banishing the echo of Fannie's words from my head, and smiled brightly at Olivia. "I am ready to see the house."

Olivia led me into the double parlor, where the partition

had been opened to create one large room illuminated by two sparkling chandeliers. Fires roared in two fireplaces decked with greenery and red ribbons. Several tables were laid with china and silverware.

The male students, dashing in their fine suits, clustered together and smiled at the girls. My pulse quickened as I searched for Eli Sevenstar's face among them.

I could not hold back the heavy sigh when I didn't find him. I looked about the entire room, scrutinizing each group, but did not see him. He had not come. Now I wouldn't see his expression when he beheld me in Olivia's fine dress. There would be no opportunity to speak to him. In truth, there was nothing left to look forward to.

"Is this where we shall eat?" I asked Olivia, gesturing limply at the tables.

"No, this is where most of the students will take their supper. Let me show you the dining room."

I felt ill at ease during the meal, for Olivia was seated far away from me and I was placed between a shy teacher from the male seminary and Dr. Stewart. The teacher seemed quite old, nearly thirty, and as an algebra teacher had nothing interesting to say. He stuttered a few words before lapsing into pained silence, and I had little desire to coax him back into conversation. The doctor, on the other hand, turned to me during the first course. His friendly blue eyes put me at ease.

"I must visit Lucy Sharp again tomorrow. I trust she is resting properly? You haven't given her too much schoolwork, have you?"

It was the first time I'd seen him smile. When animated with humor, his narrow face was even more handsome. I smiled back, feeling a pleasant flutter in my stomach.

"We haven't burdened her overmuch," I said, hoping to sound ladylike and clever. "She was a healthy girl before the accident, so I'm sure her leg will heal quickly enough. It's her mind I have concerns about."

His smile faded. "What do you mean?"

I considered his earnest face and wondered how much to tell him. Miss Crenshaw had not trusted the doctor with the full details of the accidents, but when I looked in his eyes, I felt sure he would keep our confidences. "The dreams, the sleepwalking, the little accidents—they're all blamed on a . . . *phantom*," I murmured. "And it's not only Lucy who's losing sleep over it. They all think Ella Blackstone has come back to haunt them."

The doctor shook his head. "I knew Ella." His eyes softened. "She was a sweet girl. Even if I believed in ghosts, she's the last person I would imagine coming back to haunt her schoolmates."

"That's good to hear," I said. "I was assigned her old room, you know. Sometimes—late at night—even *my* imagination gets the best of me."

"Take heart, Miss McClure. Once Miss Sharp is up and about, her nightmares and delusions will cease. As for the rest of the girls, their holidays spent at home will cure them of this ridiculous fear of phantoms." His eyes twinkled. "There aren't many ailments of mind or spirit that can't be cured by Mama's home cooking."

"Of course," I said, chuckling to hear those quaint words spoken in his clipped Northern accent. "I am much reassured, Dr. Stewart."

I would have been glad to talk more with the doctor, but for the remainder of the meal, his attentions were focused on Fannie Bell at his right. I supposed they knew each other well, being brother and sister by marriage. But when I caught glimpses of Fannie's face, it seemed to me her coy smile and high color did not arise from sisterly affection for the young doctor.

With no one to talk to, my sense of being an outsider soon became oppressive. I'd been introduced to all the teachers at the male seminary, as well as the superintendent and his wife. They were polite and friendly without exception, but seemed less interested in me upon learning I was not Cherokee. There was much talk at the table of a former Massachusetts senator named Dawes and his ideas about allotment, most of which went over my head because I could find nothing interesting in it. I spent the greater part of supper staring at my plate and doing my best not to crash my cutlery into the delicate china.

Once the meal was over and the tables in the parlor cleared away, I hoped to have a chance to breathe comfortably again. Olivia and I warmed ourselves by the fireplace while the adults and students mingled throughout the parlor. I contemplated the portrait hanging above the mantel, that of a young girl who looked much like Fannie, only a little kinder, and a little less vibrant.

I turned to Olivia. "Is that Fannie's sister? The one who died?"

"Yes, that's Sarah."

"Did you know her?"

"We were in the same year. She was very different from Fannie." She sighed. "We all envied her when we learned she was to marry the doctor."

"Did all the girls have a pash for him?"

"Oh yes. And still do, of course."

Olivia was called away by a student, so I wandered out into the center hall on my own. To the right of the dining room was the library—my favorite room of any house. Walking past the group of girls clustered by the staircase, I paused at the doorway. The dying fire left the room a little chilly, and thus it was empty.

This library was much grander than my papa's, but still had that comforting odor of books and pipe tobacco that had soothed me back home when Papa was alive. I walked along the shelves, letting my fingers trail across the spines of books about history, politics, and agriculture. There was little fiction to be found, and what I did see was of an "improving" nature. There was no Shakespeare. Perhaps this explained something about Fannie and Larkin.

I did find a book on the Cherokee language and syllabary, which I pulled from the shelf to page through. The letters of the alphabet were foreign and familiar at the same time, many of the shapes similar to those of the English alphabet but adorned with curious curves and curlicues. Some of the shapes looked more like Greek than English. Was this a language taught at the seminary? Did the students write or speak Cherokee in any of their classes? I'd never heard of it if they did.

I was so wrapped up in sounding out the syllables in my head that I did not hear him enter.

"Is Sequoyah's book really that much more fascinating than the party?"

Eli Sevenstar leaned against the doorframe, glass in hand and a lazy smile on his lips. Heat instantly came to my cheeks, and I clutched the book in both hands to keep from dropping it. Taking a breath to cool down, I returned the book to the shelf before turning to face him again.

"I didn't know you were here tonight, Mr. Sevenstar. I did not see you before."

He ran his fingers through his hair, leaving a piece standing on end. "I stayed here last night with Larkin and was a little late coming down." His smile widened. "Why? Were you looking for me?"

"Of course not! I just . . ."

"I ask because . . . I've been looking for *you.*"

The cursed heat was flushing my neck and cheeks again. When did the room grow so warm? And why did my fingers ache with the longing to smooth his hair back down? It was much easier when all I wanted was to kick him.

I lifted my chin, playing the cool lady. "Is there something you wanted to ask me?"

"Not really. I just like talking to you. Especially when you're not surrounded by an army of students."

"Why would you want to talk to a teacher?"

He looked at me for a moment, as though considering how best to answer the question. "Maybe it's because you don't seem like a teacher."

My heartbeat quickened. "Why?"

"You don't have that look—the tight frown that says you've forgotten how to have fun." He abandoned the doorway and stepped into the room. "And you always look as though you're keeping a secret." His voice lowered. "A very delicious secret."

This was dangerous. In so many ways. I clasped my hands tightly to keep them from trembling. "Perhaps we shouldn't be talking in this way. In this room. Alone together."

"Why not?"

He stepped closer and leaned against the bookcase. A familiar odor arose from him—was it brandy? Whiskey? It reminded me of Papa. The seminary boys were expected to be teetotalers, but I suspected dandies like Larkin Bell would partake from time to time. I wasn't going to be a frowning schoolmarm about it, especially when he was smiling that smile. My stomach fluttered at the darkness of his heavy-lidded eyes, while my thoughts wandered to rivers and the sea. Had he looked at Ella this way? If so, how could she have resisted?

He leaned in, lowering his voice to a whisper. "What are you thinking?"

I can't say what I'm really thinking. "That Larkin Bell is a bad influence on you."

"Who's to say it's not the other way around?" His mouth curved in a mischievous grin. "Are you upset because I've been drinking? Is that why you don't want to be alone with me?"

"No, it's not that. Um, it's really that I shouldn't be alone with you because it's inappropriate."

"Why?" He leaned in even farther.

"Because—"

"Would it be *inappropriate*"—he glanced at my mouth— "if I kissed you?"

I stared at him for a long moment, unable to look away. He held my gaze, his eyes wide and unblinking. Those eyes glittered with challenge, but they communicated something else too—something that made me bend toward him ever so slightly.

The gentle chiming of the clock broke the spell. "O-o-of course it would," I stammered, taking an awkward step back. "I can't believe you would suggest such a thing to a teacher. I should . . . In fact, I really must—"

"You're not going to give me a demerit, are you, Miss McClure?"

His mocking tone made me flinch. Was that what this was all about? It wasn't *me* but the allure of the forbidden? My face flamed with anger now.

"Do you think it's amusing to tease me like this? Do you get some sort of *thrill* from making suggestive comments to teachers?"

His brow furrowed. "No, not at all."

"You distress me by talking in such a way."

He stepped backward. "I'm terribly sorry. I thought . . . Well, I'm not sure what I thought." He ran his hands through his hair again, a gesture that softened my anger. "I'll leave you in peace." He gave a quick bow and turned to walk out of the room.

Wait.

I longed to speak it aloud, to keep him near so I could explain. Tears of frustration sprang to my eyes, and I had no handkerchief. Real ladies always carried handkerchiefs, didn't they? What an impostor I was.

Of course it would be that moment that Miss Crenshaw chose to enter the room with Dr. Stewart. Dressed in heavy black satin, she seemed more than ever like an overgrown crow come to scold me.

"Miss McClure, are you well? Was that Eli Sevenstar who just walked out?"

"Yes, it was," I replied, wiping at my eyes with a gloved hand. The doctor looked away, as though he ardently wished to be elsewhere.

Miss Crenshaw frowned. "I'm not certain it was proper for the two of you to be alone together."

I stared at her, noting her stiff spine and pursed lips. Why was it that every time I made a misstep, she was there to remind me of it? And why couldn't she have the decency to speak to me in private?

"No, Miss Crenshaw, it wasn't proper at all. Now, if you'll excuse me—" I swept past both of them, not caring that I might cause offense.

I haunted Olivia's side for the remainder of the evening, merely nodding and smiling as she carried on conversations for the both of us. I nearly succeeded in not looking for Eli, and therefore barely noticed him standing with Larkin and a small group of the senior girls. His voice, rising and falling in that teasing way, did not pique my interest in the least. Nor did I care to know which particular girl he'd focused his attentions upon, nor what it was exactly that caused her to laugh so prettily.

On our way out, Olivia was called aside by Miss Crenshaw. I did not wish to join her in conversing with that woman, but neither did I wish to walk past Eli Sevenstar, who stood near the door with Mr. and Mrs. Bell. Where was I to go? Eli had thrown me so completely off guard that I was relieved when Fannie called out for me to join her where she stood with an older gentleman.

"Miss McClure, you must meet Mr. Greening of Arkansas. He knows many families in Van Buren. Perhaps he knows your parents? What are their names again, miss?"

I nearly choked.

The man raised his finger. "No, don't tell me—I've remembered! It's Edward and Margaret, isn't it? They had a daughter who went to a fine school in Columbia, Tennessee."

"That would be me!" I could have fainted from relief.

The man, red-faced and grinning, reached out to shake my hand. His eyes conveyed no suspicion. "I'm pleased to make your acquaintance, Miss McClure. I was telling Miss Bell how my memory plays tricks on me. I haven't been back to Van Buren in a while, but could have sworn I heard McClure's daughter was going to marry a Tennessee man, and yet here you are in Indian Territory!"

"Yes," I blurted awkwardly. "Here I am."

Fannie's eyes were wide with affected concern. "Did you break off with your fiancé, Miss McClure?"

"No, no, indeed, Miss Bell. There was no fiancé. Mr.

Greening must be confusing me with another girl—a cousin, perhaps."

He frowned. "Well . . . I suppose you must be right. I was just so certain . . ." He trailed off, fiddling with his mustache in consternation. I looked past him to see that Eli Sevenstar had departed. My path to escape was now clear.

I said good night to them, and to Mr. and Mrs. Bell. Then I rejoined Olivia, leaning heavily on her arm as we walked down the porch steps.

"What's the matter, Willie? You look as though you've received the most terrible news."

"I'm just tired," I said.

She patted my arm. "For all their fun, parties can be exhausting, can't they?"

Chapter 13

I'D LOOKED FORWARD TO GOING to Olivia's house at the end of term. The prospect of shedding the role of "Miss McClure, seminary teacher" to just be a girl visiting her friend pushed me through those final days before the holiday. Anyone as sweet as Olivia must have cheerful parents, and I was curious to spend time with a proper family, one in which everyone laughed and teased and scolded out of love.

I relied on this visit to help put Mr. Sevenstar from my mind. I welcomed any distraction that could keep me from reliving the conversation at the Bell home, for I wearied of tearing his sentences apart and examining each word as though it were a specimen under a microscope. It was a fruitless endeavor.

But during the final week of term, Miss Crenshaw called me into her office. I stood for a long moment, wondering what new trouble I'd brought upon myself, as she finished arranging papers on her desk. Finally, she looked up at me.

"Miss McClure, you have provided me with only one grade report this semester, and it was woefully spare in details. If you had read our catalog carefully, you would know that I expect a report at the end of each month. I must be apprised of those students who fail to maintain a passing grade, for they should be kept in study hall on Saturdays until they raise that grade."

"But all my students have passing grades, Miss Crenshaw," I said.

"You say that, but in all these weeks, you have turned in grades for only *one* examination!"

I stared down at my clasped hands. "I'm afraid, um, that I've fallen a bit behind in my marking, miss."

"I thought as much." Her mouth curved into a grim smile. "That is why I am insisting you stay at school over the holiday break."

I gasped. "But, Miss Crenshaw—"

She waved her hand to silence me. "Yes, I'm sure you had wonderful plans, but your students should be your first priority. And that means getting your grade book in order." She reached across the desk to pick up a letter. "I've also been in communication with Lucy Sharp's parents. Dr. Stewart has advised that she *not* travel home for Christmas because it would put too much strain on her leg."

"And you wish me to play nursemaid to her?"

Miss Crenshaw raised an eyebrow. "You were going to be here anyway, so I can't see how it would be a problem for you to keep an eye on the poor girl." She set the letter down. "That is all, Miss McClure."

"Yes, Miss Crenshaw," I mumbled.

Olivia pouted with disappointment when she heard the news. We shared some sharp words about the principal in private, but in my heart I knew I had only myself to blame. I'd often thought of staying up all night to work through those stacks of compositions, especially when the tapping at my window kept me from sleep. But when I looked at the papers, I didn't have the slightest idea how to mark them. I knew which ones were good (only a few of them) and which were bad (all the rest), but the problem was explaining *why* a paper was bad and what must be done to fix it. I could remember my teachers covering the pages of my compositions with red pencil markings—instructive words that blurred together when I tried to read them. I envied those teachers now, for at least they'd had *something* to say.

I took comfort in the fact that, at the very least, I would have plenty of time to finish my marking during the long, lonely holiday. I needn't fret and rush. And I had Lucy to keep me company. Along with Jimmy the cook, we were the only ones to remain after everyone else had been conveyed to the train station or fetched by family.

We set up a bed for Lucy in a quiet corner of the library so I would not have to help her up and down the stairs each day. With Jimmy's assistance, I dragged in two comfortable chairs from the parlor and set them before the radiator. When I wasn't working at a table, I sat quietly with Lucy.

The peace and silence settled into my bones—this was what I'd been missing ever since those long-ago days of playing quietly in Papa's library. Now that we were rid of the grueling daily routine, time took on a suspended quality. There was no need to rush or worry. I banished Eli from my mind, refusing to allow his *ungallant* behavior to disturb my new tranquility. No terrible dreams plagued me, nor any screams or bumps in the night. Even the late-night tapping at my window ceased. I hadn't slept so well since before Papa died.

Before heading out for her own holiday travels, Miss Crenshaw had reminded me that I must work with the music teachers to put together a dramatic performance lasting no more than ninety minutes and reflecting the school's strict adherence to propriety. The prospect of herding the girls into a public performance should have terrified me, but instead, I was excited to finally put Papa's teachings into action. Though Crenshaw hadn't suggested it, I'd seized upon *As You Like It* as the best candidate for staging. A few parts would have to be trimmed back or dropped altogether, but that didn't trouble me. Cutting down the text was a wonderful distraction from marking, and I'd never been overly attached to Touchstone and Audrey's bawdy romance anyway.

Lucy sat in her chair, sullen and quiet.

"Lucy, would you help me copy out scripts? We don't have the funds to purchase several editions of the entire text, so I'm copying out each part with the proper cues. My papa once told me that's how it was done in Shakespeare's day."

"But we do *A Midsummer Night's Dream* every year," she said, peering at my work. "The girls know it already."

I left the table to sit next to her. "I want to do *As You Like It*. What part would you like?"

"Me?" She snorted. "I'm no actress."

"How do you know? You were quite good when we performed poetry."

"That was different. There were no parents or townspeople watching. Besides," she said, tapping her splinted leg, "I've got this to worry about." She glanced over at the book in my lap. "What's the play about? Is it sad?"

"Not at all. It's about two female cousins who must don disguises and escape to the forest. One of the girls must dress as a boy, which proves interesting when she encounters the young man with whom she fell in love while at court."

"And he thinks she's a boy? Seems like he would recognize her if he'd been paying attention. Is he under a fairy's spell?"

"There are no fairies in *As You Like It.*" I thought for a moment. "Shakespeare wanted to show us how people get wrapped up in the idea of love and hardly see the person at all. That's how my papa explained it to me."

Lucy sighed. "Wrapped up in the idea of love—that sounds like Ella."

"In what way?"

She frowned.

"You *can* talk about her, Lucy. Her ghost is not going to jump out of the cupboards at us." I couldn't help grinning. "At least, not in the full light of day."

She took a deep breath. "Ella was a dreamer."

"How so?"

"I never thought Cale was good enough for her, but I still felt sorry for him when it looked like she would throw him over. She wanted something from a fairy tale and couldn't see what was right in front of her."

"Was she courted by other boys at the male seminary?"

"Fannie used to tell her she needed to find a lighter-skinned boy, a boy with better prospects, but whenever she caught Ella smiling at her brother, Larkin, she'd spit fire. And yet Ella still trailed after them." Her nostrils flared. "Used to make me so mad."

"Because she left you behind?"

After a moment she nodded. "I don't like talking about it." She sighed, then gestured toward my books and papers. "Which scenes should I copy out?"

"Oh, good! Why don't you start with Rosalind's part? I know you are quick and write a fair hand." I gave her arm a squeeze and rose to fetch more paper.

On Christmas Day we were entirely alone. Jimmy stayed long enough to make sure we had plenty to eat before setting out to visit cousins on the outskirts of town.

I'd never seen snow on Christmas, and it looked like Tahlequah would be no exception. It was nippy out, though—chilly and wet—so we huddled up with extra blankets in front of the struggling radiator and ate our breakfast of cold biscuits and preserves.

"It's too quiet," murmured Lucy.

"I like it," I said.

"I don't know. It's a heavy sort of quiet."

I gave her a sidelong glance. "Do you wish you were home with your family?"

"It'd be noisy *there*." A smile flickered at her lips and then vanished. "But, no, I don't." She bit at her fingernail, then looked at me. "Do you know how hard it is for a primary to make it to the upper school?"

"I think so."

"Well, it's even harder for a primary-turned-upper-school girl to go back home. My ma and pa don't speak good English, Miss McClure. They're proper Christians, but aside from that, they keep to the old ways. When I come home, they stare at me like I'm a stranger. They get shy and tongue-tied. And sometimes they seem angry with me. I don't understand it. They're the ones who wanted me to get an education!"

"Maybe they worry that you look down on them?"

"But I don't! I just don't like the way they act queerly around me now. Sometimes it makes my stomach ache to be home."

"Well, you're talking to someone who'd prefer never to go home again." It slipped out before I could think, so I quickly stood to forestall questions. "This newfangled steam heat is not as cozy as a fire. What would you think about some mulled cider?"

I was in the kitchen, warming my hands over the pot of cider, when I heard a shout in the distance. The sound was faint, but it had to be Lucy. I clutched my skirts and ran through the dining hall back to the library.

She was sitting up in her chair, her face pale with alarm.

"There was a banging on the door!"

I took a deep breath to calm my racing heart. "It's probably someone from town, Lucy."

The banging came again, making us both start.

"Should we ignore it?" Lucy looked ready to hide under her blanket.

I laughed shakily. "We're not going to cower in the library every time someone comes to the door. I'll go see who it is."

The corridor was so chilly I had to grit my teeth to keep them from chattering. Pulling my shawl tight, I turned the corner into the vestibule. Through the glass windows I could see a tall form standing outside the doorway. I breathed a sigh of relief. It was a man, not a ghost.

I opened the door to find Dr. Stewart peering at me from under his hat, soaked by the rain and clutching his medical case to his body.

"I came to check on the patient," he said, teeth chattering. "Actually, I came to check on both of you—Christmas is no time to be alone."

"Come in at once!" I cried, ushering him into the vestibule and shutting the door. I'd forgotten he would be alone on Christmas, his wife having passed and his own family far away.

He seemed to read my thoughts. "I've been invited to the Bells' for supper tonight, but I had the morning free and thought I'd stop by and bring you some Christmas cheer." He reached within his case and brought out a colorful tin. "It's candy my family sent from Chicago. Very fine stuff, but I couldn't eat it all myself."

I grinned. "I've just made hot cider, and Jimmy left us a loaf of gingerbread. You must come sit by our radiator. It's not as festive as a fire, but better than standing in this freezing vestibule."

Lucy's face brightened at the sight of the doctor. She opened her mouth to speak but then ducked her head shyly.

"See, it's only the doctor come to keep us company," I said, pleased to see the happy flush spreading over her cheeks.

After he'd given me his coat and warmed himself before the radiator, Dr. Stewart offered to bring another chair from the parlor. He was shivering when he returned. "I was going to ask why you didn't sit in that cozy parlor, but now I understand. It's terribly cold in there!"

"Yes, we much prefer it in here. It's still chilly, but the books seem to provide some insulation."

Lucy still smiled shyly at the doctor. With his ordinarily pale cheeks broadened by a grin and reddened with cold, he seemed quite animated. The damp air made his hair curl, and his eyes glittered a bright blue. I could see why Olivia sighed when she spoke of him, and how Fannie might yearn to take her sister's place as his wife. He was a handsome man and very gentlemanly. A little reserved, but improving upon acquaintance.

Best of all, I need not feel wicked for admiring him.

When I returned from the kitchen carrying a tray loaded with gingerbread and mugs of steaming cider, I found the doctor closing up his medical case. Lucy's eyes followed his every move.

"Our patient is doing quite well," he announced. "A few more weeks and she'll be able to walk on that leg again. It was a clever idea to set her up on this floor for the nights. Keeping her off the stairs saves stress on the fracture and encourages swifter healing."

He spoke quickly, almost as though to cover his unease. Was he nervous here with Lucy and me? No doubt we were staring.

I cleared my throat. "Have a seat, Dr. Stewart. Would you take some cider?"

We sat quietly for a while. I racked my brain for sensible topics of conversation, inwardly cursing Lucy for her dull silence. Finally, after a few false starts in which we both tried to speak over each other, the doctor gestured toward the piles of paper upon which Lucy and I had been copying scripts.

"It looks like the two of you have been hard at work on some new project."

"We're copying scripts for *As You Like It*," said Lucy, suddenly bold.

"Ah, for the spring play!" He glanced again at the papers, his eyebrows raised. "No Oberon and Titania this year, then? It is nice to have something new."

"Do you enjoy Shakespeare, Doctor?" I asked, a trifle eager.

He nodded. "The histories, particularly. I am quite fond of the Roman plays—*Julius Caesar, Coriolanus,* and the rest."

"I find those plays in my volume of tragedies."

"But they are based on history. Shakespeare made great use of my favorite book, Plutarch's *Lives.*" He smiled. "I'm certain a young lady would prefer the comedies."

I *did,* but something in the way he spoke made me want to

deny it. I'd never minded before when Papa said such things, but the words made me a little prickly after my battles in the classroom. "The sophomores read a portion of *Julius Caesar* earlier this term. It's a very bloody play, but one can't help being swept away by Antony's funeral speech, right along with the crowd." I paused, hearing the words so clearly in my head. "My father played Mark Antony once, you know."

His eyes glinted. "Your father was an actor?"

The breath caught in my throat. "Oh, it was only in school," I said quickly, "but to this day he still trots out the old 'Friends, Romans, countrymen' at parties and such. He's quite the ham." I looked down and laughed—a high-pitched sound that seemed to echo throughout the room. I expected to find both the doctor and Lucy staring at me in wonder, but when I looked up, they were contentedly sipping cider.

Dr. Stewart swallowed and wiped his mouth with a napkin. "You might share Plutarch's *Antony* with your students, Miss McClure. I'm sure they'd be interested to learn how closely Shakespeare's version of the funeral oration follows his narrative." He paused. "Those were days when men took matters into their own hands rather than talking endlessly and getting nowhere." He set his plate upon the small table near his chair. "I would be happy to stay longer, for it's been a pleasure talking with you both, but unfortunately, I have patients at the asylum to attend to."

I shivered. "That sounds most unpleasant, Dr. Stewart."

"It's part of my contract, Miss McClure—I attend to patients at both seminaries, the insane asylum, and the jail." He smiled thinly. "I would love to be a man of leisure, free to fill the day with reading and sport, but instead, I am forced to work for my living."

"But your work is important," said Lucy earnestly.

His mouth softened. "Of course." He stood. "I do thank you both for your hospitality. You have cheered me on this cold, wet day. But now I must take my leave."

Perhaps we were fools to be so easily moved to giddiness, but hours after the doctor left, Lucy and I were still smiling at the memory of his visit. If only there'd been someone to whom we could boast of it!

I awoke to darkness and distant screams. The chapel again? I sat up in bed, listening. It seemed to be coming from directly below me. *Lucy.* The ghost had found her.

Heart thudding, I scrambled to light the lamp and then pulled my wrap about my shoulders. By the time I'd reached the stairs, the screams had subsided into sobs. The downstairs corridor was so cold I could see my breath in the lamplight. When I reached Lucy, she was sitting up in bed with the covers clutched to her wet face.

"Lucy?"

"It was the water! I was drowning in it, so heavy I couldn't swim to the top. Something was holding me down, Miss McClure—pinning me to the riverbed!"

I looked around. There were no overturned tables or chairs. The pictures on the wall still hung where they had earlier that day. The only odd thing was the bitter cold, but that could be blamed on the faulty radiator.

I sat on the edge of the bed. "Lucy, it was only a dream." An older teacher might have pulled her into an embrace to console her, but it seemed awkward for me. So I smiled and patted her hand. "It was a terrible nightmare, I know, but that's all."

She wiped her face and looked at me, her eyes still frightened. "She knows it was my fault."

"Who?"

"If she knows it was my fault she's dead, she should know how sorry I am, shouldn't she, Miss McClure?"

"How was it your fault?"

But she only shook her head and burst into tears once again. I could get no more details from her that night. I did bring an end to her crying, however, by offering to sleep in the parlor. She settled back into bed once she knew I'd only be a few steps away.

I made up a pallet on the settee, shivering at the cold in the room. When I turned down the flame on the lamp, the velvety darkness engulfed me. I crawled under the heavy pile of blankets but could not fall back to sleep.

For some time I lay awake and wondering. Was pain causing Lucy to become unhinged in the mind? Or did she truly believe she had something to do with Ella's death? What would make a girl my age wish for another girl's death? I thought daily about flaying Fannie Bell alive, but if she were to drown, I wouldn't blame it on myself for thinking ill of her.

The room grew warmer, as though the steam radiator had suddenly redoubled its efforts. The panicked tightening of my muscles gradually eased. Perhaps it was because Lucy slept across the hall, but I did not feel alone. Why did the girls find this room so off-putting? It was quite cozy, indeed. I snuggled into my blankets, feeling toasty warm and well protected . . . almost as though someone watched over me.

Chapter 14

I WAS WARM AS A KITTEN curled up against its mama. So warm and safe in the heavy darkness. Eli lay behind me, cradling my body against his chest and stroking my arm. His touch made my flesh tingle. His breath feathered my cheek.

My eyes opened. I blinked at the darkness.

It had been a dream. A beautiful, scandalous dream.

But still I felt the weight of someone—or *something*—next to me. The hand continued to stroke my arm, sliding up to my neck and cheek, nearly covering my mouth before my limbs finally unfroze and I leapt off the settee.

I clutched at the matches near the lamp, knocking several to the floor. Then I held still and listened, but the only sound to break the silence was my heavy breathing. No one was there. I clutched at my blankets, felt them come away from the settee without resistance. The air seemed to grow colder by the second. Pulling the blankets around me, I found a match and with trembling hands lit the lamp.

The settee was empty.

Nearly crying with fear, I dragged my blankets into the library and laid them next to Lucy's bed. I could not bring myself to extinguish the lamp. A long night of restless tossing on the hard floor followed. I woke first the next morning and quickly folded up my makeshift pallet, spared the trouble of explaining to Lucy.

I returned to my bed after that, and neither of us was troubled again for the remainder of Christmas break. But I could not forget Lucy's face when she woke from her nightmare, pale as a corpse in the lamplight. Nor would I soon forget the feel of that ghostly hand on my body.

The students returned from their holiday rested and cheered, as though the time away had helped them forget the nighttime terrors at the seminary. I was delighted to see Olivia looking pink-cheeked and plump with Christmas ham. She immediately launched into tales of family arguments, odd cousins, and endless farm chores. When finally spent, she asked about my holiday at the seminary.

"Did you get all your marking done?"

"Almost all of it," I lied. "But that wasn't what occupied my mind the entire time." I told her of Lucy's dream and my strange haunting in the parlor.

Olivia's eyebrows rose in alarm when I described the phantom hand that nearly covered my mouth. "What do you think it—she—meant to do?"

"I don't know. Smother me? But why be so tender at first?"

"It's very odd. I wonder why such a thing happened in the parlor and never in your room—*her* old room." She looked thoughtful for a moment. "We must try to make contact again. I brought a little surprise with me that might help us."

"Shall we meet in my room again?"

She narrowed her eyes. "Considering your recent encounter, I think not."

"Where, then?"

We stared at each other, and then both spoke at once.

"The *parlor.*"

That night—or perhaps I should say early the next *morning*—Olivia and I crept down the dark staircase and through the chilly corridors to the parlor. As soon as we'd closed the two doors, Olivia pulled a candle and matches out of her carpetbag and struck up a little flame. Taking the utmost care to keep quiet, I drew two chairs around a small table, and Olivia set the newly lit candle upon it. Then she drew something wide and flat from her bag and placed it upon the table next to the candle. It was a wooden board, stained rich brown and lacquered to a gloss. I touched the cool wood, tracing my fingers over the letters and words stenciled upon it.

"This is your surprise?"

"It's a talking board," she whispered. "It should be much more efficient."

Somehow, the words *séance* and *efficient* did not pair well in my mind.

She dug around in her bag and pulled out one last item—a

small triangle with stubby little legs at each corner. She set it upon the board and gestured for me to sit.

"You put your fingers lightly on the planchette." She rested her own fingers upon the triangle. "See how it glides around? When it comes to a stop and seems to be pointing at a letter or word"—she indicated the *yes, no,* and *goodbye*—"we know we're getting somewhere. But you have to hold your fingers very lightly on the planchette. *You* must not move it—the spirit will do the moving."

"How do we get it to . . . talk?"

"We'll ask it questions, of course. But first let's say the Lord's Prayer."

I'd never understood what God and ghosts had to do with each other, and how being prayerful would help the ghosts reveal themselves, but I dutifully whispered it along with her.

"Now," she continued, "we must clear our minds. Focus on the candle flame and try to empty all the thoughts from your head. We'll move the planchette in a figure eight until it wants to move on its own."

We were quiet for a moment, our eyes following the moving triangle.

"You already thought up some questions?" I whispered.

"Yes. Now concentrate!"

I shifted my gaze to the flickering light of the candle, focusing to keep my fingers and body relaxed. The only sounds were our breathing and the faint sputter of the candle wax melting. The triangle glided silently over the board. After a moment, I felt a tingle spread along my fingers. I looked up and saw Olivia staring back at me, her eyes wide.

"Is there anyone in the room with us now?" she whispered.

The planchette continued to move in its figure eight, but after a moment, I felt a pull, as if another hand was upon the strange little triangle. The tingle climbed up my arms to my scalp as the planchette moved toward the full-moon symbol, pointing to *yes*.

I looked up and met Olivia's gaze again. Her brow furrowed in concentration.

The planchette returned to its figure-eight pattern. Olivia took a deep breath and asked the board her next question.

"Are you a former student?"

My heart pounded as the planchette continued its leisurely path over the center of the board. Then I felt that pull again as the triangle pointed once more to *yes*.

"Is it you, Ella?" It burst out of me before I could even think the question. I gasped as the planchette jerked downward and came to rest upon *goodbye*. I glanced at Olivia, who frowned at the board. "What does that mean?"

"You upset the spirit. One should never be confrontational with the talking board."

"But I only asked if it was Ella—how is that confrontational?"

"It was too forceful, Willie. The spirits often balk when you attempt to pin their identity down like that." She took a breath and smiled. "Let's start again. Try to be patient."

Once more we said the Lord's Prayer and concentrated on clearing our minds as the planchette traced its figure eight back and forth along the middle of the board. I stared at the candlelight and tried so hard to think of nothing that my head began to ache. Finally, the tingling began again. Olivia spoke in grave tones.

"Is there anyone in the room with us now?"

The planchette pulled toward *yes* before returning to its figure-eight pattern.

"Are you the spirit who was with us before?"

Again the planchette pulled toward *yes*. Olivia looked at me and gave a tight smile of triumph. But in her eyes was a warning— *Let me do this.*

"How did you die, spirit?"

The air in the room immediately chilled, and I could feel every hair on my body rise as the flesh prickled with goose pimples. The planchette began to circle more quickly, moving to point at the *r*, followed by *i*, and then *v*. It paused in the middle of the board.

"Did you drown in the river, poor spirit?"

The planchette moved to *yes* and continued circling in its figure eight.

"Spirit, what is it that you want?"

The triangle circled back and forth for a moment. But then I felt the tingle, the wooden piece pulling, and slowly it made its way to the letter *h*. I held my breath as it moved three letters to the left and pointed at *e*. After that it swooped toward the right and landed at *l*. It paused for a moment and I gulped, wondering where it was taking us. Finally, it made a dip back to the left and down to the second level of letters, coming to a stop at the letter *p*.

Olivia nodded. "Do you need our help, spirit?"

The planchette moved slowly to point at *yes*.

"How can we help you?"

The planchette shuddered ever so slightly, then moved slowly upward and to the left, pausing at *d*. Then it slid downward and pointed at *o*. Olivia and I glanced at each other—it was going to tell us what to do!

A creak of the floorboards in the corridor brought the planchette to an eerie halt at the middle of the board.

"Someone's coming," I hissed, taking my fingers off the triangle, which felt strangely lifeless now. "Put that back in your bag!"

"I have to say goodbye first," said Olivia, moving the planchette down to the word spelled out at the bottom of the board. "You shouldn't have taken your hands off, Willie—we have to do these things properly or there'll be more trouble."

"Just put it *away*," I said.

Olivia shoved the board and planchette into her bag, which she then slid under the settee. As we both stood up, I could see the dim glow of lamplight through the crack under the door.

"How does Miss Crenshaw *always* know when something's going on?" I hissed.

"We should have planned for this," whispered Olivia. "Shall I blow out the candle?"

"She knows we're here." I picked up the candle. "I'll do the talking—she already hates me, so I'll take the blame."

Olivia opened her mouth to protest but snapped it shut again as the door opened. I braced myself for the sight of Miss Crenshaw, her frowning face eerie in the lamplight. Instead, it was Jimmy. His eyebrows shot up at the sight of us.

"Sweet Jesus!" he cried. "I thought to find a ghost, not you two!" He ran a hand over his sleep-smashed hair. "What you doing here?"

"Keep your voice down, Jimmy," I said, gasping with relief. When I'd caught my breath, I launched into the lie I'd concocted moments before the door had opened. "I heard a noise in the parlor but was too frightened to check it myself, so I roused Olivia and made her come down here with me."

Jimmy shivered. "I felt somethin' strange in the air. Coulda sworn I heard whispers."

"All the way from the kitchen? That's impossible," said Olivia.

"Oh, it happens all the time, miss. I'm always hearing and seeing them ghosts." At our gasps he nodded knowingly. "Sometimes it's people from town who had a bad death. Or slaves from the Bell plantation who died before the war. Other times it's those seminary girls."

I stared at him. "Seminary girls?"

"More girls than Miss Ella Blackstone have died at the seminary, you know. Sometimes the girls sicken and die, what with the typhoid and all." He shrugged. "It happens—doc can't cure everything. But," he said forcefully, "that Blackstone girl didn't die natural."

"You mean because she drowned?" I whispered.

"That weren't no accident, I tell you. And this place has had a queer feel to it ever since."

Olivia crossed her arms. "What do you know about Miss Blackstone, Jimmy?"

"Nothing." He bit his lip and stared at the ceiling. "Except she used to sneak out at night pretty regular."

"And you didn't tell Miss Crenshaw?"

He shook his head. "Them girls can be vicious when you cross 'em."

Olivia looked ready to launch into an inquisition, but I was getting nervous. "We can't stay here much longer, Olivia, or Crenshaw's sure to find us." I turned to Jimmy. "You'd best get back to your room, Jimmy. We'll talk to you later."

His expression went blank. "I don't know anything more, miss. Swear to God."

"We'll see about that," I said, and waved them out of the room.

Chapter 15

THERE WERE NO MORE SÉANCES after that, for Miss Crenshaw's gimlet eye was always upon me. I wondered if Jimmy had told her something. He certainly did his best to avoid me.

My nights were taken up with marking anyway. Sure enough, Crenshaw had confronted me the moment she returned. And I'd had no choice but to confess the truth—I'd made *some* progress with my grade book, but most of the compositions and exams remained unmarked. She'd trained her withering gaze upon me for several terrifying moments. When she finally spoke, allowing me one week to get my business in order, I nearly fainted with relief.

When Olivia found me hunched over my desk, the compositions stacked all around me, she'd sighed in exasperation. Then she briskly explained the rubric she used to mark her students' written work, demonstrating how it could be applied to English compositions. In the early-morning hours, I blessed her for simplifying the process, and for once I was glad of the tapping at the window—it woke me when I grew drowsy.

Once I'd returned all the student papers—and dutifully shown my grade book to Miss Crenshaw—I could finally distribute the scripts for *As You Like It* to the juniors and seniors. The principal frowned when I informed her of my choice—a play never performed by the seminary girls before. But when I showed her the scripts and explained the cuts I'd made, she nodded primly and gave her blessing for us to continue.

"Keep in mind, however," she said in ominous tones, "that I'll be watching."

Casting the play took several days and involved all the upper-school English classes. To me it was much like a holiday, for one couldn't conduct actual lessons when there were readings to be done, parts to be assigned, and set designs to be planned.

Fannie made it clear from the start that she expected the part of Rosalind. She read for it and nothing else, and it was whispered she had the entire part memorized before the second day of auditions. She read beautifully.

But I cast her as Orlando.

I told myself that Fannie, the tallest girl in the seminary, would be the best romantic hero. But my heart knew I just couldn't let her have the prize. Why did *she* deserve the best of everything—she who treated everyone else so badly? I would set limits on her even if no one else dared.

"You all knew some of you would play male parts," I said when she gave me a darkly mutinous look. "Orlando is the romantic lead—it's a wonderful role, Fannie."

"But I played Titania last year—as a *junior*!" She crossed her arms. "Perhaps I'd rather play nothing at all."

"That's fine." My heart pounded. "You may work with the sophomores on set design."

"Why are you punishing me?"

I took a deep breath. I would have loved nothing better than to ban her from the production altogether. How satisfying it would be! But . . . that was something a petty schoolgirl would do, so I choked back my pride and tried to imagine how Papa would convince her. He certainly wouldn't wheedle or beg. He would *direct*.

"Fannie, you are tall and carry yourself with dignity. You have a commanding presence when you read. I cast you as Orlando not to punish you but because I thought your talents would be put to best use in that role."

She stared for a moment, jutting her chin out. Then she looked about her, as if seeing for the first time the anxious faces of all her classmates. Did she see how much they dreaded her temper? How much they wanted this to be resolved?

Finally, she lifted her hands in surrender. "Fine! I'll play Orlando. I hadn't thought the fate of the world hinged upon it." She looked at her classmates, her face determined. "But I warn you now—I'm going to upstage each and every one of you."

I sighed in relief. "Thank you, Fannie. That settles just about everything, for Lucy Sharp has agreed to manage the scripts and act as prompter during rehearsals. There's only one other item of business. Before Christmas, when the seminary boys came to serenade, I went up to the third floor and found the primaries dancing."

Most of the girls looked confused, but Alice nodded. "Sometimes they put on little performances, and we go up to watch them."

Fannie snorted. "I'm sure *I* never do."

"It's very sweet to see them dance and sing," cried Alice. "Don't you think so, Lucy?"

Lucy shrugged her shoulders lightly, her face a blank.

"I tell you this because it gave me an idea," I said, affecting teacherly confidence. "Why don't we invite the primaries to dance for the audience at the beginning of act four, right after intermission?"

The girls stared.

"Why would we do that?" asked Fannie.

"Well, they danced very prettily. And . . . I'm sorry for them, for they must feel rather lonely up there . . . from time to time."

Lelia gasped. "Oh, I see what you mean—they could dance as the forest people." She giggled. "It could be very quaint."

"They *could* perform the Green Corn dance," said Alice. "It's a summer dance, but I don't see why they couldn't do it in April."

"Oh, not that rubbish," said Fannie. "Surely you don't want to put everyone to sleep with that tiresome old custom? The very idea makes me yawn."

"Do you have a better suggestion, Fannie?" I asked.

She smiled. "I think we mustn't take it all so seriously. We should make it fun. I like Lelia's idea of using the primaries to represent the quaintness of the forest people." Her eyes brightened. "I know! Oh, it would be so amusing."

I'd rarely seen her so animated—at least about something remotely related to school. "What, Fannie?"

"They could perform a *warrior dance*. Surely Lucy could teach them something." She gave a sly glance at Lucy, who stared at the ground and said nothing. "And," she continued, "we could dress them in buckskin and put feathers in their hair."

"And give them bows and arrows to carry!" cried Lelia.

Alice raised a hand. "Or hatchets?"

"Would our audience enjoy it?" I asked.

"Oh, there's no doubt," said Fannie. "As long as Miss Crenshaw will allow it. She rarely lets the primaries out of the attic, you know."

"It's not an attic," said Lucy, speaking for the first time. "It's the third floor, and I'm certain they think it a refuge from girls like you."

"And *I'm* certain I don't know what you're talking about," said Fannie, raising her chin. "Anyway, it will be great fun. We *are* putting on a comedy, after all."

"Since you are so keen, Fannie, I'll put you in charge of the primaries."

Her eyes flashed with panic. "But—I have a whole new set of lines to learn!"

"You may choose some sophomore and freshman girls to assist you." I stood tall, for it felt very teacherly indeed to delegate. Certainly it would do everyone good to have Fannie well occupied. "Who better than you," I continued, "to make sure this performance will be charming?"

•   •   •

The next Saturday I chaperoned a group of junior girls in charge of costumes for the play. The weather was unseasonably warm, and thus everyone was cheerful as we set out. We were on the hunt for woodsy-looking fabric appropriate to the Forest of Arden.

At Foster's store we encountered Dr. Stewart, which sent the girls into flirtatious sighs and giggles. "Hello, ladies," he said, sweeping off his hat. His blue eyes were merry. "Buying material for dresses today?"

I allowed them to explain their quest, standing by as they effused about romantic forest attire. The doctor nodded and smiled very attentively, but when his eyes turned glassy, I directed the girls toward the bolts of fabric. He grinned at me over their heads, his eyes grateful, and I blushed with pleasure.

We'd just found a fine rust-colored cotton, which the girls proceeded to unroll for experimental draping, when out of the corner of my eye I noticed a tall figure standing a few paces away. I turned to find Eli Sevenstar, hat in hand.

For the past few weeks, I'd forced him from my mind—so effectively, in fact, that I'd become convinced my schoolgirl crush had waned. And yet there I was in Foster's, heart leaping and cheeks burning at the mere sight of him across a room.

"Excuse me a moment, girls. Stay right there." They looked beyond me to Eli, their brows wrinkling. But at that moment I didn't care what they thought. I casually stepped toward him, taking care to keep a bit of distance between us. Larkin Bell stood at the front of the store, talking with Dr. Stewart. It seemed we would be watched from all sides—but that didn't mean we'd be heard.

"Did you wish to speak to me, Mr. Sevenstar?" I asked, keeping my voice low.

"I did." He cleared his throat. "I owe you an apology."

My heart, still leaping, began to sing a little too. "I am listening."

"Before Christmas, at the Bell home, I took liberties in the way I spoke to you. It was inappropriate, I know that now."

The words sounded rehearsed, but his eyes crinkled with genuine worry. I could not look away or feign indifference.

"I accept your apology," I said quietly. "I only wish I'd known, as a student, how much words could hurt a teacher, even if they were only meant in jest."

"I meant to tease you . . . as a friend, not as a teacher."

I lowered my voice another notch. "It pleases me that you might think me a friend."

His eyes widened, but before he could say anything more, I said goodbye and turned back to the girls, who were doing their best not to stare. In the distance I heard Larkin Bell, his tone peevish, asking, "What was that all about?" I did not hear Eli's response. I didn't need to. I'd seen the look of relief, and of hope, in his eyes. And at that moment I didn't care that I was a fool for encouraging him to hope at all.

As I walked toward the post office to mail my usual payment to Mother, I saw Fannie coming toward me. She walked with bold strides, her face determined. I considered postponing the errand but couldn't bear to give her the satisfaction of knowing I did so because of her. She said nothing, but waved for me to go ahead. Mindful of her standing behind me, I kept my envelope facedown when handing it to the clerk and hoped she didn't notice the extra coins I passed along with it. A sense of misgiving chilled me when I turned to find her studying my face. Giving her a stern nod, I brushed past to walk out the door. Her eyes had been sly, her brows arched in challenge. Fannie Bell was up to something, and whatever it was didn't bode well for me.

When we returned to the seminary, I carried one of the many packages of material up to the third floor. Mae sat with her friends in the alcove, all of them giggling companionably. Her expression sobered when I beckoned her to the corridor.

"I have the fabric for your costumes, Mae. Do you wish to see?"

She led me to her room, where I spread the caramel-tinted cloth upon her bed.

"Mind you, I couldn't find actual buckskin. I suppose we shouldn't have been able to afford it if I had. Miss Thompson told me you girls could work on the costumes in your sewing classes. The dresses should be simple tunics—modest and comfortable. Miss Thompson has some ideas."

Mae nodded.

"How are the dance rehearsals coming along?"

She grimaced. "Miss Fannie doesn't know much about warrior dances."

"Oh well, it's meant to be lighthearted fun."

"Still, I don't see what a Cherokee dance has to do with Shakespeare, but I suppose you know more about that."

"None of us is terribly concerned with historical accuracy," I said quickly, "and neither was Shakespeare."

I'd tried to dismiss her concern, but a vague sense of unease settled over me. I looked away, my eyes drawn to the curving wall of the turret and its three windows.

"You have more windows than I do, Mae. It makes your room much brighter." I walked toward them and looked out upon the seminary's front lawn. "Do noises outside your window ever wake you at night?"

"No, miss."

"Oh," I said, strangely disappointed.

She tilted her head. "But I heard voices once."

"What voices?"

"A girl's voice. I think it was Ella. She was talking from her window, right below mine."

"Who was she talking to?"

"Don't know. A couple of times, when the moon and stars were bright, I saw her running from the school."

"Where was she going?"

"To the river, I think." She shivered. "It made my flesh creep to see her run off in the dark in her white nightie. She looked like a ghost already."

I walked back down the stairs to Lucy's room, planning to cheer her with talk of costumes. She sat on her bed frowning over my volume of Shakespeare's comedies. Though she tried to smile when I showed her the samples of cloth, her distraction was obvious.

I gestured toward the book in her hand. "What's wrong, Lucy?"

"I've been reading through *As You Like It* again. Listening to rehearsals has got me to thinking."

"Thinking of what?"

"Miss McClure, I don't *like* this play!"

I hadn't expected that. To be honest, my face flushed with sudden anger. But I took a breath and thought for a moment before speaking. "What don't you like about it, Lucy?"

She sat up straighter, her face suddenly animated. "Well, for one thing, I don't like this Duke Senior. I suppose we're meant to feel bad for him because he's exiled, but he's having a merry old time in the forest with all his friends. Does he ever think of the danger his daughter's in back at court? No!"

I blinked at the ferocity of her words. "Perhaps he thinks a young lady would be much safer at court than in the woods."

"But he knows what sort of person his brother is! Why leave his dear Rosalind in the hands of such a villain? My pa isn't perfect, but he wouldn't leave me behind like that. He wouldn't *forget* me."

"Nor would mine," I murmured.

I stared at the wall behind her, my mind drifting to the past when Papa was absorbed in his local theater ventures. During the good times, he'd invite the actors to the house—to *our* study. While they drank and laughed, I would sit in the corner, blinking against the thick clouds of pipe and cigarette smoke. And when the production was in trouble, Papa would lock himself away with his whiskey for hours—days, even.

But I'd never felt *forgotten*. Actors and productions came and went, but Papa and I always had each other.

"That's not all, miss," Lucy continued. "It's Rosalind and Orlando who truly bother me. They don't know each other. They're only *pretending* to love, as if it's some sort of game. You can't love someone you've only spoken to for a few moments. Why doesn't Shakespeare write about lovers who grew up together, who've known each other all their lives? I'm sickened by this 'love at first sight' nonsense—it's all shine and no substance."

I started to give examples of the bard's other lovers—Beatrice and Benedick, for instance—but stopped when I saw tears in her eyes. It wasn't Shakespeare who was upsetting her. It was Ella. Ella and her fairy-tale notions of love. Ella running to the river and forgetting those who loved her.

"Are you thinking about Ella?"

She sighed. "It's coming up on a year since she died. Next week the boys will come to help plan the graduation celebration, and I don't know if I can bear it without her."

I patted her hand sympathetically, but I knew there was more to her morose attitude than that. It seemed about time to confront what truly bothered her.

"Lucy, why did you say her death was your fault?"

She opened her mouth but said nothing. After a moment she pressed her lips together, shaking her head.

I tried another tack. "Why did she go to the river that night? It's quite a walk from here."

Lucy took a deep breath. "At first, she'd go there to meet Cale."

This didn't shock me, considering what I'd already learned from Jimmy and Mae. Back in Columbia I'd known girls who sneaked out of the Athenaeum on warm nights all the time. Some were foolish enough to be caught and punished, while others were far more clever. "You say it was Cale, *at first*? What happened?"

"I told you Ella broke off with him?"

I nodded.

"Well . . . there was someone else."

"Who?"

"I don't know. All the boys liked her. But Fannie teased her for loving a poor full-blood. Was she going to work a farm for the rest of her life? She told Ella the finest girls married richer boys. *Whiter* boys."

She paused, her face crumpling. Impatience tempted me to shake her until she spat it all out, but "Miss McClure" had to wait until she'd regained her composure. Finally, her breathing calmed.

"Go on, Lucy."

"Last spring she was restless," she said quietly. "Ella nearly jumped out of her skin when I said her name. She'd slipped out of the school at night in the past but was doing it more often to meet this new boy. It went on for months. I thought she'd get us both expelled. And every time we saw the seminary boys in town, Cale would take me aside and ask questions. I grew up with the two of them—they *both* were my friends. I was pulled in opposite directions, you see? When she told me she was going to meet this . . . whoever . . . and that everything would be fine afterward . . . I snapped."

"How?"

"I told Cale where she'd be."

"Why? Did you mean to punish her?"

"Maybe." She bit her lip. "But I didn't want her to die! He was shaking with fury, so angry that I'd kept the truth from him for months. He said I'd betrayed him. He grabbed my arm so roughly . . . I truly thought he might hurt me." Tears glistened in her eyes. "And I sent him to her! Am I responsible for what happened to Ella?"

"No, Lucy. Of course you're not." I thought for a moment. "What about the telegram Eli Sevenstar received? It said something about Cale trying to stop her. Did he try to stop her from meeting this person—someone who ended up causing her death?"

She frowned. "I always figured Cale got to her first. And when the other one got there, no one was about."

"And when this other boy heard about Ella's death, he wouldn't have said anything for fear of being suspected." I paused, thinking through the implications. "But what if Cale never went to the river? What if he tried to stop her, like the telegram said, and she laughed him off? Pushed him away? Perhaps he was so angry, so deeply hurt, that he just walked off in the middle of the night."

"Who killed her, then?"

"Maybe it was an accident."

"You think she walked into the river and fell over? She could swim, you know."

"Well, I still wonder if she drowned herself."

Lucy shook her head forcefully. "I said it before—that wasn't in her nature. Misfortune hit her hard all her life, and she always came through it. That's what I loved about her." She swallowed hard. "It makes more sense it was Cale. The other one loved her, and she chose *him*."

That night thoughts of Ella and her secret lover kept me awake. Fannie had pushed the poor girl toward the fairer-skinned, wealthier boys. But she didn't encourage Ella to make a play for her own brother, at least according to Alice and Lucy. It was more likely to be one of his friends.

Eli, for instance. He'd admitted to loving Ella in front of everyone. He'd even copied out a passionate poem for her, which she'd not had the decency to throw away. The thought made me more than a little sick.

I fell into a restive sleep, dreaming of Ella. I'd never seen a photograph of her, but in my dream she had long black hair, flowing loose, and skin the color of milky tea. She sat in the parlor, talking to a boy without a chaperone. I needed to interrupt them, to scold them for such impropriety, but I was frozen in place. Ella's eyes flashed, and as she tossed her long hair, I saw who sat so close to her, whispering seductive words of rivers and the sea.

Eli Sevenstar, of course.

Chapter 16

"HAVE YOU SEEN THE GIRLS' FACES?" Olivia nodded toward the three Bell cousins conversing in a tight group near the staircase.

"They seem nervous," I said, noting Lelia's tight-lipped frown. Fannie held her chin high, but her eyes darted toward the chapel more than once. "I thought they would look forward to hosting the boys tonight."

"It's usually a festive gathering, but you know this night also marks the anniversary of Ella's death. I expect they fear the ghost might make an appearance."

I studied Fannie's haughty face. "Do they think one of their group might be targeted?"

Olivia nodded. "If they were desperate enough to stage an exorcism, they must feel vulnerable. Fannie behaved wretchedly to poor Ella."

"But she's already been attacked."

"She fears a worse punishment awaits her. I think that's why she's avoiding the chapel until it's absolutely necessary to go in there." She took a breath and closed her eyes for a moment. "There's a powerful energy in the air tonight, don't you think?" she whispered. "Perhaps we could try another séance later?"

I shivered. "Crenshaw's always watching me these days."

When the male students arrived, I did my best to maintain a teacherly reserve—at the very least I tried not to be obvious in searching the crowd for Eli Sevenstar. But the instant his eyes met mine, I could not look away. He did not smile, and I wondered if walking through our doorway took him back to the previous year's gathering—the last time the male students had seen Ella Blackstone alive. Did this night bring back memories of their courting? Did he still mourn her? The words from that poem echoed in my mind. Ella had gone to the river to meet someone, and it wasn't Cale. A question hovered in my mind.

Was it you, Eli?

I could never bring myself to ask it.

Eli and Larkin Bell joined a small group of junior girls in the parlor, but I could not follow since Miss Taylor already patrolled the room with one of the music teachers. Olivia and I walked the halls instead, making sure no girl wandered into a dark corner with a boy.

Once the meeting officially convened in the chapel, we took our places near the door as directed by Miss Crenshaw. Eli slumped in a chair, his back to me, and spoke to no one as the students took their seats. I settled into my own and prepared to endure the slow passage of time until the meeting was over and I could see Eli's face again.

After a tepid exchange of ideas, Fannie Bell rose abruptly and stood before the group. If she'd previously felt any nervousness about the chapel, it was not evident as she boldly outlined her suggestions for the graduation festivities. Occasionally, I saw a hand tentatively raised, but Fannie pointedly ignored all attempts at interruption. I couldn't help rolling my eyes. Fannie was supposed to be the one *listening* as the juniors offered ideas. Olivia seemed absorbed by this unfolding drama, but I allowed my mind to wander. I cared little about the events Fannie planned, for in the end I would merely stand at the edge of their circle as the students celebrated. My thoughts turned instead to the play and how I might direct Alice to affect more confidence in her exchanges with Fannie. Alice's sweetness was an asset when Rosalind shared scenes with her cousin Celia, but a detriment during the witty banter with Orlando. . . .

Eli suddenly stood. We were an hour into the meeting—not nearly time for refreshments—and yet there he was, turning away from the group and walking past me toward the corridor. I glanced back to see Fannie staring after him. No one else seemed to notice, not even Miss Crenshaw, who sat at the front of the room marking math quizzes. I turned questioning eyes to Olivia. She merely shrugged her shoulders, looking as perplexed as I felt.

"I'll go round him up," I whispered, my heart pounding even as I tried to keep my expression matter-of-fact. I was merely a teacher going after a stray pupil, after all—nothing for anyone to be concerned about. With a final glance to make certain Crenshaw was still absorbed in her work, I slipped from the room.

The first floor was deserted, the freshmen and sophomores having withdrawn to the dining room for study hall. The primaries kept to the third floor, as usual.

When I reached the vestibule, I heard the soft click of the front door closing. Did Eli intend to walk back to the male seminary alone? After a moment's hesitation, I followed him, pulling my shawl snugly about my shoulders as I opened the door and stepped into the chilly night air.

He stood under my window, his back to me. The gas lamps blazed, so I stayed within the shadow of the building's grand archway.

"I know you're there," he said.

My heart lurched. "What are you doing?"

"I couldn't listen to Fannie anymore. I just . . ."

I took a step toward him. "You just what?"

"I don't give a damn about planning a party for graduation. No one dares speak about what happened a year ago. Maybe no one cares anymore."

"Do *you* still care?"

He turned at that, staring at me for a long moment. His eyes were unreadable. Finally, he glanced up at my window and frowned. "That was her room."

"It's mine now." He must have forgotten Fannie teasing me about it in front of everyone, for his eyebrows lifted.

"You're in Ella's room?" He moved closer, his dark eyes thoughtful. He searched my face intently. "You're nothing like her."

A cold knot tightened in my stomach. I was no great beauty—I knew that. In comparison to Ella, I must have seemed quite dull and plain. Tears came to my eyes, but I couldn't let him see. I tugged at my shawl and turned away.

"Don't leave," he said, placing his hand on my shoulder.

I flinched at the sudden contact but allowed him to turn me back around. I couldn't look in his eyes, couldn't bear to see mockery there.

"I should go," I whispered.

"You misunderstood me." He traced a finger along my cheek. "Ella was lost in a dream, changing her mind from day to day. You are steady, and I trust you. I just wish . . . I knew how you felt."

At those words, I looked up. "About what?"

"About *me*." He twined a loose tendril of my hair around his finger.

"But . . . I can't feel anything about you. I shouldn't be out here with you. I'm a teacher."

He smiled. "You have the eyes of a girl. You followed me out here, and when you look at me with those eyes, I can't help seeing you as a girl." He drew closer, and without thinking, I leaned in to meet him. "For months I've thought about kissing you," he whispered, "and it's not part of some prank to rile a teacher. I think about it because *I want to kiss you.*"

His face was inches away. He smelled vaguely of spirits, which made the knot in my stomach tighten again. Drinking at

Larkin's home was one thing, but at a seminary function? If he were caught, the punishment would be stiff—perhaps even expulsion. But more worrisome at that moment was the thought that he'd been drinking to cloud his memories of Ella, to dull the pain of her loss. The very idea made me want to shake him.

Or kiss him.

"What are you thinking?" he whispered.

My cheeks flamed as though he'd read my mind. I couldn't meet his eyes, so I stared at his mouth instead. Such a handsome mouth. How terrifying and yet how lovely to be kissed by those lips!

Still, he did not come closer.

The longer we stood so near, the more powerfully a strange certainty gripped me: if I kissed him, I might exorcise those memories of Ella. If I didn't, I would shrivel up and die a coward.

So, I took a deep breath . . . and pressed my mouth against his.

His lips, cool and soft, curved into a smile.

The reality of what I'd done struck me like a hammer and I pulled away. Eli's arms were around me in an instant, and I gasped as he buried his face in my neck.

"Finally," he murmured, his lips brushing my ear.

One hand moved down my spine, while the other gently cradled the back of my head. The shock of his body touching mine, his breath on my flesh, clutched the air from my lungs. I softened against him as he kissed my neck, my cheek, and then covered my lips with his own.

At first the kiss was slow and tender, but as my breath

quickened, his mouth pressed harder, parting my lips. I'd never been kissed before, and in my wildest dreams I never expected to be kissed like *that*. It was thrilling . . . and a little frightening.

I broke the kiss, gasping for air and shivering.

Eli frowned. "Are you cold?"

"I've nearly dropped my shawl." I fumbled at the scratchy wool, staggering as I stepped on a stray end. Once I'd tugged it from under my foot, Eli smoothed the fabric so that it fit snugly around my neck. His hands lingered on my shoulders.

I shivered again.

"What is this between us?" he asked wonderingly.

"I don't know." I glanced back at the school. The clock tower loomed above us, sending a different chill through my body. "But I could lose everything if we're seen out here tonight." I pulled away and began walking toward the side door.

He was at my side in an instant. "But why? You're not *my* teacher. And I doubt you're that much older than me."

"Miss Crenshaw is very keen on propriety. It's important that I keep this position. I don't know where I'd go if I lost it."

He was quiet for a moment. "It will be different when I graduate."

My heart swelled. But in the next moment all my lies came back to me—how could I possibly explain them? It would be easier to let him forget he'd ever had feelings for me. "You should walk back through the front door," I said primly. "I don't want anyone to see us entering the school together."

"No one will see us coming through the side door," he murmured. "Once we're inside, you can go ahead. I'll stand back for a bit."

When we reached the door, he grasped my hand and pulled me around to face him. The moon cast a pearly light on the pronounced angles of his face. As he leaned in, I heard the creaking of the side door.

"You've surprised me yet again, Miss McClure."

We jumped apart, Eli dropping my hand as we both turned toward the building. Standing in the doorway in her crow-black gown, a forbidding smile on her face, was Miss Crenshaw.

Chapter 17

"Miss Crenshaw, I—"

She held up her hand. "I'll deal with *you* in a moment." She turned to Eli. "Mr. Sevenstar, you can expect demerits for this, as I will be giving a full report to your principal. Now go back inside, before my temper gets the best of me."

Eli looked at me questioningly, but I merely shook my head. With a deep sigh, he walked past Miss Crenshaw into the building.

Once he was out of sight, she looked to me. "There is no way you can explain this, so don't try. As I said, I am surprised. Shocked, even. He is a *student*, Miss McClure! I should terminate your contract this very moment."

"Please don't, miss," I whispered. "He walked outside during the meeting, and I merely went to fetch him back in. There was nothing untoward in our meeting." I bit my lip at that lie.

The principal shook her head. "I've always had the most

trouble with my youngest teachers. Too friendly with the students, too preoccupied with being admired. Your utmost concern should be to maintain the best example of propriety for your students."

"I always keep the students in mind—"

"Miss McClure, our very reputation is at stake! Don't you realize what we are trying to prove here? Cherokee girls *deserve* to move in the same circles of society as white girls. Don't you see how your behavior undermines this and serves to prove the very stereotypes of primitive carnality we are fighting against?"

Having no worthy reply to that, I bowed my head in defeat.

"You may consider this your final chance, Miss McClure," she said, her mouth grim and thin-lipped. "And I only extend it in deference to our students, who have suffered too many disruptions of late. There is just the slimmest hope you will continue teaching here beyond this term. Your behavior will decide the matter. Now get back to your room at once."

After that, my leash shortened dramatically. I was not allowed to go to town with the girls, and even socializing with teachers was frowned upon. Miss Crenshaw walked beside me during our daily exercise, and I was expected to remain in my room or work in the library during those rare periods of leisure afforded to teachers. Late-night visits with Olivia were strictly forbidden, and I didn't dare bend the rules for fear of snapping the final straw of Crenshaw's patience.

But one night after supper, Olivia finally managed to corner me out of Crenshaw's sight.

"What is going on? Why has Crenshaw been shadowing

you these last few days?" She leaned in. "Are you *in trouble*? I knew you shouldn't go after Eli Sevenstar on your own." She paused, then raised an eyebrow. "What happened?"

I sighed. "I only meant to find him in the corridor and suggest he return to the meeting, but he went outside instead."

"And you *followed* him?"

"I went out to fetch him—as a teacher should, yes? Only Crenshaw happened to be at the side door when we came in, and she was right huffed when she saw us."

"Of course she was! You were gone so long. She asked me where you were, but I kept my mouth shut. Willie, what were you doing out there?"

I stared at the floor, imagining her horror if I told her the truth.

"We were just talking," I finally said.

"About what?"

"About Ella . . . and how strange it was that no one would speak of her death. It really was nothing, Olivia." I glanced at her, knowing too well how lame the words sounded. She frowned but could say nothing more when we heard Crenshaw approaching.

In truth, I was almost glad for Crenshaw's punishment, as it saved me from having to make a more thorough explanation to Olivia. I cared too much about her good regard to confess the truth of how I'd spent my time with Eli Sevenstar. I'd been alone with a boy outdoors at night—not just a boy, a *student*. How could I explain? A real teacher would have ordered him back to the chapel and immediately reported him to the principal. She would not surrender to her secret fancies and fall straight into his arms.

Working seemed the best way to take my mind off an uncertain future—and Eli. I kept on top of my lessons and marking. We made great strides in our rehearsals for *As You Like It,* since the seniors seemed to crave distraction. The girls used their domestic science class for fitting and sewing costumes, showing me their progress after supper every few nights. They were too busy to notice I was being punished, taking for granted it was my choice to devote every minute of the day to schoolwork.

I could only assume Miss Crenshaw was very sly when reporting Eli's infractions to the male seminary principal, for there wasn't a hint of gossip concerning me. One morning during recess, I did hear the seniors chattering about how Crenshaw had caught Eli with a girl the night of the meeting. At one point, Fannie looked directly at me, and I feared she might speak my name. She must have seen me follow Eli out of the room. But she held her tongue, and their talk turned instead to possibilities among the freshmen and sophomores.

No one but Fannie looked at me with suspicion, and perhaps I'd imagined the knowing gleam in her eyes. Most of them would never suspect a spinster teacher of something so daring and romantic. I almost wished they would.

By mid-March, Miss Crenshaw had loosened my leash enough to allow me into town for play rehearsals. Tahlequah surprised me yet again by having its own opera house—an impressive brick building, longer than it was wide, with twenty-foot ceilings. Row upon row of seats led to a wide stage draped with a handsome red curtain. I confess it shook me a little to see the students upon the stage and hear their voices echo in the empty auditorium. I'd thought we'd be performing in a meadow somewhere, with only teachers, students, and a few school officials to watch us make fools of ourselves. But, no, this was to be an *event*. According to the girls, we'd be making fools of ourselves in front of the entire town.

On our second visit to the opera house, we arrived just as a group of male seminary students wrapped up rehearsal for an upcoming oratory contest. The girls instantly launched into giggles and flutters, and my own heart did a somersault in my chest when I saw that Eli numbered among them. When he and Larkin took seats in the audience to watch our rehearsal, the girls' tittering took on an edge of panic.

"You mustn't stay and watch," cried Alice, "for Miss Crenshaw wouldn't like it."

"She wouldn't mind, as we've got a chaperone," Eli said, gesturing toward me with a grin.

"We're working on the end of act three," I said, my heart thumping. "It won't make any sense to you."

"Oh, let them stay, Miss McClure." Fannie's eyes were cunning. "As I think you know, Mr. Sevenstar's been under lock and key for ages now. Would you send him back to prison so soon? How cruel." Before I could wonder exactly what she was hinting at, Fannie grinned and clapped her hands with delight. "I know! Let's show them the primaries' dance—they'll love that." She pointed at the seated boys with a dramatic flourish.

"But you boys must leave afterward so the rest of us can rehearse in peace."

The primaries wore their everyday clothes, but the seniors had stashed their quaint props, crafted in domestic science, under the stage. Suddenly there was a flurry of activity as feathered headbands and bows and arrows were distributed among the primaries. The young girls shook with nervousness, their faces grim. But as the older students clapped a rhythm for them, they regained their composure and, with grave dignity, started the pattern of their dance.

I sneaked a peek at the boys. Larkin was grinning, but Eli looked confused. When the girls began their warrior whoops and kicks, he stood abruptly and walked out of the auditorium.

My mouth fell open. Did he want me to follow as I had that night at the seminary? Surely not, unless he wished to be expelled.

I turned to Lucy. "What's wrong with him?"

"He seemed angry," she said, raising her eyebrows. "I wonder why."

I searched her face. "Lucy, is there something you're not telling me?"

"If you want to know why he left, you'd best ask *him*, Miss McClure. He can't have gotten far."

"But I don't have time to talk to him."

Lucy shrugged.

I looked at the stage and then back to the door. "Keep an eye on things for a moment," I said over my shoulder to Lucy. "I'll return before they're done."

I shouldn't be doing this. Why am I doing this?

I found Eli pacing the lobby, his back to me.

"Why did you walk out?" I asked. "I'm sure you've hurt their feelings."

When he turned, his face was flushed with anger. But he said nothing.

"At least do me the courtesy of explaining before you stalk away," I barked.

He took a breath. "What are you *doing* with those primaries?"

"What do you mean?" I crossed my arms, anger quickening my pulse. "Do you think they aren't good enough to be included in our play? Is their skin too dark for them to grace the stage?"

"That's not what I meant." His eyes narrowed.

"What *did* you mean?"

He turned away.

I took a breath and tried to speak calmly. "I can't know what horrible thing we've done unless you tell me. Was it the dance?"

"You think you're doing them some great favor, don't you?"

"I wanted them to be included. Seems to me they're more like prisoners than students."

He turned back to face me. "But why make them do that ridiculous dance?"

"It's supposed to be amusing—they are playing the forest people, and we thought it would be charming to dress them up as warriors."

"This was *your* idea?"

I frowned. "Partly. Fannie had the idea for the dance, and I agreed to it." I took a deep breath. "I don't understand why it makes you so angry."

He paced a few more steps, then turned back to glare at me. "No Cherokee ever dressed like that, danced like that, or made those awful noises." He ran his fingers through his hair. "You could have staged the Green Corn dance and not made such fools of those girls."

"But Fannie told me that was a tiresome custom."

He snorted. "If she could, that girl would drain the last few drops of Cherokee blood from her veins. She thinks anything traditional is tedious and backward. Don't you see it was a trick? She plays Shakespeare while the full-blood girls perform a parody of our heritage. How could you not see that she's poking fun at them?"

"I'm sorry," I said stiffly. "I suppose I am ignorant about what is offensive to your people."

"My people," he muttered. "Does *anyone* want to see their traditions made ludicrous on the stage?" He sighed. "Did you ask the primaries what they wanted to perform?"

"No," I said quietly. "But they didn't complain."

"Of course they didn't. They wish to please their teachers." He shook his head. "I can't believe you fell in so easily with Fannie's plan."

"Now you're crossing a line," I said hotly. "I don't appreciate being lectured by a student."

He flinched. "I thought we'd moved beyond that."

"You think because you . . . *kissed* me, you can scold me as though I were a child?"

"You kissed me first," he hissed. His jaw tightened as he stared at me. "I don't know what to think anymore, *Miss McClure*."

Before I could say another word, he turned and walked out the door.

I stood there for a moment, breathing deeply to fight the tears and calm my thudding heart. Then I dragged myself back into the auditorium and tried not to cringe as everyone stared. Mae and her friends stood at the edge of the stage, their arms hanging awkwardly at their sides and ridiculous feathers drooping. I gestured for Mae to come down to me.

"He didn't like our dance," she said before I could speak.

I sighed. "No, he didn't."

"On the outside he looks progressive, but inside"—she tapped her chest—"he is traditional."

"What does that mean?"

"Ask him."

I looked beyond her to the other primaries, then met her gaze again. "You don't like that dance, do you?"

She shrugged.

It would have been best to think things through. To consult Olivia or even Miss Crenshaw. But when I looked at Mae, I saw her dancing as she had the night Eli sang to me under my window. And that decided it.

"Mae, I'd like you and the group to make your own dance, just as you did that night the boys came to serenade. We'll use the same music, for it's too late to change that, but you decide the steps. And let's get rid of those feathers and arrows. I really don't care anymore about what's progressive or traditional. I want you to dance from your hearts as beautifully as you did the first night I met you." I smiled. "How does that sound?"

"Sounds good, miss," she said with a grin.

Chapter 18

NO MATTER HOW I TRIED TO RESIST IT, my thoughts often turned to Eli Sevenstar. Every night I meditated upon his scathing words at the opera house. His anger made me bristle, but it also shamed me. I'd been thoughtless and gullible—so eager to get Fannie under control that I'd never questioned her motives. In the end I'd *given up* control rather than taking it. And I would have brought pain and embarrassment to so many girls had Eli not been bold enough to speak his mind to me.

But who *was* this boy, and what did he really want from me? The Eli I argued with at the auditorium was a passionate idealist—too good for a liar like me. But the Eli I kissed that cold, dark night in late February—a boy with the effrontery to kiss a teacher on the very doorstep of her school—was a shadowy, seductive creature. He'd said he could trust me, but I wondered how to feel the same about him.

I was considering this question late one night, as I had

every night since my argument with Eli, when a tremendous boom—like a cannon exploding—nearly sent me leaping straight up in the air. Through the wall I heard a muffled scream. I waited, rubbing my arms to smooth the violent prickling of hair. Just as I'd caught my breath, a flash of lightning illuminated the room, and moments later the thunder clapped again as the rain crashed against the windows.

Olivia had warned me about spring thunderstorms. "They don't roll gently over this part of the country," she'd said, and after the first few storms of the season, I was forced to agree with her. And yet being prepared didn't make the experience any easier. How could anyone keep from jumping when the thunder crashed like a cluster of iron pots falling on your head?

Sleep was out of the question, so I lit my lamp and retrieved Swinton's *Studies in English Literature* from my desk. I could at least prepare for Monday's class while the racket continued. I was nearly finished with "Thanatopsis" when I heard it. In the pauses between thunderclaps, just audible over the slapping of rain on the windows . . .

Tap, tap.

I hadn't heard it since before the night Eli kissed me.

Tap, tap . . . plink.

I set the book down and walked toward the window. Easing the curtain aside, I peered through rivulets of rain into the darkness. *Something* was out there, and it made the hair on the back of my neck stand up. Perhaps it was only the electric charge to the air, but I felt certain a presence lurked outside— something separate from the storm.

I flinched as a solid object struck the window. A thin crack snaked across the glass. I leaned closer, squinting. The lightning flashed, brightening the night sky and illuminating the grounds of the school.

But I saw nothing aside from the lampposts and trees in the distance.

The thunder crashed again, making my heart leap. I shook my head and leaned in, counting the beats until the next flash. When the lightning came, I focused my gaze on the ground under my window.

A figure stood there—the dark silhouette of a man.

I cried out in alarm and jumped back from the window, taking cover behind the chiffonier. Could it—he—have seen me? I gasped for air, the furious pounding of my heart making me light-headed. Had I imagined it?

Just then the thunder clapped so loudly my teeth vibrated, and with the noise came the crashing of glass. As the cracked window shattered inward, tiny daggers of glass sliced my right arm. I took an awkward step backward and fell upon the floor. The rain blasted through the window, splashing my face. I rolled into a ball, hands over my head, and screamed until I was hoarse.

A pounding at the door brought me to my senses, shutting my mouth.

"Miss McClure?" It was Crenshaw's voice. "Are you all right in there? I'm coming in, so don't be frightened."

The door opened, and I heard the swish of nightgowns and the padding of slippered feet as more than one person approached.

"Good Lord," Olivia cried, "the sleeve of her gown is soaked with blood!"

"The window has shattered. I've never seen the like," Miss Crenshaw said.

I felt a hand on the back of my head, a gentle touch. "Willie, can you sit up? You're soaked, and I don't want you to catch a chill. We must get your wounds seen to."

Slowly I uncurled my body and allowed Olivia to prop me upright.

"Can you manage the stairs to the infirmary, child?" Crenshaw's voice was unusually tender.

I nodded.

"Good. I'll get Jimmy to move your furnishings away from the window. We'll get that glass replaced as soon as possible. In the meantime, you may stay on the third floor."

Olivia tucked her arm under my left elbow and helped me to my feet. Then she pulled the shawl around my shoulders and, with a smile, told me to lean against her as we made our way upstairs.

None of the cuts on my arm was terribly deep. Nurse Gott applied a salve to all but one, which she quickly stitched herself. She then gave me a sleeping draught, but before it took hold, Miss Crenshaw prompted me to confirm what happened.

"I'd been looking out at the storm." I swallowed, avoiding the principal's penetrating gaze. "I . . . had just pulled away—the lightning flashed so brightly—when the window shattered inward."

"The chiffonier provided some protection, it seems," Olivia murmured.

"I'm still perplexed that such a thing could happen," said Miss Crenshaw. "Jimmy found no evidence of anything having been thrown through the window. And why only your right window, Miss McClure? It's downright odd."

I ignored the meaningful look Olivia directed at me.

"I can't begin to explain it, miss," I said with a yawn. "Perhaps it was cracked already? All I know is that I'm powerfully sleepy."

"Of course you are," Miss Crenshaw said briskly. "Miss Adair and I will leave you to rest, shan't we?"

Olivia glanced back at me almost longingly. I knew she wanted to stay, to glean more details that would flesh out her understanding of the ghost. But sleep weighed heavily on my eyelids, and I could hardly move my mouth to speak. Seeming to understand, she smiled and followed Miss Crenshaw from the room.

I did not dream that night, most likely an effect of the drug. All I remember is sinking gratefully into velvet darkness and then, a moment later, opening my eyes to find Mae sitting next to my bed. The curtains had been pulled back to allow the morning light to illuminate the room. I blinked at the grittiness in my eyes.

Mae's look was grave. "You've slept a long time. Miss Crenshaw asked me to watch you."

I rubbed my eyes. "What time is it?"

"After eleven o'clock."

I sat up quickly, then grimaced at the pain in my right arm.

"I slept that long? Why did no one come wake me? Am I missing classes?"

"It's Sunday, miss."

"Oh yes, of course." I grinned at Mae in relief. She did not smile in return, nor did she speak. Her eyes were red-rimmed, but I couldn't tell if it was from sorrow or fatigue. "Is something wrong, Mae?"

She shrugged. "Didn't get much sleep. That storm kept me up half the night."

I leaned toward her, searching her face. "Are you sure that's all? Did you . . . *see* anything out the window last night?"

A knock came at the door, making us both start.

The door opened and Olivia walked through. She nodded at Mae, who stood without saying a word and left the room. Olivia gathered her skirts and sat upon the now vacant chair next to me. Ordinarily, she would have been at church, but that morning she must have stayed at school out of concern for me. I smiled at her, my heart swelling with gratitude.

"How's the patient feeling?"

"Sore," I said.

"I've come to coax you downstairs. The rain has washed away the humidity and the sun is shining gloriously. We could sit outside under the awning and watch the girls return from their church services."

"I would love to. Just allow me a moment to make myself presentable."

It was nearly noon by the time we were settled on the front porch. The vast blue sky and cool breeze pushed the horrors of the previous night to the back of my mind. My thoughts turned instead to Eli Sevenstar. It was impossible to harbor any feelings of resentment toward him on such a fine day. He'd been perfectly correct in speaking so directly to me that day at the opera house—he'd intended to protect the primaries, not hurt my feelings. The next time I saw him, I would somehow communicate my understanding. Perhaps we would have an opportunity to speak again after the performance of *As You Like It*—he would look kindly upon the dance now that I'd put the matter in Mae's hands, wouldn't he? I imagined his smile, his eyes shining with pride, and felt a pleasant tingle down my spine.

I'd just started to drowse in my chair when our peace was interrupted. Three girls in fine hats trudged up the boardwalk toward the school.

"Here come the Bells," murmured Olivia.

I straightened in the chair and pulled my shawl tight as though to shield myself from Fannie's disdainful gaze.

But as Fannie drew near, her eyes didn't meet mine. She stared into the distance, her expression grim, but at the same time . . . triumphant? Lelia and Alice whispered together behind her.

I glanced at Olivia, who stared at the girls with raised eyebrows. "Is everything all right, ladies?"

"No, Miss Adair," said Alice flatly.

Her blunt response set the flesh on my arms to prickling.

"Come sit down," said Olivia. "If something is wrong, we want to hear about it."

The girls hesitated, then slowly approached and took seats near us.

"Well?"

They were quiet a moment, each looking anywhere but at Olivia. Finally, Alice nudged Fannie. "You'd better tell it, Fannie. It was your brother who told us the worst of it."

Fannie clasped her hands in her lap and looked directly at Olivia. "There was a lot of whispering in church today. After the service, Larkin took us aside and explained." She paused, glancing sidelong at me before returning her gaze to Olivia.

"Please go on, Fannie," Olivia prompted.

The girl took a breath. "Last night, a body washed up on the bank of the river. Larkin said that a fisherman found it early this morning."

Olivia gasped. "How horrible!"

"The body had been weighed down with rocks," Fannie continued, "but the violence of the storm broke it free from its constraints, and . . . it washed ashore."

"Who was it?" I asked. "Does anyone know? Not another student, surely?"

"Oh yes," Fannie said, nodding, "a student. But not a female seminary student." She could not meet my eyes. "It was Cale Hawkins."

The words echoed in my head. "What?"

"Larkin talked to the man who found him," said Alice. "He told us the body was much decayed, but they identified him from an engraved locket Ella gave him." She shuddered. "He'd been in the river for many months. You know what this means, don't you?"

I shook my head, trying to dislodge the fog that had settled over my brain.

Alice's eyes were wide. "Cale has been dead all this time. He never went to Texas, like Eli said."

"But . . . what about Eli's telegram?"

Fannie turned her eerie gaze to me. "It must have been a lie, Miss McClure. I bet that Hawkins boy was already dead when Eli claimed he got the telegram."

"Has anyone talked to Eli? What does he have to say?" I couldn't contain the flood of questions. "How did he explain himself?"

They were all staring at me now.

"*We* didn't see Eli Sevenstar," Fannie said, assessing me with knowing eyes. "But when my brother talked to the fisherman, Eli was with him. Larkin told us Eli turned pale as a ghost when he heard the news, and afterward he said he wasn't going to church." She leaned forward, her eyes locked with mine. "He told Larkin he had to *get out of town* for a while."

I stood up then, banging the backs of my legs so hard against the chair that it flipped over. Immediately, I regretted the sudden movement, for my head was spinning.

"Sit down, Willie," gasped Olivia, standing up to take my arm. "You're not well."

"I just can't—"

The last thing I saw as I sank against Olivia was Fannie's smug little smile.

When I came to my senses, I found myself back in the infirmary bed. My first thought was one of sympathy for poor old Jimmy, who must have carried me up two flights of stairs. I sat up to find Olivia sitting on the chair next to the bed. When my eyes met hers, I remembered.

He lied.

I thought of Eli's letter to Ella, of Lucy's confession to Cale that Ella was meeting someone else, and I nearly choked at the sudden drought in my throat. Three people had been at the river that night, and two were dead.

"There was no telegram from Cale," I croaked. "Eli lied about it."

She nodded sadly.

"Do you think Eli . . . that he . . ." I trailed off with a sob.

"You showed me the note, Willie. Eli loved Ella quite passionately at one time. Perhaps he never stopped loving her. But *she* never stopped loving Cale. Something horrific happened at the river that night. Fannie said . . ." She gulped before continuing. "After you fainted, Fannie said the body showed signs of violence—a deep wound to the head."

I thought of Eli's arms around me, his lips on mine. "Oh God," I cried, the bile rising in my throat. "How could he do it, Olivia? How could he . . . *hurt* them . . . and act so innocent?"

"I'm as shocked as you."

"How could he lie to everyone? To *me*?"

"Willie?" She leaned in and took my hand.

The sobs racked my body so violently I could barely breathe. I tried to compose myself, but when I lifted my face to Olivia, I saw her eyes widen and it choked me once again.

"Were you . . . ?" Her brow furrowed. "Did you . . . have *feelings* for him?"

I stared back at her without speaking.

Her brow furrowed. "Oh, Willie."

Unable to face her dismay, I pulled the covers over my head.

The chair creaked as Olivia stood. I knew she had no choice but to go straight to Crenshaw, for I'd just confessed the unspeakable. Soon I would be riding the coach back to the train station. I'd been a fool to think a few stolen moments meant Eli Sevenstar cared for me—and was worth caring *for*.

I waited for the door to shut behind her but instead felt the mattress sag as Olivia sat on the edge of the bed. Her hand went to my face, pulling the coverlet aside. Gentle fingers pushed the tear-soaked hair from my eyes.

"I'm sorry, Willie," she murmured. "I didn't know for certain. I'm so very sorry."

Chapter 19

MISS CRENSHAW SUSPENDED UPPER-SCHOOL CLASSES during the week following the discovery of Cale's body, announcing to a chapel full of pale and weepy girls that preparations for the play must move into full swing. Inwardly, I blessed her for providing this distraction, for I could not imagine holding class after such a shock. In any case, there was much to do before the big event. Drama and music rehearsals filled each day, along with scenery and costume adjustments. Soon the girls would crowd into the kitchen to prepare treats and plan every last detail for the reception to be held on the capitol building lawn after the play.

With so much to do, there was little time for any of us to contemplate the horror of Cale's death or Eli's betrayal.

After all my undignified sobbing in the infirmary, I turned numb. During the day I kept busy with the students, running lines and blocking scenes again and again. The repetition was soothing. I knew the girls were being pushed to the breaking point, but I didn't care. For the first time, I was an efficient teacher—ruthless, even. The power I wielded over my students distracted me from truths I couldn't face.

At night I listened for the tapping sound, but it never came. Strangely enough, I missed the steady noise that had been my companion during long nights of agonizing over Eli. If Ella had been trying to contact me, why was she silent now? Because Cale's body had finally been found? I thought back to the night of the storm, cringing at the memory of shattering glass, and wondered who had stood below my window. A man? Or a phantom?

No funeral was held for Cale. According to Olivia, his parents drove up in their wagon and took the body away. He would be buried on their own land. A few words of commemoration were spoken at the following Sunday's seminary chapel service, but only a fraction of the girls were in attendance. Perhaps the churches in town took more time to remember him. For so long he'd been the wild boy who left town when Ella died—a boy many had thought responsible for her death. I hoped someone took the time to eulogize him properly. But were there enough words to wipe the dark smear from his memory?

I knew the students whispered of Eli Sevenstar, but I didn't listen for the details. Just hearing his name was like a knife in my heart. Olivia shared the tidbits of information she came across, conveying the specifics in a detached manner so as not to upset me. From her I learned that the sheriff and his men had searched the town and surrounding countryside but could find no trace of Eli. As far as they could determine, he'd packed a small bag and left the same day Cale's body was discovered. He'd not taken the stage to Gibson Station, nor had he boarded the train. His parents claimed not to have seen him, and Larkin Bell knew nothing.

Eli had simply vanished.

If I'd had my way, I would have operated in my unfeeling manner until the end of term—pushing the girls through the spring play and then pushing them through final examinations. That way I'd be too busy to think overmuch . . . or feel. But Olivia wouldn't allow it. True to form, she had to *talk* about everything, and I could no longer rely on Crenshaw to forestall our late-night visits.

"You still haven't told me exactly what happened that night of the storm," Olivia said one evening, after inviting herself to my room. "You were screaming in terror. Was it just the window shattering? Or was it more?"

I moaned pitifully.

"Willie?"

"The tapping came again that night. I hadn't heard it for a while."

"Ella's tapping." She glanced at the window, her expression thoughtful. "Are you certain it wasn't just the storm?"

"Something hit my window, Olivia. A pebble was thrown, and it cracked the glass."

She blinked. "Who? Did you see someone?"

I thought back, trying to remember the sequence of events. "I stood by the window, waiting for the lightning so I could see. In the first flash, I saw nothing. Not a soul near the school. But in the next flash . . ." I trailed off, my pulse thumping at the memory.

"You saw someone." Olivia leaned in, her eyes gleaming.

I shook my head, recoiling from the memory. "I hardly know how to put this, but it didn't seem like a person. It was a shadow, shaped like a man, but somehow not *human*." I met her gaze. "I know it makes no sense. I've told myself the rain was playing tricks with my vision. But, really, it had nothing to do with my eyes. Some deeper sense, something in my blood, told me it wasn't a man that stood below my window. And you know what? I think Mae saw it too."

"You don't think it was Eli?"

"I can't imagine why Eli would be standing underneath my window on the very night that Cale's body washed up on the bank of the river."

"Cale . . . ," Olivia murmured. Then she gasped, and my heart pounded to see the color drain from her cheeks.

"What about him?"

"It was *Cale*," she said in a whisper.

I flinched. "Oh my God."

"We've had it all wrong," she said. "The tapping on the window—it has been Cale all along!"

I considered this. "But the accidents in the school—that *must* have been Ella, right? She was angry with Fannie and Lucy, so her spirit turned vengeful."

Olivia raised an eyebrow. "Did it? I confess that notion always troubled me. You never knew Ella. She was so good-natured. Flighty, yes, and far too starry-eyed about romance—

I think she drove the boys quite mad at times. But she was not one to hold grudges."

"Dr. Stewart said something similar once," I murmured. "But that still doesn't explain the hauntings in the school."

"Actually, it's starting to make sense to me." She took a breath. "I must calm down, so I can explain." She lowered her voice, speaking slowly. "You've been plagued by that tapping noise on your window for so long—perhaps that's what drove the students from the room in the first place. With so much spirit activity, one would think we could have contacted Ella in her own room. But we couldn't, and it's because the spirit has always been Cale, and he couldn't actually be *in* a girl's room at the seminary—"

"Wait," I broke in. "Can't a ghost go wherever it wishes?"

She frowned. "I can't say for certain, but according to my grandmother, revenants return to familiar places, and they often follow the same paths—the same rules, even—that they followed when alive. Cale never would have been allowed upstairs at the seminary; therefore, he could only communicate from the outside. Didn't you say that Ella often left the school at night? What if Cale came to her window and threw pebbles, much like what happened the night of the storm? That would explain the tapping, wouldn't it?"

"And the encounters downstairs?"

Olivia held up her hand. "Let me think a minute." She frowned in concentration. "If we catalog all the accidents, you'll see they occurred in places where male students had free access—the lower landing of the staircase, the first-floor water closet, the chapel . . ."

"And the parlor," I said, shivering at the memory of ghostly hands on my neck.

"It all makes sense. Except . . ." She paused, her frown deepening. "Why would Cale hurt Lucy? They grew up together—I think they may have been cousins."

A shiver snaked down my spine. "I know why," I murmured. "Lucy told him Ella was meeting another boy at the river, but by that point the dalliance had been going on for *months*. Cale was furious."

Olivia nodded. "He felt betrayed. The three of them were very close."

"Lucy feared he'd hurt her for keeping the secret."

"And so he did, but not in the way she expected."

I sat still, considering her theory. "All along, the ghost has been trying to tell us that *two* people died that night?"

"And Eli was responsible."

I cringed.

She patted my hand. "Once Eli is found, the revenant will be at peace. And so will we." She sighed. "We were close to the truth on the night of that first séance, you know. You must have suspected something when you found that note in your room," she said. "I wish you'd said more, but I suppose you had to be circumspect, considering your own feelings for Eli."

"At that time, I suffered from jealousy rather than suspicion."

Olivia was quiet for a moment, her eyes thoughtful. "What happened the night of the graduation planning meeting? Why do you think Eli went outside?"

"He said it was because he couldn't stand to hear Fannie

talk anymore. He seemed angry that no one acknowledged the anniversary of Ella's death." I glanced at Olivia. "But maybe it was guilt that forced him from the room?"

"Did he act like a guilty man?"

I said nothing, my skin prickling at the memory of how boldly I'd kissed Eli, and how he'd pulled me to him.

"Willie, you're blushing!"

"I don't want to talk about it." I put my hands to my cheeks, willing the flesh to cool.

"Of course," she said gently.

"I'm afraid Fannie suspects something . . . about my feelings for Eli."

Olivia's eyes widened. "Why?"

"She looks at me knowingly whenever his name is mentioned."

"Surely it doesn't matter now. You don't think she'd go to Crenshaw now that we know"—she faltered for a moment—"now that Eli is gone?"

"Oh, I could imagine her giving Crenshaw quite an earful." I looked at her. "Olivia, why haven't *you* lectured me on impropriety? How can you be so accepting of my feelings for Eli Sevenstar?"

Her expression sobered. "I *don't* accept them. I could never condone a teacher having romantic feelings for a student. But that doesn't mean I'm not sympathetic. I'm not blind, Willie. Those boys aren't much younger than us, after all."

"That's true."

Eli was *older* than me, but I couldn't tell her that.

Olivia breathed a dramatic sigh. "So many teachers are

doomed to spinsterhood. I look at Miss Crenshaw and wonder if I'll share her fate. She seems content, but sometimes she must despair at the loneliness of her life, don't you think?" She looked down. "Part of me is envious that you had a taste of love, even if it didn't end well."

"Didn't end well? It's not as though he spurned me for another. He is a liar and a . . ." I couldn't say the word.

"I know, I know. But secret romances are so . . . *soul-stirring,* even when the hero turns out to be a villain."

"I used to think so," I said dully. "Now I am quite sick of secrets."

Olivia merely nodded, smiling sadly.

How I wished I could unburden myself by telling her everything from the very beginning! But I couldn't. Once I told her the entire truth, there'd be nothing left of the friend she knew, for that girl was a creature made up entirely of lies.

Chapter 20

THE DAYS LEADING UP TO the performance dragged on, with most of us dreading the inevitable failure of a Shakespearean comedy during such dark times. Instead of improving with practice, the girls' performances grew increasingly stilted. Entire pages of lines were skipped during rehearsal. Arguments broke out, and tears were shed. Panic gripped the girls by the throat, and I hardly knew how to encourage them. What promises could I make? My spirits were just as depressed as theirs, if not more.

When Miss Crenshaw announced a forthcoming visit from Dr. Stewart during morning Chapel, the sudden burst of lifted spirits was quite palpable throughout the school. Even I, accustomed to numb perseverance, felt a thrill of excitement. As soon as the girls heard the doctor would be conveying an invitation, they fell to primping and hair arranging. I spent a fair amount of time in front of the mirror myself.

As Miss Crenshaw settled the juniors and seniors in the study hall, I caught Olivia's eye. When she joined me, I threaded my arm through hers so that we could find seats together. Dr. Stewart, smiling shyly, stood next to the principal as everyone took her place. Once all were silent, Miss Crenshaw nodded to him. He cleared his throat.

"Our community has suffered a blow lately. No doubt your spirits have plummeted, and I hope to do something about that. Over the Christmas holiday, I spoke with Miss McClure and Miss Lucy Sharp about the spring play." At his words almost every head turned to stare at Lucy and me. Out of the corner of my eye, I saw Lucy raise her chin a little higher as the doctor continued. "I learned you were attempting something new—a Shakespeare play that's not been performed at the female seminary before. As a man who is fond of Shakespeare's works, I commend you. And I wish to commemorate this new production, and provide a welcome distraction from recent events, by inviting all juniors, seniors, and teachers involved in the play to my home, on the Wednesday evening before the performance, for a celebratory supper."

The girls clapped their hands, prompting a blush to spread over the doctor's cheeks. I couldn't help leaning forward in my seat to stare at him. He really was most handsome when smiling.

"But, Dr. Stewart," Miss Crenshaw said, her expression apprehensive. I sensed the collective intake of breath from the girls. "A school night? I fear this may not be appropriate—"

"Not to worry, Miss Crenshaw," the doctor interrupted with a smile. "I promise to have the young ladies back to the seminary in plenty of time for their evening rest." He paused for her reply and nodded vigorously when she smiled in acquiescence.

The girls cheered.

Curiously, his expression sobered. "I expect one thing in return," he said in ominous tones. The girls quieted. "But it's something I think will prove helpful to you. Miss McClure, I wish you to stage a few scenes after supper—as practice, you see, as well as entertainment for those who have worked behind the scenes and are not performing." He gave a dramatic pause. "Well, what do you all say?"

At once the girls cried out their approval, clapping again and whispering among themselves. Olivia was grinning and I found myself clapping too, for finally, at long last, there was something to look forward to.

The doctor's house was a tall structure with elegantly angled eaves and a snug little porch. Its wood siding gleamed with a fresh coat of white paint, as did the dainty fence that enclosed the property. Olivia told me the style was "Queen Anne," which was considered very fashionable for Tahlequah. Inside the house we found upholstered furniture, floral wallpaper, and Oriental carpets on the gleaming oak floors. A butler and two maids, all solemn-faced negroes, were in attendance.

"Such a fine little home for a country doctor," I murmured to Olivia as we looked about. "Like something out of a fairy tale. Are those permanent servants? I wouldn't have thought his wages would allow for such a luxury."

"Rumor has it that Mr. Bell paid for the servants when

Sarah was alive and continues to do so now," Olivia replied. "He built this house for his daughter, you see. Sarah was his favorite and always received the best of everything. I'm sure it pleased him to think of his grandchildren growing up here."

"And now that will never happen."

"It still might," she said, nodding toward the doctor. He stood next to Fannie Bell, who held her chin high and stared down at those who walked past. I almost felt embarrassed for her, but also a little sickened by the thought of her snaring him. He was too good for her—a man dedicated to healing, not to lording his wealth and superior breeding over everyone else.

"Although," Olivia continued, "I've heard whisperings that Miss Bell has caught the eye of a wealthy young lawyer in town—one with aspirations to a political career."

"A white man?"

She tilted her head. "Mixed-blood, with progressive ideals."

From what I could tell, "progressive" meant to think as a white person, so it was practically the same. I wondered which was more important to Fannie—blood or money?

The sound of laughter distracted me from such thoughts. It seemed every spare inch of the reception room was filled with swishing skirts and fluttering fans. Dr. Stewart took pains to greet each guest individually, and as he took my hand, he smiled so warmly that I blushed.

"Miss McClure, you look radiant this evening."

He almost made me forget I was wearing Olivia's dress again. "Thank you, Dr. Stewart. I think we all are improved by our surroundings tonight. Your home is very lovely."

His mouth turned down slightly. "It is a testament to my late wife's good taste. I fear I cannot take any of the credit."

I could think of nothing appropriate to say, but my heart went out to him. I squeezed his hand and smiled. Immediately, his eyes brightened. As he moved on to greet the next cluster of admirers, I could still feel the warmth of his fingers on mine.

"He seems to feel very comfortable with you, Willie," said Olivia, when we were alone again.

"He has an easy way with everyone, I'm sure," I murmured, fanning my face.

As I watched him greet the students, it was hard to believe I'd once thought him thin and gray-faced. He seemed an entirely different person now—golden rather than pale, his hair curling softly about a face that didn't seem quite so narrow as before. That deep burgundy waistcoat brought the warmth of color to his cheeks. And he was wonderfully tall, taller than Papa even, so that all the girls had to crane their necks to look up at him. It was difficult *not* to indulge in hero worship when looking up at his face, framed as it was by the nimbus of golden hair. It brought to mind a line from Shakespeare, though I could not remember the play.

A bright face that cast a thousand beams upon me, like the sun.

Again I fanned my hot cheeks, embarrassed to be carried away by such romantic nonsense. But what danger was in it? He was a grown man, not a student. And I was a grown woman . . . for the most part. Looking at him made me feel like one. He may not have truly fancied me, but at least I didn't have to feel guilty or improper about fancying *him*. I needed this distraction. In fact, I craved anything that helped banish Eli Sevenstar and his betrayals from my mind.

At supper I was seated next to the doctor as a guest of honor. Fannie, sitting at a separate table in the parlor with other students, frowned most unbecomingly. *Make up your mind,* I thought, and smiled back at her. Then I turned to the doctor, intent on playing the coquette and engaging him in flirtatious banter. Unfortunately, he was occupied with Miss Crenshaw, who was unusually animated that evening. Still, he did smile when he looked my way. A few times he spoke, usually to offer another piece of bread or something equally meaningless. I stammered in reply. I hoped Fannie wasn't watching then, for undoubtedly I looked a fool.

A leisurely period followed supper, while the servants cleared the tables out of the parlor and placed chairs in two rows in the dining room. Miss Crenshaw encouraged the girls to stretch their legs or practice lines before the performance, but most of them clustered in groups for conversation, content to stay near the doctor. Olivia made eyes at me from across the room, beckoning me to her, but I wanted to walk about the house and learn more of the doctor from his surroundings. I returned to the reception room and glanced up the staircase, admiring the polished oak banisters. Two junior girls were walking down the stairs, and they smiled to see me.

"You simply must see Mrs. Stewart's sewing room, Miss McClure. She had a most impressive Singer sewing machine. It's the cleverest thing you could imagine," said one of the girls. She frowned. "Too bad there's no one to use it now."

I made polite murmurings of excitement as I took the

stairs, but in truth I cared little about sewing machines. *I'm more curious to see the private areas of the house.* My cheeks burned at such a thought. Did I hope to gain insights into the doctor's character by gazing at the counterpane upon his bed?

To my relief, the upstairs rooms were unoccupied. The sewing room and guest bedchamber, though pretty enough, held little interest for me. The doctor's bedchamber, however, required a pause for admiring the bed frame and furnishings, all made of intricately carved wood, as well as the brick fireplace topped with a gleaming oak mantel.

But it was the adjoining room that made me gasp in delight.

It was a study much like Papa's, with shelves lining the walls and a great leather chair sitting in the corner. At one end was a wide desk, very tidy except for a stack of anatomy books. At the other was a window looking out over the back garden. Such a window would provide a lovely prospect in the daytime.

I walked about the room, lightly stroking the spines of books, straightening the inkpot and blotter, and breathing in the scents of wood polish and leather. The only odors missing were those of spirits and pipe, but I did not mind their absence. Unlike my papa, Dr. Stewart would not cough so terribly from the smoke, nor would he lapse into childlike incoherence after taking too much liquor.

The books near the desk were all to do with the doctor's work—heavy medical tomes that did not interest me. But to the left of the window I found familiar titles. There was a handsome three-volume set of Shakespeare, much more costly and in better condition than my own. I gently pulled the collection of comedies from the shelf, paging through to re-visit old friends. The engravings were charming. I was tempted to sit in the chair and lose myself in my favorite stories, but the performance was to begin soon. So after breathing in its leathery scent one last time, I placed the volume back on the shelf.

The shelves held many other classics of English and American literature, as well as works in French. I could not make out the titles of the latter, for we never could afford the additional tuition for French courses, but they were lovely little books nonetheless. As I moved on to the translations of great works in Latin and Greek, one in particular caught my attention. It was positioned quite near the leather chair, and thus I could imagine the doctor reaching for it often. Plutarch's *Lives*.

I looked behind me to make sure I was still alone, then slipped the book off the shelf. I flipped to the table of contents and found the chapters on Antony and Brutus. Perhaps it would prove entertaining to compare them to Shakespeare's *Julius Caesar*, as the doctor had once suggested. I scanned the pages of dense print. It soon became clear that Plutarch would strain my powers of concentration to the very limit, so I closed the book and lifted it back to the shelf.

That was when I saw it—an elegant little volume perched face out behind the larger books. The cover design of wilted flowers caught my eye first, but when I saw the title, my heart leapt in my chest.

POEMS
Emily Dickinson

I reached into the bookcase to work the smaller book out from behind the others. I set it on top of Plutarch, intending to study its table of contents. Instead, it fell open about a third of the way through, where a folded piece of paper had been placed between the pages. I gasped to see the poem marked by the paper. The title—"The Outlet"—was unfamiliar. The text, however, brought a familiar flash of heat to my cheeks.

My river runs to thee:
Blue sea, wilt welcome me?

Feeling light-headed, I turned back to the inside cover page and saw the name scribbled there: *Charles Stewart.* Only the *C* had a distinctive loop at the top that made it resemble a lowercase *e.*

The folded paper, a creamy linen of good quality, looked to be a letter. My fingers itched to unfold it. I glanced behind me one more time and then carefully spread the letter open with my right hand.

I read the first few lines, then skipped down to the signature. My stomach convulsed. I read the letter all the way through.

Dearest Charles,
   You have not done right by me, failing to meet me
at our usual place and time after refusing to set a
date for our wedding. I can live with this secrecy no
longer. It is a slow poison that devours a little more
of my heart each day. Soon enough our secret will be

*obvious to everyone, so please let us make our love
known before scandal tarnishes it forever. I have
given you everything, and all I wish in return is to
take care of you. I will leave school so that we can be
married. You cannot wish me to go home and confess
how I have been used and abandoned by a man
whom everyone respects and admires.*

*Meet me Friday night at our usual place. If you
don't come, I will have no choice but to go to Miss
Crenshaw and explain why I cannot continue at the
seminary.*

Yours forever,
Ella

Hardly knowing what I was doing, I slipped the letter into my bodice. Then I carefully set the book at the back of the shelf and placed the volume of Plutarch in front of it. As I did, I heard footsteps behind me.

I turned to see Dr. Charles Stewart standing in the doorway.

Chapter 21

HE STOOD VERY STILL, his expression unreadable. Had he seen which book I returned to the shelf? Was the spine of the Plutarch properly aligned with all the others? Or did it protrude, betraying me? I dared not look. If he didn't already know what I'd done, he certainly would begin to suspect if I looked at that book.

I breathed in slowly and forced a smile. "You have such a lovely library. I could spend days on end here!" My voice was pitched a little too high—I hoped it did not ring false.

After a moment—a span of time that could have been an eternity but was probably only a few seconds—his mouth widened into a charming smile. "As I said before, my wife planned everything about this house. The study was her special gift to me." He stepped forward, and I willed myself not to back away. "I've been looking all over for you."

He reached out and touched my temple, tucking a stray

piece of hair behind my ear. His eyes were deep blue, and for a moment it seemed he meant to kiss me. And despite what I'd just read, it seemed I was about to let him. He leaned in, but his lips went to my ear rather than my mouth.

"The girls are ready to perform their scenes," he murmured.

I gasped. "Of course! I got lost in your books and completely forgot."

He offered his arm, and I stepped forward to wrap my own around it, praying the letter in my bodice would make no crinkling sounds as I moved. Its sharp corners poked my flesh. Had he seen it when he leaned in? Could he see it now? His shoulders were relaxed and he smiled pleasantly, but when I glanced briefly at his face, I thought there were tiny beads of perspiration lining his upper lip.

For the rest of the evening, I was in a daze. The girls had prepared three short scenes and performed them well, with only minor missteps or forgotten lines. There was much laughter, and usually at the appropriate places, but I couldn't bring myself to pretend the same amusement. *Let them believe the director's grim face is from nervousness,* I thought.

I watched Fannie closely. Her former coolness was gone, for she now searched out the doctor's eyes when she wasn't performing. He kept his face trained on the other actresses, never once meeting her gaze. Still, I couldn't help but wonder. Was she his next target among the students? Was she being misled just as Ella had been before her death? Surely not. Fannie, the only living daughter of the doctor's wealthy benefactor, was the perfect replacement for her dead sister. Ella, on the other hand, had been a poor nobody.

The thought that he might have killed Ella sent a cold chill down my spine, for I couldn't imagine him hurting a young woman. Perhaps, despite what Lucy said, he'd driven her to suicide. If that were so, who had done violence to Cale?

And why had Eli lied about the telegram he received from Cale?

It was all too much—I couldn't make sense of it.

As the girls took their bows, I rehearsed the moment in the library over and over in my mind but could not be sure the doctor had seen what I'd done. It was possible the book was in place before he saw me. He had behaved in a perfectly pleasant manner. He had not seemed disturbed, aside from the perspiration on his lip. And that could be attributed to the warmth of so many people in a small house.

But it was only a matter of time before he discovered the letter was missing. He would know what had happened then.

And he would have to do something about me.

Olivia took my arm as we made our way to the wagonettes. "You seem distracted, Willie. In fact, you went quite pale as the girls were performing." She gave me a gentle squeeze. "You shouldn't worry—they did just fine."

I leaned over to whisper in her ear. "Come to my room later—I have something to show you." She opened her mouth to speak, but I held up my hand. "We can't talk about it here."

As I waited in my room for the school to settle into the quiet of late evening, my mind turned once again to Eli. Why had he lied about the telegram? And where was he now? A possible answer made my stomach lurch with panic.

Had the doctor silenced him?

Finally, a soft knock came at the door. I rushed to open it, waving Olivia inside. Once she was seated next to me on the bed, I handed over the folded letter. Mouth in a grim line, she unfolded the paper and read. I watched her eyes widen and her mouth drop open. Like me, she read the letter several times. Her eyes found mine.

"Where did you get this?"

"I took it from the doctor's study."

She gasped. "Was it lying on his desk?"

I explained how I'd spied the volume of Dickinson's poetry hidden behind the larger volume of Plutarch's histories. "This letter marked a particular page—a poem titled 'The Outlet,' which began 'My river runs to thee.'"

"The poem in Eli's note!"

"Not Eli's note. Dr. Stewart writes his initial *C* with a loop."

"Oh no. 'C.S.' rather than 'E.S.'?"

"Exactly."

Olivia's face crumbled. "But this is terrible! The girls admire the doctor so much. We all thought him the perfect husband for Sarah Bell, and he was absolutely *broken* when she died." She stared at the letter. "It's appalling to think he seduced poor Ella and got her with child. Why couldn't he just marry her?"

"And break his tie with the Bell family? Think of his house, Olivia! Think of those servants. If he'd married Ella, he would have lost his position and the patronage of the Bell family. They would have been forced to leave this town."

"So he killed her?"

"And Cale. I'm sure he's had his eye on Fannie Bell ever since. He certainly never discouraged her obvious pash for him."

She stared into the distance. "What can we do? All we have is this letter and the note to Ella. It doesn't prove he killed her."

"It's a start."

"What about Eli Sevenstar?" Olivia asked. "If the doctor killed them, why did Eli run?"

"He must have been scared. He did lie about that telegram, after all."

"Maybe he went in search of some way to prove his innocence?"

"Or . . . maybe something's happened to him." I raised my eyebrows even as my eyes began to fill with tears.

"Oh no," she moaned.

"I need to show this to the sheriff as soon as possible." I wiped my eyes, then took the letter from her. "The doctor might have seen me take it."

"Willie!"

"I know. This may not be the smartest thing I've ever done."

She took my hand. "You can't go to the sheriff alone. He doesn't know you from Adam, but he's known my family for a long time. I'll go with you." She paused. "Should we speak with Miss Crenshaw first?"

"Oh Lord. I forgot about Crenshaw. I forgot about the play and the picnic and *everything*."

"That play means everything to the girls." Olivia sighed. "The entire town looks forward to it each year. Should we wait . . . just a few days? We could talk to Miss Crenshaw on Sunday."

I shook my head. "Crenshaw doesn't trust me. I'm not sure she'd believe a word I said, even with you backing me up." I thought for a moment. "And if she *did* somehow believe me, I'm afraid she might try to sweep this scandal under the rug. You know how keen she is on propriety and maintaining the school's reputation."

"But surely, if something terrible has happened to Eli—"

I held up my hand. "I know! That's why we must go straight to the sheriff and not waste any time explaining to Crenshaw. I'll go to church with you on Sunday, and afterward we'll find him. That way it'll be quiet."

"What are you going to do in the meantime?"

"Oh, the doctor can't get to me *here*." I forced a brave smile. "But I'm not above putting my chair under the doorknob at night, just to be safe."

I could not sleep after Olivia went to bed, for our conversation continued to echo in my head. Was Eli dead? Would I be the next target? Desperate for distraction, I walked down to the parlor and sank into the settee. Hands shaking, I struck a match to light the candle stub I'd brought with me. I'd taken pains to be quiet, but on that night I was past the point of worrying about propriety or keeping my position. The memory of the doctor whispering in my ear, perspiration dotting his upper lip, shook me to the core. And I felt the ghost should know this.

It did not feel strange to speak to the darkness. I knew he was there and did not wish to hurt me.

"What should I do?" I asked in a whisper. "The doctor has the power to make me vanish entirely. No one would come for me. No one would hold the school accountable for my disappearance." I laughed bitterly. "The McClures wouldn't know what Miss Crenshaw was talking about if she wrote to them. My own mother would never know what happened to her only daughter, because even Olivia doesn't know who I really am."

The room grew colder with each word I spoke.

"I would simply disappear, Cale. If that man gets to me, I'll become a ghost like you. Would you—" I broke off, not sure how to ask. "Can you watch over me?"

The candle flickered, but that was all.

Chapter 22

I WAS AWAKE AND DRESSED EARLY on the morning of the performance. As soon as breakfast was cleared, I gathered the girls together for one last read-through of the play. I was a mediocre classroom teacher at best, but as I listened to them recite their lines, I allowed myself some satisfaction in being a passing fair director. Not that this soothed my nerves—or theirs.

Shortly after ten o'clock, Miss Crenshaw swept in, walking straight for me with the usual frown on her face.

"I have a cable for you, Miss McClure. Pray do not let it distract you from your duties. The girls must be ready to depart by eleven o'clock."

"Of course, Miss Crenshaw. Thank you." I took the telegram from her and stared at the name scrawled upon it— it still shook me to see Angeline's name on items meant for me—before turning back to the girls. "Perhaps you should all go upstairs to don your costumes now," I said, trying to keep the tremor from my voice. "Please be back in thirty minutes."

"But, Miss McClure, we wish to know your news!" Fannie was standing next to me, her eyes bright with curiosity. "Such a historic day, for this is the first communication you've received since you arrived."

Miss Crenshaw cleared her throat. "I distinctly heard Miss McClure ask you to don your costumes. All of you—upstairs now!"

Fannie frowned but dutifully followed the others as they moved toward the corridor in a fit of whispers and giggles. I glanced back at Miss Crenshaw.

She returned my gaze for a moment. "I will leave you to it, Miss McClure," she finally said. "The wagonettes will be ready at eleven."

I nodded, clutching the unopened telegram as she turned and walked from the room. When finally alone, I took a seat at the nearest table and stared at the envelope. Had Mother finally found me? I supposed this was as good a time as any for my entire world to come crashing down upon me.

I opened the telegram. The short message was transcribed in bold cursive.

Meet me at seminary after play. Have information. Eli.

It took me several minutes to absorb the shock—I had to read the message many times, running my finger across the page and sounding out each word as though I were translating a foreign language. *Eli was alive.* He knew something important. He'd not abandoned us. Relief flooded my body, leaving my arms and legs wobbly. It would take several more minutes before I could safely stand.

I longed to tell Olivia, but she'd already departed for the opera house to supervise final preparations.

I could get through this with Eli's help. I only had to figure out how to meet him without arousing unwanted attention.

As the girls paced back and forth behind the stage, running lines and cursing softly to themselves, I peeked between the curtains at the crowd assembling in the auditorium. Everyone wore their best day clothes, the schoolgirls in white with flowers in their hair and the boys in fine pinstripes and bowlers. Even the teachers had taken particular care with their appearance and seemed especially lighthearted. I scanned the various groups of adults, giving a quick wave to Olivia when she raised her head. I did not see the doctor anywhere. I clung to the faint hope that he feared exposure was imminent and thus had decided to stay away.

Someone tugged at my sleeve. "Miss McClure?"

I turned to find Lucy, her lips quivering. "What is it, Lucy?"

"Alice is having the vapors, miss—she can barely breathe and says she can't go on the stage."

"But we're only minutes from curtain! Where is she?"

I followed her to where Alice stood in her fine court gown, gasping into a paper sack. Her brown eyes, already huge with panic, were made larger by her spectacles. Lelia had her arm around the girl's waist, but Fannie stood off to the side, frowning. The bodice of Alice's costume was straining with each ragged breath she took.

"Alice, what's wrong?"

"Oh, miss!" she said between gasps. "My dress . . . has shrunk."

"But it's the same dress we fitted for you two weeks ago."

Fannie shook her head. "It's the blasted ghost making her a nervous wreck. Alice dreams of Ella's ghost ruining her performance. She's been eating late at night—says it calms her."

"Can't help it." Alice glared at the taller girl from behind the sack. "Now I'm . . . too plump . . . to play Rosalind!"

"And you thought strangling your waist in a corset would solve the problem?" I threw my hands up. "No wonder you can't breathe, all sucked in like that."

"Please don't . . . tell Miss Crenshaw." She breathed into the sack. "I can't . . . do this. Lucy . . . will have to."

Lucy gasped, and all at once it seemed every girl was wailing in panic. I frowned at them, wishing for silence so I could *think*. Papa never shared stories of actresses who balked at the last minute on opening night. In his tales of treading the boards, he'd always been eager to step in front of the audience for the first time. He never spoke to me of those who weren't. No doubt he'd had little patience for "weaklings" who struggled with stage fright.

I turned to Lucy. "Miss Sharp—"

"Oh no, miss!" she interrupted. "I can't do it!"

"Listen to me," I said soothingly. "You and Lelia take Alice to the dressing room and get her out of the dress *and* that corset. Rip out the seam in the back and sew in a panel. Use any material you can get your hands on. Lelia, rip up your petticoat if you have to. Doesn't matter what color it is—her cape will cover the gap."

"Yes, miss," said Lelia and Lucy in chorus before guiding Alice toward the dressing room.

I turned to Fannie. "While they're working on the dress, you help Alice get her breathing back to normal. Run some lines with her." She opened her mouth, but I held my hand up. "There's no time to argue. Do you want to cancel the performance after all our work? Could you bear the humiliation?" She frowned and shook her head. "All right. Do as I say, then."

Alice breathed much easier, and seemed a little less green in the face, when she returned. We already were ten minutes overdue to begin, so I patted them all on the back and gave the signal for the curtain to rise.

We'd rehearsed in full costume a week ago, and I'd nearly cried at how many mistakes marred the performance. But this day was magic. Yes, there were awkward moments and mishaps, and Lucy had to prompt a performer more than once. These things were barely noticed by anyone but me, however, for the girls had thrown their hearts into their roles and the crowd was mesmerized. Despite her nerves and vapors, Alice was bold as Rosalind—at her best while playing the heroine disguised as a boy. How the crowd delighted in her!

But the true revelation was Fannie as Orlando—with her dark hair tied back and her slim height draped in a belted tunic over a narrow skirt, she was a heroic adventurer as well as lovelorn sop. The audience broke into cheers when she took Alice by the hand and cried, "If there be truth in sight, you are my Rosalind!" I held my breath while watching her, and then held back tears as she took her bows at the end.

The primaries' dance was also a triumph, but I could take no credit for it. They wore their plain brown tunics but had adorned their hair with flowers and greenery. Their dance was mystical and sinuous, like nothing I'd seen before and yet somehow timeless. Everyone in the audience seemed surprised—both mixed-blood and full. My heart ached with pride . . . and something strangely akin to envy.

When the girls came backstage after their final bows, their faces shining with the certainty of their success, I felt my heart might burst. I'd meant to congratulate every performer, to re-mark on each girl's particular triumphs, but all I could do was stand stupidly as the tears poured down my cheeks. The girls came to me then, trying to kiss and hug my tears away. Fannie stood stiff and proud behind the others, so when they stepped away, I took her by the hand.

"Miss Bell, you were glorious!"

Her somber face broke into a wide, unaffected grin. "I was quite good, wasn't I? I thought it'd be such a bore to play Orlando, but it turned out to be great fun to swash a buckle like that!" Then her smile wavered and her eyes grew serious. "You're being very kind to me, Miss McClure. I'm afraid . . . you won't feel so kindly later."

"What do you mean?" I asked, confused, but before she

could reply, her friends swept her away into hugs and laughter, and Olivia was by my side congratulating me. I had little time to ponder Fannie's words as the other teachers approached, followed by several of the parents who lived in town. Even Miss Crenshaw made an effort to praise the performance, saying with quiet restraint, "It all came off rather well, Miss McClure." When I beheld the astonished pride in her eyes, my heart sank. At that moment, she thought well of me and felt certain we'd upheld the reputation of the school she loved so much. All too soon, that reputation would take a heavy blow, and I would be the one to blame.

At Miss Crenshaw's urging, I herded the girls toward the wagonettes so that they could go back to the school and change out of their costumes. The picnic could not begin until they had made their triumphant return in their best spring dresses. The girls giggled and sighed as our wagons pulled up to the school.

"Careful with your costumes!" I called out as they bounded from the wagons, ignoring the driver's offer of assistance. Alice was first to reach the door. The girls crowded behind her, eager to get upstairs and change into their fine dresses.

Alice groaned in dismay. "The door is locked, Miss McClure!"

I gestured for them to part so that I could get through. "It shouldn't be. Miss Crenshaw assured me we'd be able to get in."

"Well, I can't turn the knob." She tried again, then quickly pulled her hand away. "And it's *freezing*!" She faced me with wide, panicked eyes. "Oh, miss—not again!"

I tried the knob myself, and it was cold indeed. Pulling my sleeve over my hand, I tried again. "I don't think the door is locked," I said quietly.

"It's the ghost," whispered Lelia, an announcement that immediately prompted gasps from the group.

The nape of my neck prickled, but I fought the urge to back away. I needed the girls changed and gone.

I turned to face them. "You mustn't be afraid. If this is the work of a ghost, it will only feed on your fear. We are in the full light of day, and I assume we are all awake." One girl giggled. "Nothing can hurt you unless you let your imaginations run wild."

I turned back to the door and grasped the knob again. *Let me in, for I am trying to help you.* After a moment, the knob turned with a jerk and the door came open. The vestibule was freezing cold, but no phantom figures leapt out of dark corners.

"Go upstairs and change—it might calm you if you keep someone else near at all times."

Shivering, the girls trooped up the stairs. I followed them to the landing and then stood to wait, feeling like a guard on watch. Something was different, but I could not put a name to it. There was a familiar charge to the air, an energy that lifted the soft hairs on my arms and the back of my neck. And yet I was not exactly frightened. It was more that I was on edge, wondering if I'd missed something obvious.

Hardly knowing why, I walked to the kitchen and opened one of the utensil drawers. Knives glittered in a partitioned wooden tray. I held my hand above each one, as though testing the air. Finally, I carefully grasped a small paring knife and slipped it into my pocket, blade up. Then I returned to the foot of the stairs.

At all other times, the girls would have taken ages to change and primp, but today they were quick, and within minutes were filing back down the stairs. It was time to put my hastily contrived plan into action. I followed them to the doorway before making my announcement. "Girls, you should go on ahead. There's something I must take care of."

Alice cocked her head as though confused. "But you'll have to *walk* back to town by yourself! Shouldn't we wait for you?"

Several of the girls frowned. They were eager to get to the picnic and away from the school.

"I was *attempting* to be discreet," I said, "but if you must know, my monthly has come upon me early. I really must stay behind for a bit, but I will join you as soon as possible. Now go enjoy yourselves—you deserve it!"

No one wished to argue. They made their way down the steps toward the wagonettes and loaded up quickly. After waving them off, I walked around the school exterior in case Eli had been hiding while the girls were with me. But he was nowhere to be found. I checked my brooch watch. Nearly half past three o'clock—the students would not return for at least two hours. I would wait for Eli in the parlor.

I walked back up the steps to the entrance door, which had closed behind me while I saw the girls on their way. Pulling my sleeve over my hand once more, I put my hand to the knob.

Again, it was cold and unyielding. This time I spoke to the ghost aloud, begging him to let me in. After concentrating for several moments, I felt the knob turn. But it moved sluggishly, as if against its will. Finally, the bolt retracted and the door swung open slowly.

On the other side stood Dr. Stewart.

Chapter 23

WHEN I STUMBLED BACKWARD, he grabbed my arm. I screamed, but there was no one to hear me. He jerked me into the building and shut the door. The vestibule was so cold our breath steamed in the air. The doctor gripped me with both hands, pinning me against the door. His face was damp with sweat, but his eyes were icy.

"Don't struggle, Miss McClure."

"You are hurting me!" I fought him, trying to reach for the knife in my pocket, but he held my arms firm.

"If you would only be still, I could explain myself."

My arms ached—he was much too strong for me. "Eli Sevenstar is meeting me here—he'll not let you hurt me."

He shook his head, a slow smile spreading over his face. "Mr. Sevenstar is not coming."

"Yes, he is—" I broke off as the realization dawned. "*You* sent the telegram."

"I did. Clever, wasn't it? I saw how you two looked at each other at Foster's store. If memory serves, you spent an unladylike amount of time alone with him at the Bell Christmas party too."

All the blood in my body seemed to drain to my toes. My knees buckled, but he forced me upright against the wall. His eyes were terrifyingly blue.

I swallowed hard. "Are you going to kill me?"

"It's tempting, for I'm certain everyone would blame your disappearance on Mr. Sevenstar." He looked away, as though considering the options. "But I'd rather not. I mean to give you a choice."

"What choice?"

"You took something of mine. I want it back."

"That's all?"

"And you must leave here. Today. As soon as the letter is in my hand."

I stared at him. "What did you do to Eli?"

His eyes widened. "I have no idea what you're talking about. Now stop being a fool. I've worked too hard to let a nobody like you take it all away from me." He squeezed my arms even tighter. *"I need that letter."*

I gasped at the pain. "All right. It's upstairs."

"I'll follow you." He released my right arm and shoved his hand against my neck. "But I need you to stay calm. Any sudden moves and I'll have no choice but to hurt you."

A memory came to me of Fannie's screams as he shoved her shoulder into place. He knew the human body intimately—if he could heal it, he also knew how to harm it. How could I stop him? Cale's spirit had no power past the first floor. It was up to me. But I couldn't bear the thought of actually using the knife in my pocket—the very idea of the blade sinking into the doctor's flesh made my stomach lurch.

So I merely nodded.

He smiled and removed his hand from my neck, gesturing for me to walk before him in a parody of gentlemanly grace. I stumbled toward the staircase.

When we reached the first landing, a distant explosion made us both jump.

The doctor jerked me around to face him. "What was that?"

Cale, please help me. I could hear water gushing—so much that it had to be from more than one pipe. "Sounded like it came from the water closet."

"Keep walking."

The explosions continued with each step I took, sounding from as far away as the kitchen. The dank odor of stagnant water wafted by my nostrils. At this rate, the burst pipes would flood the floor by the time I went back downstairs. *If* I went back downstairs. I put my hand lightly on the knife in my pocket, praying for the courage to use it.

The doctor pressed against my shoulder. "Hurry."

We'd reached the second floor. I went to my door and opened it, stepping inside quickly with the thought of slamming the door on him. But he shouldered his way through, pushing me onto my haunches.

"This is my last warning. Stop your foolishness and get the letter."

Stifling a sob, I crawled over to the bed. Careful to keep my back to him, I slipped my left hand under the mattress. I touched the folded note first, then the heavy paper of Ella's letter. I pulled the letter out. At the same time, I reached with my right hand for the knife in my pocket. I needed to rush at him, to throw him off balance. But the best I could do was push myself to my feet and thrust the knife toward his face.

He stepped back, his mouth widening into a grin. "Well, look what you've been hiding."

"If I give you the letter, you'll just kill me!"

He nodded slowly. "Probably."

"But if you leave now, I won't hurt you."

He laughed. Then he lifted a hand and crooked his fingers, beckoning. "Come on, then. Do your worst."

Tears welled in my eyes. I had to do something. He was an animal, a crazed beast that needed to be put down. If I could wound him, I'd have the chance to run. With a cry of rage, I lashed out with the knife.

I was too slow. He grabbed my wrist, squeezing until I let go the knife. Keeping his eyes on me, he reached down to pick it up. Then he ripped the letter from my left hand. After quickly scanning it, he refolded the paper and placed it and the knife in his own pocket.

In one breath, we were both completely still, staring at each other. In the next, his hand was in the air.

I heard as well as felt the crack of his knuckles on my head. Before I could scream, before I could take a breath, I fell hard against the wall and sank into darkness.

Chapter 24

I WOKE TO THE CHILL of cold water soaking my skirt up to my thighs. Opening one eye, I saw the shadow of the doctor's head in a blinding flash of sunlight. His hands were gripped under my arms, and my heels dragged along gravelly mud. He'd carried me to the river—slung over his back, I thought vaguely— and was now pulling me into the water.

Everyone was at the picnic. Not a soul knew I was about to die.

I kicked and scratched with all my strength, which wasn't much. He only pulled me deeper.

"You murdering bastard," I spluttered, then winced at the searing pain in my head.

He said nothing.

I tried to scream but could only squeeze a scratchy yelp from my throat.

He stopped and looked at me, and for a moment I thought there might be remorse in his eyes. Then his jaw hardened.

I took a deep breath before he pushed me under, releasing the air in slow bursts as he held me down. I kicked at his legs, but he stood firm. Through the rippled murk of the water, he looked fierce and terrible, grimacing with effort. My head and chest felt so tight I had to stop fighting—it took all my concentration to keep my eyes open and upon him. I would die looking at him. He would never forget my eyes. I prayed the sight of my face would live in his nightmares for the rest of his life.

The pressure in my lungs was like a scream begging me to breathe.

I writhed, fighting the urge. A shadow came over my left side, and I turned to see a face. A boy with black hair. His eyes widened. He reached out to me, his hand cold as ice on my skin.

I wanted to laugh.

Death was a boy with dark eyes.

I opened my mouth, swallowing the water.

He saw so much in that moment.

The past came to him first. Ella's pale face in the water—the doctor's hands pushing her down. He heard his own scream as her limp body floated away. A jagged rock in the doctor's hand sliced toward him like an executioner's blade. He stumbled, rage flowing hot through his veins. The darkness came anyway.

He focused on the present, anger flaring again as he watched this girl struggle. At least she had a chance to fight—unlike Ella—but it wasn't enough. Hadn't she asked for his help? Well, he would give that and more. When he saw her mouth open in surprise, he made his move.

He saw through her eyes. The doctor's face above his, blurred as though seen through poorly blown glass. Her body was heavy, weak, but his anger flooded through her veins, rousing it to life. He kicked again and again. Finally, he found the vulnerable spot. The doctor contorted, gasping for breath. He kicked the gut this time, and as the doctor reeled backward, he found his feet.

He slogged through the water to the still-gasping man, using his left hand to jerk the body forward by the collar. His right hand reached into the doctor's pocket, finding the paring knife. He thrust it against the doctor's neck. An artery pulsed there, ready to be opened. Ready to bleed for vengeance.

All around them the water boiled with his rage.

The doctor looked up, staring at his face. "Miss McClure, have mercy!"

He spoke, but the voice was not his own. "The girl can't hear you, Doc."

The water churned, moving in waves that slapped at the man's face as it contorted in fear.

"Oh Christ," moaned the doctor. "Ella?"

"Think again."

The doctor blinked, and then his eyes widened in recognition. "I didn't want to kill anyone! I just needed to shut her up. She didn't feel a thing, I promise. What was I supposed to do when you saw me?" The man was sobbing. "I had to protect myself."

Drawing the knife back, he tensed his arm to strike at the artery.

"Willemina!" shouted a voice on the riverbank. *A crashing of water followed as someone entered the river.*

He held his hand in the air, confused by the cry behind him. Then he stepped forward, moving away from the voice, pushing the doctor deeper into the water.

"I'm sorry," the doctor said, his voice choked by the churning water. Then his head plunged downward, as though the riverbed dropped beneath him.

His rage spent, Cale sank with the doctor into cold darkness.

Chapter 25

I OPENED ONE EYE TO BLINDING LIGHT and quickly closed it again. My body was being pulled from the water and carried toward the shore. My nose and throat burned, and I could barely breathe for coughing. Someone laid me down in the grass and gently tilted me on my side to cough up the final swallows of river water. My head was splitting, and my chest ached with each heaving breath.

I opened both eyes and saw Eli's face.

"Am I dead?" I croaked.

"No, thank God!"

He held me tight, squeezing so hard it seemed I might never get my breath back. But I didn't mind, for he was kissing my forehead, cheek, and finally . . . my mouth.

"Your lips are so cold," he murmured, covering them again with his own. When he pulled back, he smiled. "At least they're not quite so blue anymore."

I clutched at his sleeve. "I thought you were dead. I thought he got to you."

He glanced at the river, then back at me. "I was in Atoka, where that blasted telegram was sent—the one I got last year. I knew the sheriff would be after me unless I could prove someone else really sent it."

"But . . . surely you could have explained to him."

He shook his head. "I panicked at the look in Larkin's eyes. My *friend* thought I was a liar. I bet you did too when you heard about it. Everyone must have thought I killed Cale."

I looked down before he could see the confirmation in my eyes.

"It stood to reason that whoever sent it was the real killer—the person who killed my best friend," he continued. "It was a long shot, but what else could I do? I hoped someone there might remember who sent the telegram to me, 'cause it certainly wasn't Cale."

"It was Dr. Stewart," I said. "I got one from him this morning, saying to meet you."

He nodded. "I know."

"How?"

"I went to the source. The postmaster's assistant didn't want to help me at first—he acted like he didn't know what I was talking about. But when I offered him my gold pocket watch, you should have seen how quickly his memory improved. He remembered a tall, fair-haired man with a Northern accent sending a telegram a year ago. But I feared his testimony wouldn't be enough for the sheriff. I needed more."

"What got you *here*?"

"The assistant's greed. This morning he said the same man arranged to have another telegram sent, and he sold me a copy of the order." Eli's eyes flashed with anger. "That *doctor* killed Cale and Ella, and now he was going after you. I could never—*would* never—let that happen. I set out for the seminary as quick as I could."

"But the river—how did you know?"

He looked away, taking a deep breath before he spoke. "I saw the water in the school, from the burst pipes. When I smelled it, I knew where you were." He shook his head. "It sounds absurd, but I was absolutely certain you were at the river. We ran as fast as we could."

"We?" I stared at him. "Where's the doctor?"

He turned toward the river and pulled me up until I sat, leaning against him. I followed his gaze. Someone was in the water, thrashing about—a man whose head bobbed and then disappeared. There was a pause of eerie quiet as the ripples in the water widened and smoothed. Then the head burst through the surface, the mouth taking a great gulp of air. "I can't see him!" the man in the water shouted. "The water's too dark. But I'm pretty sure he's still in there, farther downstream." He pushed his wet hair back as he turned. "Is she all right?"

I gasped. "Oh my God. Toomey?" My mouth hung open as my mind struggled to form a question, a response, or even a coherent thought. How had my mother's wretched husband found me? And how had he managed to fall in with Eli Sevenstar?

Eli was frowning at Toomey. "Could he still be alive after all this time?"

I pulled at his sleeve. "Who are you talking about?"

He turned to me. "The doctor. Don't you remember?"

"I remember him pushing me under the water. He meant to drown me."

"You were about to stab him. I thought you *had* stabbed him when he went under, but you've got no blood on you."

I clutched my head, feeling dazed. "What are you talking about?"

But Eli had turned away. I followed his gaze to see Toomey heave himself out of the river, his great bulk dripping. He paused to twist his shirttails, wringing out the water. All I could do was stare as he lumbered toward us.

"He's gone," Toomey said simply, groaning as he dropped to the ground near us.

"He's drowned himself?" Eli asked.

Toomey shrugged. "I don't think she cut him, for there's no blood in the water. Looks like he slipped on a drop-off, but I can't be sure."

I stared at Toomey before turning to Eli. "What do we do now?"

He thought for a moment. "I should go to the picnic and take Miss Crenshaw aside. Explain to her in private. Then I expect I'll have to go to the sheriff."

I nodded slowly, allowing this to sink in. "I should return to the seminary to wait." I glanced at my stepfather, whose face was blank with confusion. "And Toomey should come with me."

"You said his name before. How do you know him?" Eli looked back and forth between us. "He called you Willemina, when you were . . . when you had the knife. . . ."

"I don't remember that." I shook my head, as though the motion might jog my memory. It only sharpened the pain at my temple. "Did I try to stab the doctor? The last thing I saw was him . . . holding me down, trying to drown me." Tears burned my eyes as I turned to Eli. "And then *you* were pulling me out of the water."

"You remember nothing else?" he asked. "How did you come to have the knife?"

"The knife?" The memory that came to me was hazy, as though dredged up from long ago. "I took it from the seminary kitchen. I hardly know why."

"You were holding it to that man's neck when we found you," said Toomey.

I flinched, suddenly sickened. "I have no memory of doing it. I tried to use the knife at the school, but he just laughed at me."

"You were so determined and fierce—I thought you would open that man's throat." Eli was quiet for a moment. Then he looked at me searchingly. "You spoke in an odd voice. The doctor was pleading with you."

I swayed a little as a fog came over my brain. When Eli moved to cradle me, I remembered the face in the water—Death coming for me with a gentle smile. "I can't explain it," I whispered.

Toomey waved a hand at us, his brow furrowed. "What are you two talking about?"

"Toomey, I can't believe you're here. Why *now?*" I pulled away from Eli, who was staring intently at Toomey. "It's all right," I said gently. "He's . . . my stepfather."

Eli frowned. "On the stagecoach, he asked about a Miss Hammond."

"It's a long story," I said quickly. "Too long to tell now. It simply must wait."

He started to speak, to contradict me, but the look on my face made him pause. "Fine. You'll explain it all later."

"Right now we need to get our story straight." I took a breath to steady my voice. "I found a letter from Ella in the doctor's study. She was carrying his child, Eli! That's why he killed her. But that letter is lost to the river along with his body."

"What? Carrying whose child?" Toomey's face was turning red with frustration.

"He was more of a devil than I thought," Eli said, ignoring the question. "All we can do is tell the story as it happened. We heard him confess, didn't we, Mr. Toomey? The doctor said he didn't want to kill anyone, but he had to protect himself. He said he was sorry."

"Yeah, I heard that," Toomey growled, "but I still don't—"

"And Olivia Adair saw the letter!" I gripped Eli's arm tightly. "I also found a note from him to Ella—we can take that to the sheriff."

"But we can't tell him about the knife," Eli said with a frown. "He'd never believe you overpowered the doctor. *I* still don't believe it. We'll just say you struggled, and the doctor went under the water at a drop-off."

"How *did* she overpower that man?" Toomey shouted. "I wish I knew what the heck you two were talking about." His face contorted in confusion and anger. "What sort of mess have you gotten yourself into, Willie? I find you about to stab a man in the river, and then you talk of murder and ladies with child and I don't know what."

"I realize you're confused, Toomey." *You always were slow,* I thought. "Just give us a minute to work this out and I'll explain."

As Toomey stared in disbelief, we rehearsed the story again. When satisfied, Eli stood and straightened his wet clothes. His hair was already drying in the sun. The rest of him would be nearly dry by the time he reached Miss Crenshaw and the other picnickers, for he had quite a walk ahead of him. I tried to smile encouragingly.

"Be strong," he said quietly. "I'll see you soon."

I watched him walk away, keeping my eyes on him until he was lost among the trees. Once he was out of sight, I rose to my feet and shook out my sodden skirt and petticoats. I turned to my stepfather, suddenly irritated to see him sitting there with wet shirt clinging to his bulky torso.

"Toomey, why are you here?"

"You'd best not take that tone with me, young lady, after all the grief you've brought to your mother."

I sighed. "Fine. Pray tell me why I have the pleasure of your company today."

"You're just like your father, you know? So full of yourself."

"My father was a proud man," I spat. "And I admired him for it."

"No doubt you did. And just like him, you're free with your words, but you won't *listen*. I'm sorely tempted to take you to the sheriff myself and have him lock you up." He rubbed his eyes and took a deep breath. "I'll tell you how I got here," he continued in a calmer tone. "I traveled in the coach with the young man. Mr. Sevenstar said he was going to the female seminary, so I followed along." With great effort, he heaved himself to his feet. "I was coming to fetch you, Willemina. Never expected to find you standing in a river, about to stab a man."

I rolled my eyes. "But *why* did you come? I told Mother to leave me be. How could you know I was at the school?"

"That, young lady, is an interesting story. I suppose you'll be hearing it on the way home."

Chapter 26

WE RETURNED TO THE SEMINARY to find Jimmy rolling up carpets and mopping the floors. He stared at our wild hair and rumpled clothing.

I turned to Toomey, hardly knowing what to do with him. "You look dry enough now. Why don't you wait in the parlor?"

"What do you mean to do?" His face drooped with confusion.

"I'm going to clean this mess I helped make."

After walking wearily up the stairs to change clothes and tidy myself, I returned to the first floor and took a mop to the vestibule floor. The stench of the water made me a little sick and shivery, but the work helped numb the fear . . . and the sense of impending doom as I waited for Miss Crenshaw to return. There would be no reprieve—I knew that. I was about to lose everything, and I'd brought this fate upon myself.

Jimmy stood in the doorway, frowning. "That's not proper work for a teacher, miss."

I paused to wipe my face with my sleeve. "I've a feeling I won't be a teacher much longer."

He shrugged and went back to mopping the corridor.

I worked in quiet. Odd how the seminary felt so peaceful when only an hour ago it was erupting with rage. The building stank of dank water, but at the same time it felt *cleansed*. I set my mop against the wall and walked toward Jimmy. "Do you still feel that strangeness?" He stared at me blankly—a little too blankly—so I tried again. "You told Olivia and me you'd seen ghosts before, but this time it was different."

He nodded. "The anger was thick in the air. That's what it was, you know. That's what all this is." He gestured at the water on the floor. "Wrath. I felt it, tasted it on the air, smelled its stench. I thought it smelled like death, but it was more like . . . *blood*."

"Do you still smell it?"

He sniffed the air and looked thoughtful. "Nah. I don't smell it no more. I smell that filthy water, but we'll get rid of that. The rest is . . . gone."

I threw my back into the work after that, grateful for the distraction. When Miss Crenshaw finally appeared at the front doorway with Toomey behind her, I set the mop down and made to follow her to the office.

She shook her head. "Your stepfather has made himself known to me. I will speak with him first."

She certainly knew how to stretch my nerves to the breaking point. I couldn't bear to mop the floor any longer, so I sat on the edge of the settee in the parlor—a room now warm and peaceful like ordinary parlors, but very lonely. Not even a ghost to keep me company.

Finally, the office door opened with a creak and Toomey's footsteps echoed in the corridor. He appeared at the parlor door, his eyebrows raised.

"My turn?" I asked.

He nodded slowly. My stomach sank with dread as I walked past him.

Miss Crenshaw looked gray and shrunken behind her enormous desk. She studied my face for a moment before speaking. "Perhaps we should find Nurse Gott and have her take a look at you?"

I shook my head. "I'm only bruised—there's no need to send for her. Where's Eli?"

She frowned. "Once he told me what happened, I sent him to the sheriff. He was to give his testimony quickly and return to the male seminary."

"He saved my life," I murmured.

"For that, I am grateful. It seems we all should be grateful to you and Mr. Sevenstar. Had you not intervened, we'd never have known how Ella Blackstone and Cale Hawkins died, and Miss Bell might well have married a murderer."

I must have looked surprised, for she raised an eyebrow and smiled faintly.

"Did you think I could not see how she fancied him? I may seem ancient in your mind, but I assure you I'm not blind."

I lowered my head, knowing that her smile—her brief

flash of humor—would be the last sign of kindness I would get from her.

"However," she continued with a sigh, "I have never before been so utterly deceived by anyone in my entire life. Your stepfather has explained everything—how you impersonated one of your classmates and ran away." Her eyes flashed with anger. "What were you playing at? How could you lie and insinuate yourself into our school? Our lives?"

I thought of home and my mother—of how hopeless and confining it all seemed, but how to explain that without sounding like a selfish brat? "I was so desperate to get away, Miss Crenshaw."

"Why? Because your family needed you at home for a while? Your first duty should always be to your family!"

"Miss Crenshaw, how did my stepfather find me?"

"He can tell you that."

"But I want to hear it from you. Was it Fannie Bell?"

She clasped her hands on top of the desk. "She suspected you weren't who you said you were, so she wrote to the Columbia Athenaeum. They, in turn, wrote to your parents."

You won't feel so kindly later, Fannie had said. And she'd almost looked repentant. I knew exactly when she'd mailed that letter. We'd started rehearsals for the play after that, and though I doubted she'd ever feel affection for me, I knew a grudging respect had replaced her loathing. The irony did not amuse me.

"I can't say I should never have taken you on," continued Miss Crenshaw, "or that I should have let you go the night you were out with Mr. Sevenstar. I can't say those things because of the role you have played in uncovering the truth about the doctor. But I will say that you must leave this place immediately. You cannot say goodbye to the students or teachers, not even Miss Adair, and don't you dare ask again about Mr. Sevenstar. You must pack your things and go straight to the sheriff, and after that I expect Mr. Toomey will take you home. But his plans for you are not my affair." She pulled an envelope from her desk drawer and passed it toward me. "I'd not yet paid last week's wages, but now you may consider our account settled. I care only that you are gone from here before the others return from the picnic." She heaved a sigh. "I can barely stand the sight of you."

I stared at her through the tears pooling in my eyes. From the first moment I'd met Miss Crenshaw, she'd been steely-eyed and invulnerable—not a mere woman but a battleship in skirts. Now I could see how the past few months had taken their toll. The lines on her face had deepened, and her body seemed on the verge of crumpling, as if my deceits had sapped her last ounce of strength. It was terrible to behold.

I shoved the cursed envelope in my pocket. "I'm sorry I failed you, Miss Crenshaw."

She held silent, not even nodding a farewell as I turned to leave the room.

I'd half expected a Wild West lawman with silver badge and menacing mustache, but the sheriff was a quiet man in ordinary clothes. He spoke to me first, separately from Toomey. I told the story in a straightforward manner, leaving out the ghosts, of course. I'd found an incriminating letter. The doctor realized what I'd done and confronted me. When I tried to get away, he knocked me unconscious and carried me to the river. When Eli and Toomey came upon us, the doctor panicked. And so on.

The sheriff wasn't harsh and accusatory, as I'd feared. In fact, he hardly asked any questions at all. Nor did he register surprise as I spoke, for he'd heard the same details from Eli. It seemed he accepted this version of the story—that the doctor, fatigued from having carried me to the river, lost his footing during the struggle—and never once considered that *I* might have become the aggressor. Which I hadn't, really. Whatever happened at the river, it wasn't me who pushed the doctor under the water.

He frowned and chewed his lip when I drew the doctor's note to Ella out of my bag. His brow furrowed as he read it. I couldn't tell if he was disappointed in me for keeping it or disturbed that I'd read something so unseemly. Either way, he looked at me intently as I explained how I'd found it. Then he told me to sit on the bench outside his office while he spoke with my "father."

He took a long time with Toomey. While I waited, two men with grim faces knocked at his door and stepped inside. Several minutes later, they came out again. They would not meet my gaze. When I saw my stepfather's face afterward, I half expected to be locked up for fraud, but the sheriff asked only that we stay in town for a night in case he had further questions.

I gave Toomey a questioning look as we walked away from the station.

"The body's washed up already," he said.

I shivered. "Do they need me to identify it?"

"No." His tone softened. "They'll find someone else to do that."

"Did you tell him . . . what I did? How I deceived people?"

"I told him I came for you because your mother was ill. He didn't ask for specifics."

I nodded, grateful to him and more than a little ashamed of myself. I wondered what Eli had told the authorities about me. It couldn't have been much, for we'd had so little time to discuss why Toomey would be looking for me by a different name. Miss Crenshaw would surely keep my true identity hushed up for the time being—she being so keen on reputation. But it would all come out soon enough. My heart panged at the thought of never seeing Olivia or Eli again—of never having the chance to explain why I ran away to Indian Territory in the first place. The students would be shocked, their pleasure at the success of our play spoiled. They would all think me a horrible, deceitful person, and there was nothing I could do about it.

We took cheap rooms in town that night with the intent of catching the stage to Gibson Station the next morning, if the sheriff allowed. I insisted on paying for supper and the rooms with my savings, and Toomey did not argue. In fact, he didn't say much at all.

Papa would have railed at me until I was weeping and his anger had dried up. Then he would have behaved as though nothing had happened, and I would have gone back to acting as I always did. It was different with Toomey. I thought to get a tiresome lecture at the very least, but he merely ate in silence, devouring every morsel on his plate and carefully sopping up the last dribble of gravy with his bread. The longer the silence continued, the more I felt myself shrinking, as though the clock had turned backward and I was getting younger by the minute. Soon they would have to bring me a bolster so that I could see over the edge of the table.

I'd been a teacher, earning a decent wage and taking care of myself for several months, but now I felt like a shunned child. The maddening silence made me want to leap out of my skin, to scream, to shake Toomey until some sound came out of him.

"You got the money I sent?" I finally asked.

"Yep."

The pall of silence fell over us again.

"I've been fine, you know," I continued. "I'm good at taking care of myself."

He wiped his mouth with tedious precision. "I've no doubt about that."

"So . . . you didn't need to come all this way."

"Yes, I did."

"Why?"

Finally, he looked at me. "Well, for one thing, you damn near died. But more importantly, your mother has been sick with grief and worry." He slammed his fist on the table, making me jump. When he spoke again, his voice was low and even. "I couldn't bear to see her so sad. You broke her heart, Willemina."

Part III

Revenant

April 1897

Chapter 27

WHEN I SAW THAT HOUSE ON THE RIDGE, its patched roof and drooping eaves, I felt like a revenant haunting my own past. I had returned, but not from the dead. Rather, I'd returned from life—a real, honest-to-God life—to a *place* that seemed dead. I slowed down and glanced behind me, considering the options if I were to run in the opposite direction. Toomey, on the other hand, stepped up the pace as though eager to see his wife and children.

No one waited on the porch. This was to be no sentimental homecoming. As we walked through the front door, I could hear the usual noise in the kitchen, smell the beans warming on the stove and the freshly baked bread cooling on the table.

Toomey took my bag out of my hands. "I'll run this upstairs. You go through and say something to your mother." He started up the stairs, and then paused on the third step. "Be gentle with her, Willemina. She's been hurtin'."

Stomach roiling, I made my way to the back of the house. Mother stood at the stove before a steaming pot, her back to me. I hovered in the doorway to get my bearings. Her brown hair was tidy, her dress clean, but she looked thinner and more stooped than when I'd last seen her. The twins sat under the kitchen table, playing with toy soldiers. Freddy and Hal were much bigger now, past the stage of soiled diapers and baby drool. They were nearly four years old and exploding with noise and energy. So absorbed were they in their war game they didn't notice me standing only a few feet away. I looked past them to the bassinet standing near the table.

The baby. I'd forgotten the thing that started all my troubles. I had no idea when it had been born.

At that moment one of the twins, I think it was Freddy, mimicked the sound of a cannon explosion. He did it so authentically that the baby set to crying. My mother wiped her hands on her apron and, after scolding Freddy in a soft hiss, walked over to the bassinet to make soothing noises. That was when she saw me standing there. She started so violently I thought she might scare the baby into another screaming fit.

"Willemina!" Her face paled. "I didn't hear you come in. Is your— Is Gabriel with you?"

She'd been about to call Gabriel my *father.*

"He's taking my bag to the attic," I said.

She narrowed her eyes. "What on earth happened to your head?"

My hand went to the bruise on my temple. In the mirror that morning, I'd noticed it darkening to purple. "It's nothing."

She looked at me a long time, as though uncertain whether

to launch into scolding or take me in her arms. She did neither, waving me toward the bassinet instead. "Well, come and meet your sister."

Sister? I hadn't imagined sturdy old Toomey would sire anything so delicate as a girl. As I crossed the kitchen toward the bassinet, the twins frowned at me as though I were a stranger. I resisted the urge to stick my tongue out at them for staring.

The baby was red-faced from crying but otherwise free of deformity. She had quite a thatch of dark Toomey hair on top of her head, but I decided not to hold that against her. She stopped fussing when she saw me, her eyes widening at the sight of a strange face.

"When was she born?" I asked.

"December twenty-sixth," replied Mother. "We named her Christabel, what with her being born so soon after Christmas."

"Little Christabel," I murmured, reaching down to her tiny hand. How could I not smile when she wrapped all five fingers around my own?

"We've been worried about you, Willie." Mother still looked down at the baby.

"You needn't have. I was fine. Toomey told me you were getting the money I sent."

"And it was appreciated, but we'd rather have had you with us, safe and sound."

"I suppose my labor was worth more to you than the money?"

She sighed. "You're here a few minutes and already spoiling for a fight, I see." The baby began to cry again. Mother stroked her cheek and then lifted the blanket to check her diaper.

"Well, it's going to have to wait. We'll not discuss this in front of the children."

So I helped set the table, my heart sinking as I took the plates out of the cupboard and arranged them along with cups and cutlery. It was odd to do such mundane work, and yet at the same time it felt as though I'd never left. How long would it take me to forget the person I had become at the seminary? How many settings of the table before Miss McClure's triumphs and perils faded to a ghostly memory?

I dreaded another supper eaten in deafening—and damning—silence, but my brothers made things lively. They practically wriggled with delight to see their father. After pelting him with questions, they told tales of the adventures he'd missed while away. They did not speak to me, still shy of my other-worldliness, but that didn't stop them from staring.

After supper was cleared away and Christabel was settled once more into her bassinet, Toomey took the boys to their bedroom and I dried the dishes that Mother washed.

She didn't turn to look at me. When I risked a glance out of the corner of my eye, I saw her stiff shoulders and tight mouth curved downward. I dried and dried, waiting for her to speak. Waiting for her to say the words that would stoke the flame of my anger.

But Mother did not speak. And I wasn't about to open my mouth first.

So when I'd dried the last dish and placed it on the table, I threw the rag down next to it and went to my room.

•   •   •

The stalemate continued for days. I did my chores in silence and then retreated to the attic to avoid Toomey's drooping face and Mother's coldness.

After supper I'd crawl into bed and dream of the river, my mind flashing with images of the doctor's face, pale and streaming with water. In these dreams I had him by the throat, pushing him deeper and deeper into the river. Invariably, I woke up with a start, heart pounding and body soaked in sweat. For the rest of the night, I'd toss and turn, wondering how my dream self remembered what my waking mind couldn't.

The days crawled by. Rain drummed on the roof each night, making the attic air heavy and damp. But I refused to go downstairs unless absolutely necessary, for the twins paced the house like caged animals while Toomey stared out the window. The longer it rained, the more the house felt like an asylum for the mentally unfit.

Finally, even the sun grew tired of the gloom and decided to blast the clouds and rain away. On the first dry morning, Toomey took the boys outside, and Mother perked up enough to actually speak to me.

"Gabriel will be turning the earth for spring planting this morning. He's already milked the cows, but you'll need to feed and water all the animals."

Tempting as it was to throw a fit over such a blunt request, I actually was pleased to get out of the house. It had been years since I tended the livestock, and Papa never countenanced too much rough work for his girl. But I was so eager to breathe some fresh air that I tied on my bonnet and marched out to the barn without a word of protest.

The cows were more curious than I remembered, nuzzling me with slimy noses and blowing their sour cud breath in my face. Their rolling eyes and long tongues were monstrous, and they nearly knocked me over when they mistook me for a scratching post. The chickens were small but raised a racket of clucks and squawks. My heart nearly rose to my throat when they descended upon me, for I feared they'd peck me to death as I spread the feed. By comparison, the pigs were downright gentle and merely grunted appreciatively as the slop splashed into their trough. Their muddy beds raised an unholy stench, however, and it nearly gagged me.

At least none of the animals talked back or poked fun at my clothes.

By the time every creature was fed, I was filthy and damp with perspiration. The flies were taking notice. So I washed the sweat away with trough water and climbed the ladder to the barn loft. The air was fresh and the hay smelled sweet—a perfect spot for a nap. I fluffed up some hay and settled down where I had a view out to the orchard.

Just as my eyelids were growing heavy, I heard it.

Purring.

I sat up and began to root around in the hay. A few paces away in the corner of the loft, I found a skinny cat with six kittens pounding away at her belly as they nursed. The poor mama looked exhausted and didn't even mew in protest when I stroked her handsome head. I leaned in to get a closer look at the kittens. Plump little bodies and wide-open eyes. They'd be weaned before long. When one detached for a moment, I reached in and gently lifted it to my chest. I swear the mama cat looked relieved.

Before long I had three kittens in my lap. I took turns bringing each to my face and breathing in their smell of sweet hay and clean fur. Their deep, rumbling purrs brought a warm tingle to my belly. I leaned back and let them crawl all over me until they curled up together and fell asleep on my chest. Their warmth soaked into my very bones.

In my drowsy contentment, I imagined Eli's arms around me, his hands tangled in my hair. No one had touched me since that day at the river when he pulled my body from the water. It occurred to me that before the night we'd embraced under my window, no one had held me for years. Once Papa died, Mother's arms were busy with Toomey, and soon thereafter, the twins.

It was enough to make me wonder—how long could one live without the warmth of human touch?

Chapter 28

EVERY DAY THAT WEEK I spent my mornings in the loft. When I wasn't dreaming of Eli, I sorted through my bottled-up frustrations—things I would have shared with Olivia if she'd been near and didn't loathe me for being a liar.

What would she make of my nightmares? The more I considered the matter from her point of view, the clearer it became. In those moments before I'd lost consciousness, when I was so close to death, I'd seen a dark-haired boy. Cale Hawkins. Somehow he'd reached out to me, and his spirit had guided what happened in the river. His rage—the violence unleashed on Fannie and Lucy, the very same rage that shattered my window—had somehow possessed my own body. But that rage had cooled when the river claimed the doctor, leaving me with nothing but the blurry visions of my dreams.

Once I'd imagined Olivia explaining it that way, my nightmares came less frequently, and when they did come, they weren't quite so terrifying.

I often thought of writing to her, though I doubted Crenshaw would pass my letter along. I could see her keeping it from Olivia lest it prove upsetting—she would consider it part of her duty to protect the staff after a harrowing incident. I couldn't blame her, really.

Even if the letter did reach Olivia, what would it say? How could I explain? If there'd been paper in the house, I would have written down my thoughts to see if they looked as pathetic as I feared. But Mother did not keep stores of paper for idle scribbling, so I tested the words aloud in the loft when the kittens were sleeping.

"Dearest Olivia," I always started. And then something would catch in my throat. But that day I was determined to get the jumbled thoughts out of my head. "Dearest Olivia, I hope you are well. I miss you." I paused, grappling for the right words. "By now you probably know I am not Angeline McClure, and that I was only pretending to be a teacher. I lied because . . . well, because I had a terrible home life and lying was the only way to escape it."

I could see Olivia reading that letter, gasping at the thought of my parents beating me until my only choice was to lie, steal, and run away. That would not do. The last thing I wanted was to mislead her with yet another half-truth.

"Olivia, I lied because my mother was forcing me to leave school and come home to work on the farm. The very idea of such drudgery was unbearable. My papa would have turned in his grave—"

"Willemeeeeeena!"

I jumped at the high-pitched voice. After catching my breath, I scrambled across to the wide loft window and peered over the edge. Freddy and Hal were looking up at me, stubby little figures with wide eyes and red cheeks.

"What?"

Hal tilted his head. "Who you talkin' to?"

"Nobody. What do you want?"

"Has the kitties opened their eyes yet?" Freddy asked, bouncing with excitement. "We wanna play with 'em and Mama says we can't till they open their eyes."

"The kittens are still too little. I'm afraid you'll hurt them. Now go on back to the house."

Both boys hung their heads. Then Freddy bounced again. "Can we come up there and just *look* at 'em? We'll be good, I promise."

"No, Freddy! I want to be alone right now."

"But *why?*"

"Because you annoy me. Now go on home."

Freddy looked at Hal. "What's annoy?"

Hal shrugged and kicked at the dirt.

I scrambled back to my spot in the hay, hoping they'd give up and return to the house. But after several false starts, I could not pick up the thread of my letter to Olivia. Nor could I settle into romantic thoughts of Eli again. The peace of the morning had been rudely interrupted, and I could sit still no longer.

I decided to walk the property. It seemed the only way to stay ahead of the thoughts that haunted me.

That night I stood once more at the sink with Mother, drying dishes as we did every night. My hands were busy, but my mind was far away.

I'd fully intended not to be the first to speak. And I'd held to that. But that night I couldn't keep the deep sigh of self-pity trapped inside any longer. When the mournful breath rushed out of my mouth, Mother finally looked at me.

"Are you ready to tell me why you felt it necessary to run away, Willemina?"

As if I could explain in a way *she* could understand! A year ago the thought of going home had made me physically ill. It broke my heart to be in the house without Papa, and I couldn't bear to see Mama smile lovingly at Toomey or his boys.

"You betrayed Father." I kept my eyes on the plate in my hands.

"By remarrying?"

"You barely mourned him, Mother!" I stacked the dried plate on the table with the others and stared at her. "If you'd loved him, you'd have mourned at least a year, if not more. But, no, you were married again in a month and carrying the twins not long after that. It makes me wonder . . ."

Her face was grim. "What?"

The suspicion that had wedged itself into my heart years ago now ached to be pulled out and laid bare. I'd never voiced it, but I was a different person now. A stronger person, willing to face the darkness rather than run. Taking a deep breath, I looked her squarely in the eye. "It made me wonder if you and Toomey did not wait for Papa to die."

She pulled her hands from the water and wiped them on her apron, a gesture made almost violent by her anger. "Let me tell you something about your beloved papa, Willie." Her voice was cutting. "He was a drunk and a spendthrift. He drank himself into an early grave and left me with a heavily mortgaged farm. I had nothing. No family to turn to. I thought we'd have to leave the farm and go beg on the streets of Columbia. But Gabriel Toomey, who'd always been a good neighbor, took pity on me. He helped with the harvest and shared his food. He was a good friend to us—an honest, steady man who knew how to save rather than spend."

"But Toomey is such a . . ."

Her mouth tightened. "Such a what?"

"He's an oaf, Mother! Slow and uncouth. I couldn't see why you'd befriend him, let alone *marry* him."

She laughed bitterly. "I was so taken in by your father's dandy ways—a man of the theater who wished to retire to the country and play lord of the manor. I had no idea how little he knew about farming, and how little time it would take him to go through the money it'd taken my parents *years* to save. He missed the stage, you see. He didn't find peace out here. Instead, he longed for the attention he received as a performer."

"How could you blame him?"

"I didn't blame him for missing the stage! I blamed him for taking advantage of me. And for making me suffer for *his* disappointment."

At those words I turned to walk away, out of that crypt of a house, but she grabbed my arm with her damp hand. Her fingers were strong as talons.

"No!" she hissed. "You will stay and listen."

"Mother!"

She held my gaze, waiting for me to be still. Then she took a deep breath. "Your father told me he wanted a quiet life in the country, and that is why I married him. The first few years were fine, especially after you were born, because you distracted me from seeing the truth about him. But by the time you were in school, I was begging for food on credit from the grocery. I was milking the cow and feeding the chickens and working in that garden where nothing ever grew because the birds would always get to it first. I was doing it all by myself. And do you know what your father was doing? Sitting in his study, drinking his whiskey and planning the first season of his Columbia Theater."

Her words were cruel blows, but my heart resisted them. Papa was a noble and loving man, and it burned me up with anger to hear him cast as the villain. My fondest memories were of sitting in his study while he talked to me about the theater. When he told stories from the past or shared his dreams for the future, it made me feel older, wiser—as though I *mattered*.

"Your bitterness sucked the life out of Papa," I finally replied, meeting Mother's eyes directly. "You never could find it in your heart to believe in him or his dreams, and that drove him to ruin!"

She stared at me, her face white with anger. When she

finally eased her grip, I tore away and stumbled from the room, ignoring Toomey's growl of exasperation as I pushed past him. A high-pitched wail sounded from the kitchen as baby Christabel began to cry. I barely managed to make it upstairs before my own tears came.

Chapter 29

MOTHER AVOIDED ME for the next few days, which was just fine. If Papa had been a drunk, she drove him to it—I was certain of that. Such a fretful, frowning woman would send any man straight to the bottle. Steering well clear of her, I did my chores as usual and spent the rest of my time in the hayloft.

But one day when I was washing the sweat and filth from my arms after slopping the pigs, I turned to find two pairs of eyes staring at me. Freddy and Hal stood by the trough, their freckles prominent against their pale skin. Freddy twisted his hands together, opening and closing his mouth as though to speak, but no sound came out. His cheeks flushed with color, and he looked to Hal for help.

Hal swallowed. "May we please see the kitties now, if it's not too much trouble?" His voice was barely audible. Both boys were wide-eyed with hope, but Freddy flinched when I stepped toward them.

My heart seemed to contract and soften at the same time.

"I think the kittens are ready for you now. But you must be very gentle."

I helped them up the ladder, surprised by the agility of their stubby limbs.

"Walk slowly, now," I said when we'd reached the loft, "and don't make too much noise."

"We know," Hal said softly.

The kittens had finished their morning meal and lay curled up together, their soft bodies curiously interwoven. I stroked the mama's head while the boys knelt over the kitties, crooning in delight.

"Be gentle," whispered Freddy.

"*You* be gentle," replied Hal.

They both managed better than I expected. When I saw how softly they handled the kittens, I allowed them each to take one into his lap. Already accustomed to being held, the kittens snuggled comfortably against the boys' warm bellies. Freddy giggled as his kitten stretched on its back to reveal the white fluff of its tummy. Hal seemed more entranced by how wide his kitten could open its mouth when it yawned.

Freddy glanced up at me. "Can we take them back to the house?"

Hal frowned. "No, silly! They gotta stay with their mama." He turned to me. "Right, Willie?"

"That's right, Hal," I murmured.

Freddy stroked his kitten's ear. "But Christabel wants to see them."

"She's just a baby!" Hal cried.

I laughed. "Sharing the kittens with Christabel is a sweet idea, Freddy, but they're still too young, and Christabel is barely able to sit up on her own. She'll appreciate them more when she's older."

"By then they won't be wee kitties anymore!" Freddy's lower lip trembled.

"I expect Mama Cat will have more babies in the future."

Strangely enough, the boys weren't so loathsome when they were quiet. Toys and games brought out their savagery—I'd seen plenty of evidence for that—but these tiny kittens prompted tenderness. Freddy and Hal might turn out human, after all, even with Toomey as their father.

When I heard growls erupting from their bellies, I knew it was nearing time for the midday meal. So I helped them down the ladder, and together we made our way back to the house.

Toomey stood by the side door. His face broke into a grin when the boys ran toward him, and he listened patiently as they chattered in unison about holding the kittens. After he'd shooed them in the house, he turned to me.

"Thanks for that. They've been talking about those creatures for days."

I shrugged.

His expression sobered. "Willie, you really should put things right with your mother. None of us can be happy until the two of you are civil again."

A strange and unwelcome longing tugged at my heart, but I hardened myself against it. "I've suddenly lost my appetite," I said.

His eyes were sad as he watched me turn away toward the orchard.

Everyone left me alone after that. The boys did not ask to see the kittens again. Mother avoided my gaze, and Toomey made no further attempts to coax me toward reconciliation. As long as I did my morning and evening chores, no one complained when I avoided the house for hours on end.

Problem was, that left me plenty of time to think—and re-member.

When I was very little, we had farmhands for the heavy work. Mother worked in the house—cooking, cleaning, and sewing—and I fancied myself her helper. She watched pa-tiently as I coated myself with flour in the kitchen or acciden-tally trampled the laundry while helping fold it. She even asked Papa to make me a small broom so I could work with her when she swept. And she'd taken ever so much time to teach me my first simple stitches.

Not that she always had me working. When she hung out the laundry, I danced and collected dandelions. When I bruised a knee with too much rough play, she would sing the pain away. At night, she read fairy tales to me by candlelight. On Sundays after church, she and Papa would take turns lead-ing the fat pony as I rode around the paddock.

When had things changed, and why? All I knew was that Papa began to spend less time overseeing the farm, preferring instead to keep to his study. The fat pony was sold, much to my dismay. The hired help came less often, until the day they stopped coming at all. Weeds began to grow in the garden and the animals sickened and sometimes died.

When Mama took over the farm chores, I was left to play in Papa's study. That room, hazy with sweet-smelling pipe smoke, became a refuge from Mama's wan face and scolding words. I whiled away the hours paging through books or listening to Papa recount his former triumphs on the stage. While the rest of the house collected dust and cobwebs, the study grew ever more enchanting, for it was a place to indulge in fancies without fear of reproach.

As I lay in the hayloft, looking back at those times with the inner eye of experience, a troubling thought struck me. When I was eleven years old, Papa and I became a team. Our sport? How best to evade Mother and all the duties she seemed determined to thrust upon us. We wanted nothing to do with someone who was forever tired and sour in disposition.

How could she let us be so selfish?

That night as I dried the dishes, I smothered my pride and spoke to Mother.

"Why didn't you tell Papa you needed help?"

She flinched at the sound of my voice. "What did you say?"

"Back when you worked all the time with the animals and in the garden. Why didn't you make Papa help you?"

"I couldn't *make* your father do anything," she said, still staring at the pan she washed. "I did ask him. I begged, in fact. And he promised again and again to help." She lifted the pan to scrub at the crevices.

"And?" I prompted.

"Sometimes he would put the bottle aside and work for a day or two. But he never could stick with it. There was always an excuse, for he was forever in the middle of some grand project. Before long, he'd be drunk again with his friends."

"Maybe he could only stand your critical gaze for so long," I said.

She grimaced, handing me the pan to dry. "Willie, I know you think I'm punishing you for your father's failings, but I'm not."

"I only wanted to finish school! It certainly seemed like a punishment when you told me I'd have to come home."

"It was supposed to be a temporary change. I fully intended for you to finish your schooling." She forcefully splashed the last pan into the water. "I never expected you to do something so foolish as run away."

"I took good care of myself, Mother. And I made sure to send money to make up for the lost labor. Why couldn't you just let me go? Why did you have to send Toomey to bring me home?"

Finally, she turned to look at me. "I wanted you home because I missed you and feared you might come to harm. And as it turns out, I was right to worry! We nearly lost you to that river. You *think* you can take care of yourself, but you are too much like your father in doing so—lying, cutting corners, hurting others."

I winced.

"Your father spoiled you rotten, Willemina," she continued. "It's time you learned about *honest* work and sticking to it even when the going gets tough."

I chewed my lip for a minute, stewing over this. "Will I ever be able to go back to school?"

She sighed and rubbed her forehead with the back of her hand. "We'll see. I know you have savings, but you'll need to set aside more if you're to pay tuition. Perhaps not this fall, but next."

"More than a year? That's an eternity! I'll be an old woman by then."

"In a year you might begin to learn patience."

Chapter 30

THE DAYS DRAGGED ON, clumping into weeks and then months. I heard nothing from the seminary. Nothing from Eli. The hours were filled with planting and weeding, spring cleaning and diaper changing. Beasts needed feeding, watering, and milking. Fences required mending and berries were ripe for picking. Three times a day dishes piled up in the sink for me to wash. At night, I rubbed cream into hands turned rough and callused. In the morning, I stared in the mirror at a face browned from too much sun. My body grew strong and lean, but I feared my mind was turning to mush.

For all my torments at the seminary, I missed my time in the classroom. It seemed ages since I'd discussed a work of literature, or even read a book. I was simply too tired at night to peer at the pages by candlelight. I could barely make it through supper without wishing to put my head down on the table to sleep.

There was no improving the situation through playacting. One did not "perform" the roles of farmhand and household drudge. One simply worked all day and dropped wearily into bed each night. Sundays offered a bit of variety, with church in the morning and quiet sewing in the afternoon, but overall I couldn't escape the feeling that life had become something to endure rather than enjoy.

One day, when the afternoon heat became too intense for outdoor work, Mother asked me to stay inside with the boys. I pouted childishly; it would have been much more pleasant to sit in the breezy loft of the barn. But when she brought a package wrapped in brown paper to the parlor and asked me to take a seat on the lumpy horsehair sofa, I felt a prickle of curiosity. She directed Freddy and Hal to sit quietly on either side of me. The boys' eyes were huge as she placed the heavy package in my lap.

"Gabriel found this in town," Mother said softly. "He thought it might be good for the twins."

The boys leaned in, their shoulders pressing against my arms as I untied the string and pulled the paper open. Inside was a wood board covered in the letters of the alphabet. For a moment my heart froze. Had that fool Toomey purchased a *talking board* for his own children? But, no, it was a spelling board, crafted with slots through which one could move letter blocks around to form words. The board was painted a cheerful yellow and embellished with fanciful designs. The letter blocks were round and bright red. Freddy reached out to touch one of the blocks, then hesitated. He looked up at Mother, who smiled.

"It's all right, Freddy," she said. "The blocks are meant to be touched." Her gaze turned to me. "They need to spend more time learning their letters. Gabriel thought this very clever for even the roughest of boys—the letters move along the grooves without coming out, so they won't lose them."

The twins were mesmerized, crowding closer so they could fiddle with the block letters. Freddy moved them one by one toward Hal, who chose his favorites and moved them into the inner groove. Together they pushed an assortment of letters into the center.

"*A-R-B-M-D-S,*" spelled Hal, pointing to each letter as he said it. Then he looked up at me. "What does that spell?"

"That's not actually a word," I said with a laugh. "Why don't we begin with your names? Hal, what letter does your name start with?"

And so Mother left us to it. I'd thought the boys terribly ignorant, and before that day would have doubted they could sit still for more than a minute without a kitten in their arms, but the spelling board enchanted them. They were so excited to get their hands on the letters they practically climbed into my lap, and to my surprise this did not annoy me. When they clung to my arms, smelling of grass and sunshine, I felt a pleasant pang in my heart. They were so trusting, even after I'd been nasty to them. And their laughter bubbled so freely, as though deep reserves of joy surged within them, refusing to be contained.

A shadow in the doorway caught my attention. I looked up to find Toomey leaning against the doorframe with Christabel in his arms. A smile tugged at the corners of his mouth. His eyes shifted from the boys to me, and the smile faded. He stepped back as though to retreat, but for some reason—I suppose the boys' cheerfulness infected me that day—I smiled and waved him in.

Freddy looked up and wriggled like a puppy. "Papa! Look what we got!"

"We're learnin' our words," said Hal, sitting up straight and manly.

I glanced back at Toomey, then pulled the boys close. "Show your papa how you spell your names," I whispered.

Practically before I could finish the sentence, they had leapt off the sofa, each clutching the spelling board with one hand and crying for Toomey to sit down with them. I stood and took Christabel from his arms, nuzzling her plump cheeks until she giggled. Smiling sheepishly, Toomey settled his bulk into the old wingback chair, moaning in mock torment as the twins climbed into his lap. Each tugged on the spelling board as they argued over which name they would spell first.

"You two settle down." Toomey growled the words like a bear, making the boys giggle.

I stood awkwardly for a moment. I could have taken Christabel from the room, claiming we both needed fresh air. But when I watched the boys cuddle up to their father, concentrating on the board in an obvious effort to impress him, I had no desire to walk away.

So I took a seat and settled my baby sister on my knee. She gurgled happily.

Though he did not raise his head, Toomey's smile broadened.

•　•　•

And thus I became a teacher again. Though it was nothing like the seminary, teaching the boys to read proved challenging enough. With the use of the spelling board and an old slate of mine, I taught them new words every day. Before long, they were able to sound out short sentences on the slate. At that point, it seemed time for them to learn how to write as well as recognize the letters of the alphabet.

We continued our lessons each afternoon. When the boys were especially attentive during the week, I was allowed to hitch the old horse to the wagon and drive them into town on Saturdays to buy sweets at the general store.

On a Saturday in late July, we made such a trip after a week of good progress in printing the alphabet. I stood to the side as the boys inspected all the candies and made their selections, then herded them out and toward the post office to pick up any mail. Occasionally, there was a seed catalog held for Toomey or a letter from my mother's cousin in Ohio. I never took anything thrilling away from the post office, but it was nice to walk in and be treated like a grown lady.

That day, however, the clerk handed over a packet addressed to me. The postmark, clearly stamped, was from Tahlequah, and I knew the address to be written in Miss Crenshaw's hand. My pulse quickened as I mentally weighed the thick packet. Shaking it did nothing to tell me what might be inside.

I was distracted for the rest of the day, ignoring the boys and holding the reins slack in my hand as the old horse made its own way home. As soon as we were back in the house, I climbed the stairs to my room and slipped the packet under my pillow. I would wait until bedtime to read it, for I didn't want anyone looking over my shoulder.

During supper, Mother narrowed her eyes at the unfinished food on my plate. "Are you taking ill, Willie?"

"Just a little tired," I said, though my brain was quite lively with wondering. "I think I'll turn in after the dishes are done."

When finally alone, I set the kerosene lamp on the floor and sat down with the packet. After studying it for a moment, I sliced the edge with a knife and dumped out the contents. Dozens of folded pieces of paper spilled onto the braided rug. I pushed them aside and reached for the unfolded sheet covered in Miss Crenshaw's crabbed writing. My hand shook as I read.

> *Dear Miss Hammond,*
>
> *I hope this letter finds you in good health.*
>
> *The new term commences in two weeks, and thus I write during this brief lull before the girls begin arriving and the school reverts to pandemonium.*
>
> *I know we did not part well, but I think of you often. How could I not, when the girls asked after you almost daily? I must confess that I have withheld the truth from them. I've told the students that your family suffered a tragedy and you were required to return home at once. Fannie Bell knows the truth, and I did explain to Miss Adair, for she was very concerned for you, but they both have agreed not to divulge your secret to the rest of the students and faculty.*

No doubt you think I'm perpetuating your deceit in order to preserve the reputation of the school. That indeed is a large part of it. But I also felt moved to protect you because of what you accomplished at the seminary. Yes, you struggled with discipline and only finished your marking under duress, but you also managed to convey your passion for literature to the students. And you guided them in putting on the best spring play we've ever seen at the seminary—I still hear about it from the girls' families, and even from people in town. You left a deep and positive impression on the students, as you will see when you read the notes I have enclosed.

As much as it would please the girls, I could never invite you back to teach at the seminary. In all conscience, I could not even provide a reference for you to teach at another school. But, Miss Hammond, I will provide one if you decide to return to school to obtain a teaching certificate. I strongly urge that you consider this. With the proper training and, shall we say, "seasoning," you could make a very fine teacher indeed.

Sincerely,
Harriet Crenshaw

I sat back and took a deep breath, eyes burning with tears. I'd known I would never see the seminary again. There could be no going back after all my deceits. *I knew that.* Still, it hurt to read it confirmed in Miss Crenshaw's own hand. No matter what kind things she wrote, no matter how she offered to help, the fact remained that she'd never have me back. I laughed even as my heart ached. How I'd resented that place at times! How strange to long for it now.

The younger students wrote breezy missives that spoke some on how they missed me, but mostly of what they remembered best about our class. Of the senior notes, Lucy's was the longest, dealing almost entirely with her horror at what the doctor had done to Ella and Cale. Alice wrote to thank me for pushing her to perform as Rosalind despite her panic. Lelia wrote briefly and very politely about how strange it was to have Miss Taylor teach both English and domestic science for the remainder of the term. Lelia never was a very sentimental girl.

All the seniors but Fannie wrote to me. I didn't resent her for this. She knew what she'd done and had already apologized in her own way. Her deceits and manipulations were no worse than my own, and I'd never apologized to *her*.

Olivia's letter was short, but ended on a reassuring note: *I am certain you had reasons for your deception, and my only regret is that I won't have you near me in the new term. Whatever lies you told, you were a good friend.*

I'd not had someone tell me I was a good friend since . . . before I went to the Athenaeum. And though Olivia was kind and friendly to everyone, I did believe she cared especially for me. I'd shared more of my private self with her than anyone else, and we'd endured much together. I certainly wouldn't have survived at the seminary for so long without her.

It seemed unlikely I'd ever see her again, but I smiled at the thought of one day encountering her at a séance table. God only knew how I might find her; nevertheless, I could see it very plainly. Her face would be veiled and mysterious, but I would know her voice and the touch of her hand. I would trust the words that came from her mouth, because Olivia's heart held no deceit.

I knew then what to write in my letter to her. I would share these very thoughts, finally expressing what I loved about her—*not* dwelling on what I hated about my own life.

There would be no word from Eli—I knew that too—but I still searched among the notes for a passing mention of him. Apparently, he had not asked about the mysterious "Miss Hammond," and Miss Crenshaw had not deemed it prudent to explain to him. Had he been hurt that I left without saying a word? Had he made himself forget me?

I would never know.

Chapter 31

LIFE BARELY TOOK A BREATH before returning to its usual routine. There wasn't time to mope and be wistful about the seminary. The vegetable garden and blackberry bushes were bearing at their peak, and thus Toomey and I had to spend every morning picking before the sun grew too hot.

We never spoke much when we worked together, but this no longer bothered me. Strangely enough, I'd grown quite comfortable with Toomey. I now called him by first name to his face, for he seemed to deserve at least that much respect. He worked hard, straining and sweating, but there was a curious gentleness about him. He was tender with the vegetables and fruits, careful to brush the dirt off each item and set it carefully in his bucket to keep the flesh from bruising. I knew he took special pains so Mother would have less work in the kitchen. There was a tiny bit of romance in that man, after all.

One humid August morning found Toomey and me

struggling to finish picking before we drowned in our own sweat. While we worked, Hal and Freddy chased each other up and down the rows. They were meant to be pulling weeds but couldn't keep their minds on the task. I didn't blame them and certainly couldn't complain about the breeze they struck up as they rushed by. Mother needed them out of the way while she put up preserves, and they couldn't get into much trouble in the garden with Toomey keeping an eye on them.

When I'd finished my last row of okra, I stood to stretch my back, removing my bonnet so the gentle rush of air could cool my damp head. As I faced the breeze, I saw a figure in the distance. A man in a wide-brimmed hat holding a jacket over his shoulder. He walked toward us on the dirt road, his feet sending up clouds of dust with each step. I shaded my eyes, trying to get a better look at him.

"There's a man coming up the road," I said to Toomey. "Are you expecting anyone?"

Toomey looked up and wiped his face with a filthy handkerchief. "Can't say that I am."

I turned back to the road.

And gasped.

"Who is it? Who is it?" chanted the twins in unison, jumping up and down in an effort to see over the plants.

Toomey rose to his feet with a groan and stood behind me. "Is that the boy from the river? The one who—"

"The one who saved my life? Good Lord, it is. Eli Sevenstar." I turned to stare at my stepfather. "What do I do? I look a fright!"

Toomey grinned. "Go inside and wash your face, girl. I'll

greet the boy—he won't care that I'm soaked in sweat. But you tell your mother and come right back out—he deserves some proper hospitality."

I set off toward the house in the fastest ladylike walk imaginable. As soon as the door slammed shut behind me, I broke into a run and took the stairs two at a time up to my room.

"Willie?" Mother called up the stairs. "What in heaven's name is wrong with you?"

"We have a visitor! Gabriel says to offer him some hospitality."

I pulled off my gardening smock and sweat-drenched dress, sighing as the air touched the bare flesh of my arms. I poured water into the basin for a quick wash-up. Then I unpinned my hair and ran a brush through it. It was still damp, but at least it looked tidy when I pinned it back in place. I buttoned myself into a clean dress and pulled a fresh apron over my head, tying it around my waist. One more glance in the mirror and I was racing down the stairs.

Mother stood in the front hall, fanning her overheated cheeks. Her eyes were dark, her mouth stern.

"*Who* is this visitor, Willemina?"

I hesitated. "It's . . . Eli Sevenstar."

"The boy who brought you so much trouble at the seminary?"

"I think it was the other way around." I was itching to get back outside, but she looked so concerned that I reached for her hand. "Mother, I'd be dead if it weren't for him."

She stared at me, eyes glistening. Then she pulled me close, her thin arms nearly squeezing the breath out of me. I didn't mind. In fact, I leaned into the embrace, breathing in her scent of blackberry preserves. After a moment, her arms softened, and she let me go. We faced each other, smiling shyly, until finally she spun me around and gave a gentle shove toward the front door.

Toomey and Eli were talking when I came down the porch steps. The twins were silent, standing close together and looking up with great concentration at Eli. Though he didn't turn, Eli was conscious of my approach—it was obvious from the way his body straightened and his jaw grew rigid. Finally, as I drew near, he turned his head languidly and smiled. Then, as an afterthought, he took off his hat. His own hair was damp, his cheeks reddened by the heat. Those wide, dark eyes glittered with mischief. He was the best thing I'd seen in months, and despite the muggy heat, all I wanted was to fall into him and feel his arms around me.

Toomey cleared his throat. I turned to find him frowning ever so slightly, his eyes thoughtful.

"It's hot as Hades out here," he said. "I think it'd be a good idea to take the boys inside for lemonade. We'll sit awhile on the back porch. Willie, why don't you lead the young gentleman to a shady spot?"

I grinned. "We'll join you in a minute, Gabriel."

He tipped his hat and, taking a hand from each boy, walked toward the house. Hal craned his neck to stare at us, but when I made a face, his head snapped forward where it should have been. I turned to Eli, a sudden shyness setting in.

He smiled. "Willie?"

"Short for Willemina."

"Ah, yes, I remember my confusion when Mr. Toomey called out to you."

I laughed softly. "All those secret talks we had and you never once tried to call me by my first name."

"You never seemed like an Angeline to me." He stared at me for a moment, then wiped at his forehead with the back of his hand. "It's too hot to stand here for much longer."

"Of course," I said, coming out of my daze. "Let's walk through the orchard. Or do you want to go inside?"

"I'd rather walk." He looked as though he might offer his arm but then thought better of it. We walked side by side in silence.

"How did you find me?" I finally asked.

"I did a little sleuthing. Even Fannie didn't know where you lived, and Miss Crenshaw would not tell me, so I asked around in Columbia."

I stared at him. "Did you come all this way . . . for me?"

"I'm on my way to Nashville. I mean to study law at Vanderbilt."

"Yes, of course. I knew that. I mean, I knew you wanted to study law, I just didn't know it was to be in Nashville. That's . . . close."

"So close it seemed only polite to search you out."

We fell into awkward silence again. I reached for a branch and pulled off a leaf, just to have something to fiddle with. I turned to him, prepared to say anything to break the roaring silence, but he spoke first.

"You lied to me."

His words were as sudden and sharp as a slap to the face. I fumbled for a response, but all I could do was bite my lip.

"I mean, you lied to everyone," he continued, "but you should have told me the truth. I *always* was honest with you."

I knew the betrayal he felt, for I'd endured it myself when he disappeared. But that pain had its source in the doctor's lies. I had only myself to blame for the pain I'd caused.

"I lied because I wanted to keep my position. My independence."

"Fannie said you were only pretending to be a Miss McClure. But your last name isn't Toomey, either."

"No, it's Hammond. Gabriel Toomey is my mother's second husband."

He was quiet for a moment, as though digesting this information. "He seems like a good man, and you have a comfortable home here. Why pretend to be someone else?"

I stared at the leaf, tracing the delicate veins with a shaky finger. "I was . . . unhappy. Mother needed me to quit school and help at home. So I stole someone's teaching certificate in order to teach at the female seminary. I thought it was far enough away that no one would suspect I was only seventeen and not finished with my own schooling."

He shook his head. "I took you for a student the first time I saw you, remember?"

"It seemed you found me a great deal more interesting when you learned I was a teacher. Sorry to disappoint."

"I just liked *you*." He reached out and ran his finger along my hand. His head was down, but I could see his mouth curving into a shy smile.

"I never understood why," I said, staring at our hands as they touched. I would not take his hand, but neither could I draw mine away.

"All this began with you staring at me on the train. I had to know more about such a bold girl."

I did pull my hand away then. "You're teasing me."

"And now you're being coy. I've been fascinated by you since the first moment I saw you, and you know it." He chuckled. " 'That girl is an adventurer,' I told myself."

"Turns out I was a liar, and I'm sorry for it. But if I hadn't done such a foolish thing, I never would have met you." I looked up into his wide brown eyes, marveling at the bold angles of his face, the way that lock of hair falling over his forehead made him look so boyish. I reached up to push the stray hair back into place, then let my fingers trail down his cheek. His hand gripped my wrist, pulling me closer. I'm not sure which of us moved first—it might have been me—but when our lips met, I pressed so tightly against him I thought to melt into the warmth of his body, hands, and mouth.

Shame at such boldness caught up to me, and I broke the kiss. But he would not let me go. "Come to Nashville with me," he whispered in my ear.

I pulled back to look at his face. "What are you suggesting?"

"Nothing untoward. We'll find you a respectable boardinghouse. I'll go to the university, and you'll go back to school. Fannie told me—very reluctantly, mind you—that you had the makings of a good teacher."

"And just who is going to pay for all this?"

"I will, for as long as I can. Someday I'll return to the Cherokee Nation with my law degree. My dream is to help protect my people. If you feel about me the way I feel for you, you could be part of that."

"How exactly do you feel about me?"

He placed both hands on my face and kissed me gently. "I love you, Willie," he murmured. Then he stepped back, staring at me intently. He reached into his pocket and knelt.

A flush of heat rose from my chest to my face. "What are you doing?"

He pulled out a delicate gold ring with a single pearl. "I came here with a specific purpose." He took my hand. "Willemina Hammond, will you marry me?"

Chapter 32

FOR A MOMENT, I BASKED IN THE WARMTH of his touch, the glow of those words. Then a darker thought chilled me. "But I'm not Cherokee."

"That is a defect, but I'll try not to hold it against you." He smiled. "I'm not so traditional that I believe Cherokee should only marry Cherokee. I am not full-blood, after all."

I stared at him. "Oh, stand up. I feel foolish with you kneeling before me." He obliged, pulling me to him for another kiss, but I held him off. "You said I could play a part in helping your people. What use would I be?"

"You could teach."

I bit my lip. "Miss Crenshaw would never have me back."

"Who said anything about Miss Crenshaw? The female seminary is a fine school, but best suited to girls with money and progressive ideals. Most rural families can't afford to send their children away to a boarding school, even when the

Cherokee Nation pays their tuition. And these families don't want their children to become strangers. We need schools that encourage children to keep their Cherokee language and traditions. You could teach at such a school. And someday you might train others to teach." He paused, frowning. "Everything is changing so fast. There's talk of the territory becoming a state, and the U.S. government parceling out the land that the Cherokee have held in common since the removal. We have a fight on our hands, Willie."

"You've thought a lot about this."

He laughed. "It's been a long summer."

I thought of myself in a schoolroom with girls like Lucy and Mae who were fierce, smart, and weary of being teased for their brown skin and country ways—girls who didn't want to trade their language and traditions for a good education.

"Will you give me your answer, Willie?"

I looked up at him. "You want me to come with you now?"

"Today, this very minute. I want you to pack a bag and walk with me to town. We'll catch the train to Nashville." He smiled. "I'll put it to your stepfather and mother, so it's all aboveboard. I can be very persuasive, you know."

Oh, how I wanted to be with him. The thought of him walking away without me was like contemplating the loss of a limb, or the possibility I'd never be warm again. More than one untoward thought entered my head as I imagined us free to show our affection for each other, no one frowning at the idea of Eli courting me.

But then I heard my mother's voice in my head, telling me that my impatience was overruling my good sense. That I was running away yet again. And Miss Crenshaw? She would speak of responsibility to family. I thought of the lessons with my brothers and how much progress we made each day. And little Christabel, who was sitting up and would be crawling soon. Before long, she'd take her first unsteady steps. Who would be there to catch her? To kiss her knees when she scraped them?

"I can't."

He took a step back. "I thought you wanted to be with me."

"I do, Eli. I love you most dreadfully."

His frown softened slightly. "Well, then why not come away with me? Is it . . . because I'm Indian?"

"No! It's not that at all." I clutched his arm and pulled him close again. "A minute ago, *I* was worried about not being Cherokee, you idiot." I put my hand to his cheek, smoothing the hard line of his jaw. "I made a promise to my mother—a promise that I would help at home for a year."

"But I'm sure she would understand and be happy for you."

I dropped my hand, frowning. "I lied and thieved to get away from this farm, to avoid my responsibilities. I need to put in my time. I *want* to put in my time."

"That sounds like penance. Why should you have to suffer?"

"It's not penance. Not really. My mother needs me. I have two little brothers and a baby sister—they need me too. I can't leave them . . . again. Not when we've just started to feel like a family. Perhaps next fall I can think about myself again."

He held my gaze. Finally, he nodded. "I understand . . . and I do admire you for it." He wove his fingers through mine, tightening his grip. "How do you manage it?"

"Manage what?"

"Make me love you even more by telling me we can't be together?"

I squeezed his hand. "We are still so young, Eli. After teaching almost a year at the seminary, I felt *old* and worn out. But I am only eighteen. I think . . . I have some growing up to do." I smiled. "I hope you'll still find me fascinating when I'm more 'seasoned,' as Miss Crenshaw would say."

He sighed. "I suppose it was selfish of me to try whisking you away. I've been anxious about leaving home to attend university. It seemed more like an adventure if you were beside me." His mouth curved into a sad smile. "But we *will* be together, won't we?"

"Yes."

"You'll write to me?"

I put my hand to his cheek once again. "Only if you promise to visit as often as you can."

"I'll be knocking on your door every chance I get. In fact, I'll keep knocking until you finally agree to come away with me."

"I'm counting on that," I whispered.

Then he pulled me into his arms again, and I left off the thinking and worrying. Instead, I let my body memorize the softness of his lips, the pressure of his arms wrapped around me and his body pressed to mine. My skin breathed him in, receiving his imprint like a brand scorched on flesh.

I could live a year for others. *This* was for me.

That night, after I'd put the twins to bed and watched them fall asleep, I sat in the rocking chair and closed my eyes. In my mind I saw the bookshelves full of Papa's favorite plays and novels, the floor littered with the scripts he was always consulting, revising, or criticizing as nothing better than kindling for the fire. I saw the whorl of pipe smoke rising in the air, the scent of it acrid and sweet at the same time. The smell of whiskey had been one of many comforting scents associated with Papa, but now I did not try to recall it. That whiskey had driven my mother to despair and had proved his undoing.

So I sat and remembered my papa's passion for words, his tales of fame on the stage, his dreams of a gentlemanly retirement with an adoring wife and a daughter who, with proper schooling, would catch a fine husband. He'd been a dreamer rather than a doer—hell for my mother, but I saw too much of myself in Papa not to forgive him that.

I thought of all Papa's good qualities, meditating upon all the moments we spent together, drenching myself in memories. It was like holding my very own séance. I was channeling my father's spirit—I could almost feel him in the room, see him sitting in his chair by the fire, looking up from a book to smile, or to read some wondrous or preposterous passage to me.

I opened my eyes. "Papa?" I whispered. "Are you here with me?"

Aside from the deep breathing of my brothers, there was only silence. I felt no tingle on the back of my neck, no prickling of gooseflesh on my arms. No tortured spirit chilled the room with its ache for vengeance. It was only me, two snoring boys, and my memories.

And that was enough.

AUTHOR'S NOTE

The Revenant is a work of fiction, but the setting was very real. Early in the nineteenth century, President Andrew Jackson pressured the Cherokee Nation to relocate from Georgia to what is now northeastern Oklahoma. A small group of wealthy Cherokee, seeing removal as inevitable, signed a treaty agreeing to sell all Cherokee lands east of the Mississippi in return for a large tract of land in Indian Territory. But the majority of Cherokee, who never agreed to this treaty and considered it illegal, were forcibly removed, along with other tribes, as part of a devastating migration often referred to as the Trail of Tears. The Cherokee Nation proved resilient, however, and ultimately established a flourishing capital in Tahlequah. The Cherokee National Female Seminary (as it is officially called) opened in 1851, remaining in operation until 1909. The original seminary building burned down in 1887, but the subsequent building, completed in 1889, still stands as the historic centerpiece of the Northeastern State University campus.

The seminary was a fascinating place—every bit the high-powered educational enterprise Miss Crenshaw represents it to be. And because the school accepted students from various socioeconomic backgrounds and with varying quantities of Cherokee blood (sometimes as little as 1/128 Cherokee), it did feature many of the conflicts dramatized in *The Revenant*.

In developing the story, I made great use of *Cultivating the Rosebuds: The Education of Women at the Cherokee Female Seminary, 1851–1909,* by Devon A. Mihesuah. Dr. Mihesuah, currently a professor in the University of Kansas's Department of Global Indigenous Nations Studies, noted a tension between darker-skinned full-blood Cherokee girls and the lighter-skinned mixed-blood girls—with the latter considering themselves more "progressive" than their "traditional" counterparts. However, upon speaking with Dr. Richard Allen, policy analyst for the Cherokee Nation, I learned that many Cherokee scholars feel this tension was less about race and more about class and family background—that cliques arose among the wealthier town girls, who may have found the country girls rather rustic. Either way, factions developed, just as they still do in modern schools. I did my best to explore this in a way that was both honest and sensitive.

Many of the characters and situations in the book were inspired by real people and events. Harriet Crenshaw is loosely based upon the school's legendary principal of twenty-six years, Florence Wilson. The primaries *were* housed on the third floor (with older full-bloods educated alongside younger mixed-bloods), and according to the memoirs of seminary graduates, they did stage unofficial performances there. Boys from the male seminary often did serenade the girls at night, and Tahlequah truly did have an opera house, where school plays, debates, and oratory contests were staged. Even Fannie's warrior dance—so offensive to Eli Sevenstar and others—was inspired by an 1894 photograph of female seminary students wearing feathered headdresses and holding bows and arrows. All Cherokee names were mixed and matched from lists of students and alumni found in male and female seminary catalogs.

Researching the background for this book was an engaging and eye-opening experience, and I was fortunate to have access to a gold mine of primary resources at the Oklahoma Historical Society and the Northeastern State University Archives and Special Collections. As alluded to above, I consulted photographs, school catalogs, newspaper clippings, and oral histories, along with published histories of the Cherokee people and the seminary. These sources helped tremendously in fleshing out the context within which my fictional murders and hauntings occurred. In addition to writing what I hoped would be an entertaining mystery, I endeavored to honor the Cherokees' pride in their thriving nation. I hope Willie's growing appreciation of her surroundings, as well as her deepening respect for her Cherokee colleagues, friends, and students, adequately reflects this endeavor.

Finally, legends of a ghost at the Cherokee National Female Seminary continue to this day, though no one can say for sure whether the building really is haunted, and if so, by whom.

ACKNOWLEDGMENTS

Many people deserve recognition for helping me bring this novel to publication. My editor, Michelle Frey, proved a keen critic and kindred spirit as we revised the manuscript, and I am forever grateful to her, Michele Burke, and the entire team at Knopf. (Special thanks go to the art department for the fabulous cover.) My agent, Jennifer Laughran, is to be commended for her shrewd commentary on early drafts, as well as her incredible children's book knowledge and business savvy. I owe heartfelt thanks to Vickie Sheffler and Brenda Cochran at the Northeastern State University Archives, as well as Delores Sumner at NSU Special Collections, for their generous assistance with primary resources. Brandi Barnett and Martha Bryant, critique buddies and Tahlequah residents, read the ugly first draft and saw some merit in it—to say their feedback was much appreciated is a massive understatement. Diane Bailey, Michelle Lunsford, Lisa Mason, L. K. Madigan, and Richard

Allen also read versions of the full draft and provided invaluable input. My wonderful critique group members offered insights (and many laughs) along the way—Lisa Marotta, Kelly Bristow, Dee Dee Chumley, and Shel Harrington. My friends on LiveJournal generously offered feedback to strange questions on terminology and other historical minutiae; I'm particularly grateful to Ellen Maher and Edith Cohn for suggestions that inspired the novel's tagline. This novel owes a great deal to all the teachers and students who taught me so much over the years, and I especially wish to thank Michael Shapiro for being a brilliant Shakespeare professor and supportive friend (Willie would have taken ALL your classes, Michael!). Of course, none of this would have been possible if Mom hadn't made a passionate, lifelong reader out of me, or if Dad hadn't pushed me to love learning for its own sake. I owe so much to my entire family—grandparents, parents, stepparents, parents-in-law, brothers, sisters, and my little nieces—for loving me and making me a better person. (I'm still working on the better-person part, so keep after me, you guys.) I probably should thank my cat for endeavoring so frequently to sit on me as I worked, thus keeping my bum in the chair. And saving the best for last—I thank my husband, Steve, for his faith in me, his endless support, and his shrewd insights as I wrote and revised (and revised, and revised) this manuscript. Steve, you are a better partner than I ever could have wished for, far better than I deserve, and I adore you.

About the Author

Sonia Gensler grew up in a small Tennessee town and spent her early adulthood collecting impractical degrees from various midwestern universities. She experimented with an assortment of professions suitable for a dreamy bookworm—museum interpreter, historic home director, bookseller—before finally deciding to share her passion for stories through teaching. She taught literature and writing to young adults for ten years. Today she writes full-time and lives in Oklahoma with her husband and her cat. *The Revenant* is her first novel.

You can find out more about Sonia and *The Revenant* at soniagensler.com.

A sneak peek at Sonia Gensler's next novel,

The Dark Between

Chapter 1

When Kate Poole was twelve, her body had folded easily into the medium's throne. Her limbs had been shorter, her joints more elastic. In those days she stayed cool and supple while waiting for the hymns to end.

Now, two years later, she was a leggy foal contorted in the womb, straining for freedom and the first breath of life. Perspiration soaked her chemise, and her limbs twitched and tingled.

After an eternity of singing, Mrs. Martineau's voice rose to a crescendo. In response, the sitters sang more passionately. Kate reached back to slowly lift the hinged panel, inhaled a lovely breath of fresh air, and pushed her head and arms out of the hidden compartment. Once her hands found the thick support bar on the back of the medium's chair, she slid her legs out and pulled herself up to a low crouch.

"Hand in Hand with Angels" drew to a close and the great chair creaked as Mrs. Martineau's body began to convulse. The sudden movement quieted the singers to a low hum. When the room fell silent, Mrs. Martineau spoke in her singsong trance voice.

"Dear friends, my spirit guide beckons. Do not be afraid. She wishes to show herself."

Kate heard the rustling of fabric as the sitters leaned forward. This was what they had come to see, after all. She clung to the back of the chair, bouncing gently on the balls of her tingling feet.

"The spirit will walk among you," continued the medium. "Do not be alarmed if you feel her touch. She reaches for the souls of your loved ones. She intends you no harm."

Kate rolled her eyes. The audience *loved* to feel the spirit touch—the gentlemen, especially. Some of them liked to feel back, and there wasn't much Kate could do to stop them. All part of the show, as Mrs. Martineau would say.

The medium shuddered rhythmically, rising off her seat a few inches as she did so. In response, Kate slowly rose behind Mrs. Martineau's head, hidden by the vast hood of the woman's white cloak. After another spell of twitching, Mrs. Martineau moaned dramatically and collapsed onto the table. At the same moment Kate stood at her full height behind the chair.

The audience gasped. They always did, even when they had come many times before.

Kate was a ghastly sight in the dim light sputtering from the gas fixtures—she knew this because Mrs. Martineau had once brought a mirror to the parlor so she could see her reflection in the near darkness. When Kate had looked in the glass and seen her thin frame draped in a shimmering, transparent shroud, her mouth fell open. The vision was perfectly ghoulish.

The next bit was her favorite. She pulled the shroud to her shoulders, revealing her face.

More than one lady cried out. A gentleman cleared his throat. Again there was a rustling of fabric as people shifted in their seats. Kate well knew how her brown eyes, rimmed with kohl, appeared as gaping holes against the unnatural paleness of her face. In that moment she didn't care that the luminous powder wrecked her skin, or that the wig made her scalp itch and sweat. Nor did it shame her that the costume—a gauzy wrap draped over the merest of underpinnings—left her exposed and shivering. In the dim light of the parlor, she was a wraith from a horror tale.

And she held them all under her spell.

Kate arched her back and began the slow movements of the spirit dance. The ladies rarely gave her trouble. They shivered at her touch and occasionally giggled when she sighed in their ears, but they never laid a hand on her. Once a lady had cried, "She reeks of onions!" and Mrs. Martineau had given Kate a good thumping when the sitters were gone. Thereafter she could take only bread and milk before the séances.

The gentlemen were altogether different. She could almost smell it on them—their longing to touch her. A few managed to keep their hands to themselves, but most had to claim a piece of her before she moved on. Some ran fingers through the long hair of her wig or stroked her bare arm; others probed underneath the shroud in a furtive search for her thighs. Though she'd long ago ceased to be shocked by their hot breath and wandering hands, she would never find it *pleasing* to be fondled by whiskery old fools. She often felt a powerful urge to pinch them back, but all she could do was step lightly away, sighing her sorrow as spirits were wont to do.

That night her dance lacked its usual elegance, for her right foot was still prickly and awkward. This sluggishness seemed to work to her advantage, however, for the men committed no worse acts than light pawing. The two gentlemen placed at the medium's left—attending for the first time that evening—did nothing at all. In fact, they barely looked her way as she floated past them.

Finally she returned to her place behind Mrs. Martineau. When the woman lifted her head from the table and sat up straight, Kate drew her arms together and crouched, as though melting into the darkness behind her. But just as she lifted the panel to the compartment, Mrs. Martineau spoke.

"My spirit guide has encountered a very powerful presence with us tonight. My friends, the spirit of Frederic Stanton has crossed the dark chasm to join us."

Frederic Stanton?

Kate dropped the panel, and the clatter echoed throughout the room.

"What the devil?"

She flinched at the exclamation. Robert Eliot was the medium's patron, and as such he always had the best seat at the table. The best angle for groping Kate, too. Missus would not be pleased that Kate's bumbling had so provoked him.

"This is utterly ridiculous," said a soft voice near her. She thought it must be one of the aloof gentlemen. "Mr. Wakeham," the man continued, "would you be so kind as to turn up the gas so everyone might see?"

"No!" bellowed Mrs. Martineau. "You will do great harm to the spirit!"

Roused by this sudden burst of anger, Kate lifted the panel again and thrust her feet into the compartment. A moment later a burst of gaslight brightened the room and a pair of hands seized her shoulders, pulling her to her feet.

"Here's the confederate, Thompson. Hiding in the chair, of all places."

Kate gasped as the wig was plucked from her head. She craned her neck to see whose hand gripped her upper arm. She did not know his name, but it was the younger of the two newcomers.

"I say," cried Eliot, puffing his broad chest. "You promised you would not disrupt the meeting." He directed his words to the grey-bearded fellow, her captor's companion.

Mrs. Martineau looked from the strangers to her patron. "Who is this man, Mr. Eliot?"

The bearded gentleman clasped his hands at his chest. "I beg your pardon, madam. I am Oliver Thompson. And Wakeham"—he gestured toward the man holding Kate—"is my colleague. We represent the Society for Metaphysical Research. Mr. Eliot encouraged us to attend tonight."

Mrs. Martineau's mouth twisted as she glanced at Mr. Eliot. "You invited *skeptics* here tonight?"

"They expressed an interest." Eliot's forehead gleamed with perspiration. "I've told them of your spirit manifestations, and they wished to observe. I meant to finally give them proof of the spirit's ability to communicate after death . . . but it's all gone horribly wrong."

"Thompson and I suspected fraud, Mrs. Martineau, and now we have exposed it for all to see," said Mr. Wakeham, his fingernails still cutting into Kate's shoulder.

"No, *you* have perpetrated a fraud, Mr. Wakeham!" cried Mrs. Martineau. "You and your colleague brought this girl here tonight. You planted her in an attempt to discredit me." The medium paused, her expression growing bolder as her favored sitters sputtered their outrage. She raised her hand to still their voices. "I sensed something was not quite right, but I could not put my finger on the source of the disturbance . . . until now."

Mr. Thompson lifted his hands. "This is ridiculous. Eliot, how can you countenance this woman's deception?"

"It seems the girl has tricked us all," said Eliot weakly.

Mrs. Martineau took a deep breath and looked calmly around the table. "Ladies and gentlemen—my dear friends—I have been deceived along with you. These men have tricked me and now they most certainly will slander me." She staggered back, eyelids fluttering. Mr. Eliot stepped to her side, offering his arm, and she smiled weakly at him before turning back to her audience. "I beg you all to leave me now. A dark presence has defiled our circle, and it will take some time for me to recover."

With a limp hand she beckoned her maid, who herded the sitters out. Mrs. Martineau sank back into her throne, eyes closed. Mr. Wakeham's grip finally eased, and Kate shrugged him off to step toward the medium.

Mr. Thompson sighed. "I think we're finished here. Shall we push on, Wakeham?"

"Take your little pawn with you, Mr. Thompson," called Mrs. Martineau softly.

What? Kate stared at her, but the woman did not open her eyes.

"Surely you are mistaken, dear lady," said Eliot, swabbing his forehead with a handkerchief. "This can't be the work of the Metaphysical Society."

"He's correct, of course. We've never seen the girl before." Mr. Wakeham's upper lip curled as he tossed the wig to Kate. "Eliot, I assume you're coming with us?"

"Ah, well . . ." The man shuffled his feet. "You two go on without me. I'll see you next week."

The instant the two gentlemen passed through the doorway, Mr. Eliot lurched toward Kate. "I believed in you," he said thickly, as if choked by emotion. "You seemed made of air—a creature from another world."

"If you thought me a creature of air, why'd you grope me every chance you got?"

She was pleased to see him wince at that.

After a moment he took a step closer, his eyes glistening.

"Did you . . ." He cleared his throat. "Have you come at Mrs. Martineau's bidding, as my colleagues suggested?"

Kate risked a glance at the medium. Only one eye was open, but it was trained on Kate and the message was clear. *Don't even try it.*

"I came on my own," Kate whispered.

Eliot's fists tightened. "You should be made to pay for your deceit."

"She's not worth the trouble, Robert," Mrs. Martineau whispered, still slumped in her chair.

"But she's done you great harm, so great that I should take her to the police this instant. Don't you mean to prosecute?"

"You are kind to take an interest, but I fear such action would only draw more dark spirits our way." Mrs. Martineau glanced briefly at Kate before closing her eyes again. "I will recover in time. When *she* leaves this house tonight, she will take the darkness with her, and eventually it will consume her."

Eliot nodded. "Wise words." He turned back to Kate, nostrils flaring. "If I see you again, girl, I *will* take you to the police." He moved a step closer. "Either that, or I'll deal with you myself."

Kate lifted her chin and stared back. With his clenched mouth and high color, he looked like an angry brat about to bellow. She longed to tell him so, but the insult stuck in her throat. She directed her gaze to the floor instead.

As soon as Eliot was gone, the medium's eyes snapped open. Her trembling and heavy breathing ceased, and she abruptly stood to close the door. Kate watched with numb detachment as the woman turned, the skirt of her delicate white dress flaring. In three steps Mrs. Martineau was upon her. "Fool!" A backhanded slap sent Kate reeling, and a moment later she was pinned against the wall.

"How could you be so careless? *Months* of effort to lure Eliot into my scheme, and in one night you've ruined it all."

Kate knew better than to struggle—the woman liked a tussle far too well. "You didn't wait long enough to call the spirit, ma'am. I wasn't ready."

"You were *clumsy,* idiot girl."

Kate kept her head down. "Why did you say my father's name?"

Mrs. Martineau grunted. "Your father?"

"The spirit you called. Frederic Stanton."

"I called on Stanton's spirit because the little detectives gave his name as one associated with the sitters. I'm sure it's no business of yours."

"Stanton is dead?"

"Yes, you thick-skulled creature! Frederic Stanton has been dead for years." She paused, and Kate glanced up to find the woman's eyes narrowed. "And I happen to know he had no living children."

"Not with his wife." Kate looked at the floor again.

"Have you lost your wits?" Mrs. Martineau shoved Kate's head against the wall. "Clearly you have. And now you've lost your situation as well. Your clumsiness has compromised my reputation, and the damage will be impossible to repair if you remain here. Pack your things and leave this house immediately. Take only the items you brought with you."

Kate blinked. "But where am I to go? You can't just kick me to the streets."

"I can and will. If you don't go, I'll get the police after you. See if they don't lock you up as a fraud." She paused, her face turning sly. "Or perhaps I *will* allow Mr. Eliot to discipline you. You're a frightful little criminal, after all. Shall I call for help?"

The glint in the woman's eyes forestalled further argument. "No, ma'am, I will go."

Mrs. Martineau released her and stepped away, a satisfied smirk on her face. Kate kept her back against the wall as the woman swept out of the parlor.

Kate dropped the wig to the floor. The shroud soon followed, and it took a powerful exertion of will not to trample them both. Rubbing her damp and throbbing head, she slipped out to the hall and dragged herself up two flights of stairs.

As she reached the attic floor, a shadow shifted near her door.

"Who's there?" she gasped.

"It's just me," the shadow replied, sounding more like a boy than a ghost.

"Christ, Billy! You shouldn't scare me like that."

She opened the door to the attic room and made her way to the washstand. Billy lit the lamp and sat on the small bed, watching in silence as she poured tepid water into the basin and scrubbed the white paste from her face, neck, and arms.

"You must have heard all that," Kate muttered as she dried herself.

"You've been sacked," said Billy sadly.

"Yeah." She sank onto the bed next to him. "What am I to do, Billy?"

He shrugged. "You hated working for Missus. Weren't you sick of parading about in your petticoat? And never able to come out in the daylight? Don't cry, Katie."

"I'm not crying." She wiped her nose with the back of her hand. "I *did* hate prancing for Missus, though it was a lark to scare those fools at the table." She turned to face him. "It's the time I spent with you and Tec in the kitchen, with Cook sneaking us morsels, that I'll miss."

"I'll miss it, too. You shouldn't worry, though. I'm working a new scheme, and it could bring enough to keep the two of us going for a while, at least until you find a better situation."

"You'd do that for me?"

He nodded. "Of course."

A rush of affection prompted Kate to kiss his cheek, and she giggled at the boyish fit of cringing that followed. "What's this?" She gently laid her finger on his jaw, tracing a bruise. "Has Martineau struck you?"

He shrugged her hand away. "She never touched me. It's nothing."

"This scheme, Billy—are you sure it's safe?"

"I'll be fine."

She bit her lip. For such a scrappy kid, he seemed fragile and hollow-eyed in the lamplight.

"Go to Tec's cottage," he said. "It's too late to go anywhere else. I'm workin' tonight, but I'll come by in the morning or thereabouts." His expression sobered. "If you don't see me tomorrow, you'll know someone's done me in."

"Don't say that! If the scheme is that dangerous, you shouldn't try it."

"I was only joking." Grinning, he reached down and pulled something out of his boot. "But take this, just in case." He held out a knife with a four-inch blade. The slick ebony handle shone in the lamplight. "I'd give you the sheath, but it's sewn into my boot. You'd better wrap the blade in something."

"Shouldn't *you* just keep it?" Kate shivered at the strangeness of an angel-haired child holding such a thing.

"I'd feel better if you had it," he said. "Give me something in return, and we'll swap back when I see you again."

"You don't trust me?"

"You might find a better situation and forget all about me. This way, I know we'll see each other again."

Kate's rigid spine softened at that. She looked about the room, considering her few possessions. "I don't have anything that's a match for such a blade."

"How 'bout your father's watch?"

She paused. "It doesn't work anymore."

"That's okay. It still might come in handy. You'll get it back; I promise."

Kate stared at him a moment, wondering at this request. But his wide eyes did not blink, so she knelt by the narrow bed and retrieved a muslin-wrapped parcel from under the mattress. She unfolded the cloth and gave him the watch.

As soon as it was in his hands, Billy opened it. His thin finger traced the inscription inside. "It'll do perfectly."

"So it's a fair trade . . . but only for now, right?"

"Right."

She took the knife from him and placed it on the bed. Billy politely looked away as she sucked in a great gasp of air and buttoned herself into the too-tight dress she'd worn the day she first knocked at the service entrance of Mrs. Martineau's house. The rest of her possessions—including the knife—fit easily into her mother's old sewing basket, which she clutched to her chest.

She turned to Billy, thinking to clutch him to her chest as well. "See you tomorrow," she muttered, chucking him on the chin instead. He grinned and blew out the lamp, melting into the darkness once more.

Kate stepped lightly down the stairs and through the corridor to the deserted kitchen. Without looking back, she opened the back door and yielded herself to the damp embrace of night.